DESTINY'S REBEL

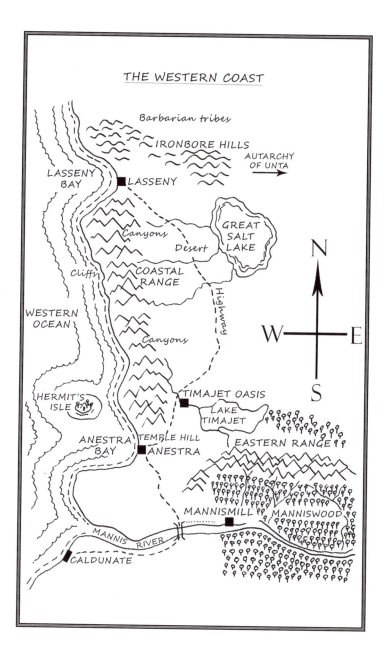

THE WESTERN COAST

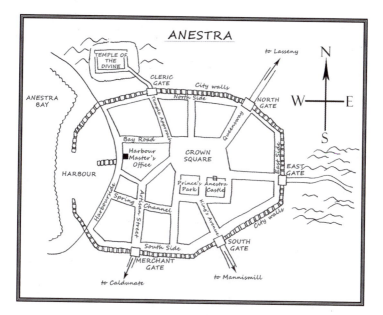

ANESTRA

TEMPLE OF THE DIVINE

CLERIC GATE

City walls

North Side

Temple Approach

ANESTRA BAY

to Lasseny

NORTH GATE

N
W — E
S

Queensway

Bay Road

Harbour Master's Office

CROWN SQUARE

East Side

EAST GATE

HARBOUR

Harbourside

Spring

Artisan Street

Channel

Prince's Park

Anestra Castle

King's Avenue

City walls

South Side

SOUTH GATE

MERCHANT GATE

to Caldunate

to Mannismill

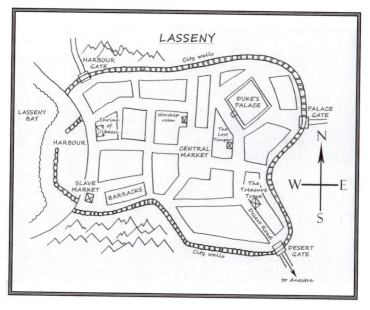

LASSENY

HARBOUR GATE

City walls

LASSENY BAY

Shrine of Ilbassi

Worship room

DUKE'S PALACE

PALACE GATE

The Lost Temple

HARBOUR

CENTRAL MARKET

N
W — E
S

SLAVE MARKET

BARRACKS

The Treasure Trove

Desert Road

City walls

DESERT GATE

to Anestra

To Ava,

DESTINY'S REBEL

Philip S Davies

with my very best wishes,

Philip S. Davies.

Books to Treasure

Books to Treasure
5 Woodview Terrace,
Nailsea, Bristol, BS48 1AT
UK

www.bookstotreasure.co.uk
www.facebook.com/BooksToTreasure

First edition 2015

Text © Philip S Davies
Design and layout © Books to Treasure
Maps © Philip S Davies & Emma Graham
Cover illustration © Emma Graham
Cover design by A J Fitzpatrick

Printed in the UK by Latimer Trend
9 8 7 6 5 4 3 2 1

ISBN 978-1-909423-32-9

CONTENTS

For Rachel (who had to be first),
for Mark and for Ann

ESCAPE

Kat had always envied those who could choose their destiny. Or find a quiet, easy, enjoyable one. Hers seemed to live as a sinking dread in the depths of her stomach.

If only she hadn't been born who she was.

Sometimes she could forget what was coming, but now it was too close to ignore. For months she'd counted down the days until her eighteenth birthday.

That afternoon, when Aunt Sirika summoned Kat to her study, the count had reached eleven.

Sirika glared at Kat through narrowed eyes. If her face was no more sour than usual, that was only because she always looked like she was chewing a lemon.

"When you are Queen," Sirika announced to her, "you will need to understand service to others."

With a curl of her lip, she plucked a flower from the vase on her desk.

"So, young Katelin, we have a plan for your last ten days as a Princess. As punishment for running away, you will work with the Castle servants. It is discipline you need, and we're going to make sure you get it."

She began to tear petals from the flower.

Kat had perfected an expressionless face to wear like a mask and get her through all that she hated. That face was on now.

"As a chance to prove you're not useless," Sirika continued, "this evening you will report to the Treasury and polish the royal silver." She leaned forward in her chair, and her voice dropped to a hiss. "You can expect the tasks to become much, much worse, you stupid little girl, because you leave us no choice but to break you."

Her tone held a veneer of reasonableness, but she was ripping each petal into shreds.

"Understand that we will crush you until you break, so why not give in now, and save yourself all that distress?"

Break her? So the punishment for running away was an excuse. Aunt Sirika and Uncle Ethabos were raising the stakes in the war of wills to come.

"We will hurt you, and humiliate you, until you do everything we say. And don't think for one moment that becoming Queen will save you. For you will still be our niece, and we will still be here, hounding you closer than your own miserable skin."

Kat couldn't tear her eyes from the neat pile of shredded petals on the desk. She considered outright refusal, and folded her arms in an attempt at defiant silence. Because otherwise she'd be shaking. They couldn't try to humiliate or hurt her as Queen, could they?

Sirika crushed the flower stem until the juice oozed through her fingers.

Kat met her Aunt's cold, grey eyes, and saw the vicious fury there. Yes, they could. And they would. Because they'd find ways to make her do whatever they wanted; they always did.

For now, it was simpler to comply. She should have expected them to take full advantage of their last days of control over her.

It had been a one-sided war until now, with all the power with her Aunt and Uncle. But as soon as Kat acquired some power of her own, the battle of wills would become merciless and cruel. There would be no escape from it. Or from them.

Once she was Queen, she'd have to find new ways to resist them. To defy them. To make them abandon their attempts to keep power over her. But she would still be a prisoner, hemmed in on every side by duty, by etiquette, by the responsibility for which she wasn't ready. And nothing would ever make up for her loss of freedom, or the chance to be herself.

So that evening Kat reported to the Castle Treasury. It was a strong-room on the lower ground floor of the Keep, ruled over by Quevelle, the Royal Treasurer. The safes and glass-fronted cabinets that lined the walls contained much of the wealth of Anestra. Kat had always been intrigued by this place, with the tales of hidden compartments behind the oak panels.

The Treasurer was a middle-aged woman with white cotton gloves and her hair in a tight bun. Kat found her berating Adisha, a dark-skinned servant girl, who was failing to polish with sufficient relish. The two of them froze as she entered.

Quevelle cleared her throat. "Ah, yes, your Highness. Consort Sirika instructed me to treat you as I would the servants. So you will assist us, please, with the cutlery for the coronation banquets."

In the middle of the room an array of silver knives lay on a dark blue cloth on the table. There were rags and jars of polish, and Adisha had started at one end.

Kat drew a deep breath. Maybe it was fitting that she should prepare for her own coronation. She tucked some dark brown strands which had escaped from her ponytail back behind her ears, donned an apron, took her place next to the other girl and began to polish.

The Treasurer inspected each piece of work before stowing the items away. At first, Kat had knives returned to her, deemed to have insufficient shine. She was about to protest, but reminded herself to hold her tongue. She polished the rejected items again.

Adisha kept shifting on her feet. Kat realised that she must have been on them all day, and was trying to ease her discomfort.

"My legs ache," Kat said to Quevelle. "Can we have stools to sit at the table, please?"

Adisha's mouth fell open. The Treasurer scowled, but before she could refuse, Kat fixed her with an innocent smile. She had few qualms about exploiting her position as a Princess when it suited the situation, to make up for enduring the rest of it.

Quevelle looked away first. "Just this once," she muttered. "They're in the storeroom."

Kat and Adisha found a high stool each and brought them back to the table. Adisha sighed with relief as she lowered herself on the stool. Kat twitched the corner of a smile at her, and they resumed their work.

Kat wasn't supposed to make conversation with the servants, but 'supposed' was one of her least favourite words.

"So you're from the Caldunate?" Kat asked Adisha.

"Yes, milady. There's more work for servants here than back at home."

"How long have you been here?"

"Nine months, milady."

Kat expected Quevelle to object to the conversation, but pressed on anyway. "And how is working at Anestra Castle? Tell me about the pay and how you're treated."

The Treasurer interrupted at once. "I don't think that's a suitable discussion, milady. More work, less chat, please."

"We can polish while we talk." Kat had made sure to keep working to forestall that objection. But if she couldn't pass the time with Adisha, what would interest Quevelle instead? "What about my royal Crown, is that here somewhere?" Kat looked around, as though expecting to see it in a cabinet. She knew it was hidden away, but enjoyed the way the Treasurer stiffened.

Quevelle's voice was stern. "The Crown of Anestra is kept safest of all. We don't have the Divine's sacred relic on display."

"The circlet has been added since I saw it last," Kat pressed her. "It will be mine in ten days' time, so I'd like to see it. Please?"

The politeness, and who Kat was, seemed to persuade the Treasurer. Quevelle sighed. "I will open the safe so you can see it, but I'm not getting it out."

Adisha's eyes were popping, and the polishing had stopped.

Quevelle walked to a wall and used her body to shield what she did. There was a click, and sliding wood, and the turning of a key. Kat was surprised to find that she was trembling. She and Adisha left their stools and peered over the Treasurer's shoulder. Quevelle stepped back.

Kat's breath caught. She'd seen her broken Crown before, of course, but it had never looked so beautiful.

She almost forgot to let Adisha see it too. In front of them, the panels had parted to reveal the open door of a safe. Inside, a glass partition protected a blue silk cushion, upon which rested a curve of ornate silverwork.

But only a portion of the Crown was present. It was about the length of Kat's hand, tall and substantial, etched and jewelled, but with jagged sides. The missing part of the circle had been completed with a plain band of silver so that Kat could wear it for her impending coronation.

This evening, it was as though it glowed with an inner light.

As though it called to her.

It was hers. Or she belonged to it.

Quevelle broke the Crown's spell by ushering them back. She hurried to relock the safe and slide the oak panels back into place.

Kat shook herself, and she and Adisha returned to their stools, exchanging grins. "Where do you think the rest of it is, then?" Kat asked the Treasurer.

Quevelle pointed to the knives and they continued polishing. Her answer would only be forthcoming when the work resumed.

The Treasurer drew a deep breath. "What do I think? Since the Crown was broken on your father's death in the last war with Lasseny, the answer has to lie there. After fifteen years of searches and questions, the person who knows the most, but won't tell, is that wretched Duke Bassikrin of Lasseny."

Kat nodded. That was what she thought too.

They fell silent and worked. The image of the Crown remained behind Kat's eyes.

The next spark of excitement was when the convoy of unpolished knives became spoons. And then at last, forks.

Kat lost track of time, but it seemed many hours later that the Treasurer dismissed them. By then her whole arms ached, from fingertips to shoulders, and Adisha endured this every day.

Kat plodded her solitary way up the stone steps to the third floor.

Apart from the aches, her first evening as a servant girl hadn't been too bad. She'd suffered worse from Uncle Ethabos and Aunt Sirika in the past, and it sounded as though she was about to do so again. Breaking her? What more did they have in store for her?

Sirika had promised pain and humiliation, and there might

even be injury. Would they stoop to a public demeaning of her? Kat trembled to think what Sirika would devise in a last attempt to subdue her to their will.

The early skirmishes were over.

The war of the rest of her life had begun.

Kat slammed the bedroom door behind her, the boom of it echoing along the landing and down the stairs. If her Aunt and Uncle heard that, good.

The bedroom was cool because the fire in the grate had subsided to ash. Her rooms were plain and functional, with a refreshing sparseness after the extravagance downstairs. Kat liked her refuge up here. Most days she didn't want to venture down at all, into all that pointless Court ritual and ceremony and etiquette that stifled the life out of her.

The oil lamp flame showed her nightshirt laid ready, but Kat was in no mood for sleep. She plonked herself on the bed and untied the ponytail in her dark brown hair.

Would they ever learn that forcing her to do things their way didn't work? The compulsion made her resist. Maybe it was too late now for them all to co-operate anyway.

She stared at the rug, but her eyes were filling, her emotions rising. A tear escaped down her cheek but she brushed it away.

Only ten more days to go and then ... then there would be no escape.

She jammed a fist between her teeth to stifle a sob or a cry. Only when she whimpered with the pain in her fingers did she allow her muscles to relax. But it worked. A fire of resolve ignited inside her.

No, Kat, no. Don't think about them. Their power over her lasted for only ten more days. Then she might have the authority to resist them. But in the meantime, she remembered the crushed flower ...

She jumped up, wiped her eyes and paced the room, rubbing

the teeth marks on her fingers. She had to do something with this time she had left. To stay here and endure would drive her insane. She couldn't give them the chance to break her.

Kat ran to the window, opened it and thrust her head out. The cool night air was delicious. She could breathe again, after the stuffy confinement of the Castle. Ah, to be out there, instead of stuck in here.

The evening's vision of the Crown was fresh in her memory, and a childhood dream popped into her head.

Her lost and broken Crown. That she'd be the one to find and restore it.

Yes!

Kat knelt and dragged from under the bed her secret store: an old chest. From it she pulled a brown tunic, trousers, boots and a dark green cloak—all of them worn and stained. She tore off the stained apron of the servant girl, and donned the travelling clothes.

She could get out of here, for one last escape. Did she dare? Yes, of course she did.

Kat fished from the chest a pack, rope, pouch of coins and dagger. From hooks on the wall she took down, with reverent care, her quiver of arrows and shortbow. She filled the pack from the drawers.

How to escape from Anestra city, and not be followed or caught this time? The harbour? A ship? Yes, she could sail somewhere and be back in time. In fact, ships on the Coast went north to Lasseny, or south to the Caldunate. If she found one going north, she could even demand that Duke Bassikrin tell her what he knew of her Crown.

She paused. It was nearly midnight and no ship would set sail until dawn. Her departure had to be in the dead of night anyway, once everyone else was asleep. She paced again, fiddling with the hem of her tunic.

The steady flame and gentle light of the oil lamp calmed her. She stopped to touch the childhood ornaments that lined the drawers and mantelshelf: a crudely painted cottage of clay, a model horse whittled from wood.

If this was a battle, was this a tactical retreat? A withdrawal, to return when she had authority? It would serve them right for calling her useless, and remove her from their plans to break her. They would be furious, of course, but then they were always furious.

She tied the rope to the leg of her bed, and then lay down and tried to dream of nothing but freedom and adventure.

Kat woke with a start. The oil lamp had burned out and a glimmer of starlight filtered through the open window.

She hadn't had The Nightmare.

Was that because she'd decided to go? Her pulse quickened.

Kat sat up, rubbed her face and re-tied her ponytail. She pulled on her boots and hoisted the pack to her shoulders. Drawing up the hood of her cloak, she slung the quiver and shortbow across her body.

A freshening breeze blew in through the window from across the sleeping city. She fed the rope across the stone sill until it reached the grass three floors below, and climbed out into the night.

Her descent would have been envied by a spider on a thread. At the bottom, she slunk back into the shadows and checked for guards. The Castle was quiet; torches flickered at the gatehouse and Keep, but the darkness of the grounds reassured her.

Ah, she loved it: her senses sharp, her body as taut as a bowstring. This was what made her come alive.

And tonight's escape route was: the chestnut tree—tall and close enough for a leap onto the outer wall. She ran across the lawn to the row of laurel bushes and eased herself between them.

Halfway up the tree she heard a shout. They'd spotted the rope—and the chase was on.

Kat scrambled through whipping twigs to upper branches and sprang to catch the parapet. Her fingers clung to ancient stone and, with a heave, she mounted the wall. She raced to the outer side, vaulted the battlements, and used the familiar cracks and bumps in a rapid descent to the street.

Cries came from the grounds and the gate, and booted feet ran along the top of the wall. Her fingers protested as Kat slid the remaining distance to the ground and sprinted for Princes' Park.

She crouched in darkness behind a hedge, drawing deep breaths to steady her nerves. She clasped raw fingers and rubbed scraped knees.

A brief smile passed over her face. Perhaps she shouldn't treat this as a game, but some childhood playfulness remained. So, escaping the Castle: one point to her. Come on then, slowcoaches. She'd see if the guards could catch her, as she stole away into the night.

Dawn had not yet kissed the eastern sky as Kat waited in a doorway on Harbourside. She huddled into her cloak against the morning chill.

Along the quay, lamps shed dim pools of light onto the cobbles and across the water. Dark blue flags, bearing the emblem of the radiant silver Crown, stirred in the half-light. A score of fishing boats rested against the harbour wall, while larger vessels had dropped anchor in the Bay's deeper waters. A heaven full of stars and a crescent moon looked down in their silent, nightly vigil.

Escaping the Castle was familiar, but this part was new.

Kat chewed her lip as she watched for the first person to leave the harbour master's office. Come on. The harbour was full. Someone had to leave today. And before mid afternoon, if they'd be so kind.

At last a tall, dark-skinned man emerged from the office and strode off along the quayside.

Kat ran after him. "Excuse me, s-sir, are you leaving this morning?" She hoped he would think that the quaver in her voice was because of the cold.

He slowed but kept walking. "Straight away." His voice was deep and his face grim.

"Where are you heading?"

"Lasseny."

Yes! "Can—can I take passage with you?"

He stopped, unsmiling, and regarded her. "You have goldens?"

Kat nodded.

"I am first mate. If you want to, you can ask the Captain."

Kat followed him to a rowing boat tied by the harbour wall. She descended the steps and boarded, while he unfastened the tether and pushed off.

In the glimmer of lamp, moon and star the boat inched towards a ship in the Bay. Kat felt the twinge of urgency. The guards could arrive at any moment to stop all ships from leaving, and search all those that remained. Would it be quicker if she paddled with her hands?

No—patience—each stroke of the oars took her closer to freedom. She allowed the gentle splashing of the water to soothe her. The Castle guards' fear of Aunt Sirika's fury would make them hesitate to wake her and report the escape. A wry smile crept across Kat's lips: perhaps she'd more time than she thought.

First light peeked from under the black and starry

curtains of the night. The rowing boat reached a double-masted galleon with a high forecastle and poop deck, and an expansive main deck between. It bore the name *Oyster Shell*, and flew the yellow and sky blue flag of the Caldunate.

As soon as they boarded, the first mate ordered all hands to set sail for the north. Kat followed him astern, wishing her boots weren't so loud on the deck. Still the heads of the crew turned. She drew her cloak closer.

As they entered his cabin, the Captain looked up from his desk.

"Captain Farag," the first mate said, "we have a passenger."

Kat swallowed and forced out: "My name is Kat, and I'm willing to pay for passage to Lasseny, Captain."

Farag's dark hand stroked his greying beard as he appraised her. "Two goldens."

That was … dawn robbery! But for this to work, she'd better get on the right side of him. Kat fished two goldens from the pouch on her belt.

"Always happy for a little extra on a trip," Farag said, as he took the coins. "Safe passage." Then he added with a knowing smile, "—and I won't ask no questions."

Kat half smiled. He knew why she hadn't haggled over the high price. He'd guessed she was running away.

The first mate led her to a cramped forecastle cabin, with space for no more than a bunk. Kat offloaded her pack, quiver and bow, but stayed wrapped in her cloak as she came back on deck. The sailors were calling and answering orders as they raised the anchor and unfurled the sails to catch the morning breeze. Kat ignored the stares of the crew and peered towards the quay. The waterfront showed the first signs of bustle but there was no obvious pursuit. The slowcoaches hadn't got here—she'd nearly done it.

Two Anestran naval vessels lay anchored in the Bay. They

looked immaculate, but Kat had heard how undermanned and ill-equipped they were. And how they never went anywhere or did anything. Their paintwork might be new, but they would struggle to hunt down the slave traders off the Coast. Typical of the Regent's complacent neglect: all appearance and no substance. Beautiful ships, not much use.

The *Oyster Shell* began to move. The sails flapped and the worn timbers beneath Kat's feet creaked. Ahead to the right on Temple Hill, the dawn light reflected off the white marble pillars of the Temple of the Divine. Its lamps shone across the darkened Bay to Hermit's Isle and the Western Ocean. Behind the shadowy hills north of Anestra, the giant saw-blade of the Coastal Range's jagged peaks stretched beyond the edge of sight. On Hermit's Isle, flocks of seabirds wheeled and chorused around its wooded slopes.

Yes, it was a beautiful city. She loved it … but if only she were an ordinary citizen, living out her life with no one trying to crush or break her.

It wasn't fair.

The stars faded as the light grew and the crescent moon was rising to its zenith. There wasn't a cloud in the sky and Kat breathed in the cool spring air, scented with the smell of the sea. She eased back her hood and her muscles began to relax. The breeze on her cheeks meant fresh air again after all of that stuffiness.

She was out of the place. Escaping not only the Castle, but also the Kingdom: a second point to her.

She took a biscuit from her pocket. This was breakfast then. What else would she miss today? History and writing this morning, and then after lunch: archery practice and a horse-ride. What would those dear old clerics think when she failed to appear for her lessons? She'd have enjoyed this afternoon though: her archery, and riding Novita. But no, Aunt and Uncle's plans to break her would have overridden the enjoyable activities.

And she could always stop talking to herself.

Kat sighed. What else could she do after so long stuck on her own?

The galleon rounded the headland and began to roll as it met the Ocean swell. Kat gripped the ship's rail. Her hands were marred by the dirt and grazes of the recent escape. If they climbed more ropes, walls and trees, they'd soon match any servant girl's.

But her escapes were improving. This was better than when she got lost in the Manniswood, or frozen up on the Eastern Ranges. She'd remember this for next time—

With a jolt Kat realised there wouldn't be a next time. All at once she remembered her lifelong fate. No, she mustn't think about it. The joy of escape struggled against the sinking dread that she always tried to master.

"Off on a little adventure then, miss?"

Kat whirled around. It was the first mate from the rowing boat. "A little adventure? Yes, something like that. And why not?"

She made herself consider him again, as he stood, coiling a rope. He had sinewy arms, a barrel chest and melancholy eyes in a face that seemed naturally grim. A sheathed scimitar hung at his belt and he lacked two fingers on his left hand.

He stared at her. "Why not? Are you sure you know what you're doing, and can look after yourself out here?"

"Well … I think I know what I'm doing … and I hope I can stay out of trouble."

"Whatever you're doing," he went on, "you'll have thought it a good day to set out. Yes, it's fine now, but mark my words, there's cloud and rain coming."

Kat surveyed the cloudless sky. Cloud and rain, right. He was either a permanent pessimist, or an expert at predicting the weather.

He might not be the first person she'd choose to trust, but who else was there? She might need to trust someone. "I'm Kat," she said, and held out a hand.

"Jersull," he said, and took her hand, but seemed awkward with the formal gesture. "Captain said he wouldn't ask, but if I had to guess, I'd say you're a spoilt young lady from a wealthy family, running away from home."

Before she could stop them, Kat's eyebrows lifted at Jersull's assessment of her. She composed her face. She could always go along with that impression because of course she couldn't reveal her true identity to anyone.

"It's none of my business," Jersull went on, "but you wouldn't know what it's like outside your safe and comfortable city."

"I know something of it," Kat replied. "More than you might expect of us spoilt young ladies from wealthy families who run away from home. I know it's better to be armed and not to travel alone. I can shoot an arrow and do my share if fighting starts."

"*When* fighting starts," Jersull corrected her. "These days we all have to defend ourselves and what we've got. You Anestrans think you're safe with your fine city and army, but outside those walls things have gotten much rougher. Gone are the days when your King kept the peace, with that legendary Old Kingdom glory and strength."

Kat turned and gazed as the morning light grew in the distance. Yes, he tended towards the gloomy. But she wished he weren't right about Anestra. The fine city and army? That was just it. Their soldiers patrolled the city walls, but little else. The Old Kingdom once stretched the length of the

Coast, but was now only the city and the lands about. And it was all the Regent's fault.

A spark of her resolve still glimmered inside. "No, things are not as they used to be," she said. "But who can say how it'll all turn out? We should try to do what we can."

"Oh, yes, well said, miss," Jersull replied, but his eyes narrowed in condescension, humouring her, as though no one could make any difference.

"Look! Hermit's Isle, look!"

Kat jumped at the terrified shout from above. Craning her neck, she squinted upwards. The lookout in the crow's-nest was flinging his arms to the west.

Jersull yelled for the Captain. Kat turned and saw the reason for his cry. The blood drained from her cheeks as she stared.

Farag dashed from his cabin. "What is it?" he shouted up. "What do you see?"

"Slavers!" the lookout screamed. "Slavers!"

Pandemonium broke out around her. The Captain and Jersull drew weapons and shouted orders. The crew were running and yelling. Some leapt to the rail to look; some ran to arm themselves; a few hurried to hide. The *Oyster Shell*'s crew began to form a grim-faced line at the rail, clutching clubs and knives.

From behind the wooded isle, a small black ship was springing its ambush. And the galleon was too slow to outrun it.

Come on, Kat, move! She sprinted to her cabin, threw off the cloak and grabbed her quiver and shortbow. She chose the height of the forecastle deck and scurried up the ladder. She'd just said to Jersull about doing her share when fighting started, but hadn't expected to prove it so soon. She slung on the quiver and readied her bow.

Kat looked out and was transfixed. A black flag with crossed swords fluttered above bulging sails as the small black ship raced closer. Figures teemed on the slaver deck like ants with their nest disturbed.

The slavers jeered and brandished their weapons. Kat waited in impatient dread, wishing her arrows were of better use against moving targets at a distance. Her stomach knotted, and she gripped her bow to stop her arms from shaking. Did slavers slaughter, she thought in sudden panic, or did they only kidnap? She wiped the sweat from her hands on her trousers. She had to get herself together. Concentrate. Breathe.

Kat fired twice above the heads of the crew as the enemy ship approached, but couldn't see if she hit any target. The two hulls collided with a splintering crunch and Kat staggered as the *Oyster Shell* lurched. The slavers threw grappling hooks to secure the ships and swarmed across.

A dozen enemies reached the rail. Cries and curses filled the air, with the clash of metal, wood and bone. Kat willed the crew to lunge and push, but more slavers were climbing towards them. The invaders gained the deck. Jersull's scimitar felled two, Farag's sword another, and a vicious melee broke out. The Caldunim crew were falling or being wrestled overboard by stronger arms.

Kat fired her first clear shot, and an enemy crumpled with an arrow in his chest. She felled another, and then remembered the command of her arms master: "Find the leader. Get the chief."

And now she saw him. A swarthy brute stood at the rail, his long hair and black cape billowing. He was directing the slaughter with the point of his cutlass, and shrieking his commands with oaths and swearing.

With her first enemies dead, a cold focus descended on

Kat. Her arrow thudded into the slaver chief's shoulder and he roared in pain. While Kat strung her next missile, he screamed at his minions to get her.

She aimed at his head … and was startled by an unearthly sight—a flicker of crimson light in his eyes. She'd no time to worry about that.

By instinct, the slaver chief ducked. Kat was quicker and her arrow pierced his neck. That should have killed him. But the crimson light—

To avoid Kat's aim the injured chief dodged and weaved, but Jersull's scimitar came from behind and felled him to the deck.

Before Kat could shoot again, three slavers swept aside two of the crew and reached the forecastle ladder. This shot had to count. Her arrow sped into an upturned face, and one fell from the ladder, screaming. With no time to reload, Kat dropped her bow and grabbed the wooden rails. She swung herself up and landed her boots on the skull of the nearest foe. He fell back too, but the third caught her ankle and stabbed a knife in her leg.

Agony shot up Kat's body and forced itself out in a scream. She fumbled to whip out the dagger at her belt, but scrabbled to hold on as the slaver heaved her forwards. Her sweaty hands slipped on the wood. She flew from the ladder and her head bounced hard off the deck.

Fog closed in, with dizzying lights. Her limbs were too heavy. Why couldn't she get up?

No, she mustn't rest … or drift away …

Rough arms grabbed her … but her body wouldn't respond.

Lifted up … and then she was falling …

＊ II ＊

SLAVERS

Pain dragged Kat back to consciousness. Her leg screamed, her head throbbed and she was soaked and shivering. Shifting to ease her muscle cramps, she winced as ropes cut into her ankles and wrists. She jerked in sudden panic to be free, but it was no use: her bonds were secure.

In a rush her memory returned. What had she done? Terror, wretchedness, rage and despair vied for control of her. She shoved them aside to assess her physical needs first.

She lay alone on a bare wooden floor. Chinks of light filtered through cracks and knotholes in the planks of a gloomy cargo hold. The slavers' ship rolled with the Ocean swell and there were voices above her on deck.

Kat rolled over with a gasp of pain. Blood coated her right trouser and boot, and it had pooled on the planks by her leg. Sickness twisted her stomach. Her shivered chill wasn't only from being soaked. She flexed her neck, and touched with bound hands where she'd hit her head. It was swollen, and blood came away on her fingers. She was parched, but the drops on her arms and face were salty. She must have fallen into the sea, and her throat burned from having retched swallowed water.

A nightmare. But with no waking up. It was real. Think.

Should she let them know she was awake? She needed to be unbound, to eat and drink, to clean and bandage her leg and head, some dry clothes and to warm up … if the slavers would allow any of this. She gained nothing by suffering in silence.

"Hey! In here! Hey!" she called. It made her throat hurt.

There were heavy footsteps at the door, a bolt was drawn back and the door opened. A scruffy head appeared, black-haired and bushy-bearded. He glared at Kat and snarled, "Shut your face. I'll get Mister Leon." He bolted the door again.

Kat's heart pounded in her ears. Who was Mister Leon? Of course, the slaver chief had been killed on the *Oyster Shell*. So who was in charge? There might be a struggle for control of the ship, but she needed the help of anyone.

The door was unbolted and a man stooped to enter the hold. The hairs on Kat's arms rose. He was small, greasy-haired and dirty. Dressed in an old frock coat and breeches, he stood there, rubbing his hands. Kat thought he was trying to look like a merchant, but was too disreputable to manage it. And she didn't like the way that he looked at her, like a starving man finding a feast.

"Are you Mister Leon?" Kat gasped, and winced as she shifted on the floor.

"I'm asking the questions," he said, in a high-pitched, nasal voice. "Your name and city?"

"I'm Kat, Mister Leon, and I'm Anestran." If he didn't correct her, he'd have answered her question.

"And your profession?" whined Mister Leon.

Which story should she tell him? "Um … adventurer, mercenary."

He grinned, and stopped wringing his hands long enough to stroke his greasy chin and wipe his nose on his sleeve. "Excellent, so maybe there's no one to come after you." He licked his lips as he examined her, from bruised head to bloodied boots, and his gaze multiplied Kat's discomfort. He said, as if to himself, "Pretty green eyes, too; we didn't see those before now. But we'll need to clean her up before we arrive." He turned to go.

Wait. She needed his help. Kat stopped him by saying, "Mister Leon, wh-where are we going and what will you do with me?" She hated that she couldn't mask her wide eyes and frightened voice.

He faced her and gloated, "Lasseny slave market."

Kat's mouth went dry. Of course. Where else on the Coast could he sell slaves? So how could she persuade a greedy slave trader?

"B-But Mister Leon," she interrupted his departure again. Then she gabbled, "As you say, you'll get a better price for me if I'm in good condition. If I could wash and bandage my wounds, and have some food and drink and dry clothes, I'll be worth more."

He regarded her, but left without a word. The door was bolted.

Kat slumped onto the planks. She was shaking, breathing fast. The bearded slaver returned after a while with a bundle of rags, a jug of water and a loaf of bread. He set these on the floor and was about to leave when Kat said, "I'll need my hands free."

The man sized her up, and then knelt to untie her wrists. He reeked of sweat, urine and she tried not to think what else. He released her hands and left to guard outside the door.

Kat deepened her breathing, trying to calm herself. Physical needs first. She rubbed her wrists and freed her ankles, gasping at the pain in her leg. She took a drink from the jug, but the water tasted brackish. She tore open the hard loaf, and found a grub wriggling inside it. Her stomach convulsed, but she had nothing to bring up.

She turned to the rags. The bundle included a shirt and trousers—both far too big for her—and other cloths. Hoping that she was unobserved, she stripped off her soaking boots, tunic and trousers. She dried herself and put on the slaver clothes, wringing out her own and hanging them on nails to dry. They'd taken her quiver of arrows, of course, and emptied the pouch on her belt.

Kat sank into numb exhaustion, as she washed and bandaged her leg and head. She drank and ate, picking the grubs from the bread and forcing herself to chew and swallow.

The afternoon became hot and stuffy with the sun on her side of the ship. The wooden hold felt too small and restrictive, a stifling imprisonment. Peering through a knothole, Kat saw a few clouds and endless white-flecked waves rolling to the distant horizon.

The endless creak of rope and timber, and the low murmur of voices, frayed her nerves further. Then close above came the sudden shouts and curses of a brawl; a scuffle, a crack of bone, a ring of steel. Something heavy crashed above Kat's head, and she panicked. She thrashed about, thumping the planks to get out.

Then silence.

Kat curled into a ball, shaking all over. She cowered and whimpered.

Don't let them hurt her. Keep that door between them and her locked. But the bolt was on their side. The guard outside would keep them out. He wouldn't let them in. Please don't, please.

Kat buried her head, pressed against the floor. She traced with her nail the grain in the wood until it grew too dark to see it. She tried in vain to find a comfortable position for sleep.

In the solitary blackness the tormenting thoughts returned. What had she done? How could she get out of this? She had to be home, without fail, in ten days' time, and become Queen. Why hadn't she stayed in Anestra? She was vulnerable, trapped. One last escape? What had she done?

Princess Rashelin ascended the steps in Anestra Castle towards the royal apartments. Her blonde hair cascaded to her shoulders and her pale blue gown swished on the stonework. She tried to face the world with calm and poise … but she couldn't do that today. This evening she was troubled. Her parents weren't going to like this.

Punishing Katelin for her running away—by making her work with the servants—had only prompted her to disappear again. Had that been only last night, and this morning? What was her cousin up to this time? And so close to the coronation! Sighing, Rashelin acknowledged the salutes of the guards as she reached the second floor landing.

An attendant opened the drawing-room doors and she entered. The room was autumn coloured, with its plush, red-brown carpets and oak-panelled walls. The low evening sunshine streaming through the wide bay windows sparkled off the crystal chandeliers, and made the air smell warm and stuffy. Balconies gave views of the city, the mountains and the sea. Deep red upholstered armchairs, polished tables and elegant furniture completed the room while maintaining the impression of space.

Rashelin crossed to where her parents, Regent Ethabos and Consort Sirika, sat and consulted with two of their ministers.

The evening light was not kind to the Regent, showing only too plainly the effects of years of overeating and drinking. His face was too red, and his eyes too bulbous and staring. He seldom gave much interest to the business of running the Kingdom, but showed his face when required and left all the rest to his wife. In contrast, the Consort, whose royal robes hung shapeless on her skeletal frame, was immaculate. Her greying hair had not a single strand out of place.

Rashelin nodded to the ministers, the Lords of Rivers and Mills, and Harbour and Fisheries.

"Mother, Father," she said. "May I have a word in private, please?"

"Leave us," the Regent ordered, and the ministers withdrew.

When the doors closed behind them, Sirika said, "Have you managed to find out something, my dear?"

"A little," Rashelin said. "After the rope and scaling the walls, Katelin seems to have gone to the harbour. A guard remembers a cloaked and hooded figure boarding a rowing boat this morning before dawn."

"The harbour?" The Consort's knuckles whitened on the arms of the chair. "A rowing boat? What on earth was she thinking? Do we know where she's gone?"

Rashelin hesitated. "The guard thinks it was a dark-skinned man in the rowing boat, someone from the Caldunate. So I checked the harbour master's records, and a Caldunate vessel, the *Oyster Shell*, sailed from Anestra this morning."

"A Caldunate vessel?" Her mother was almost shrieking. "Where is it heading?"

Rashelin bit her lip. This was the part they would like the least. "Lasseny," she said.

Sirika swore, and Rashelin winced. Her mother jumped up, paced back and forth, pounded her fist, glared at the carpet. Her father's eyes followed her.

"That wretched girl," Sirika muttered. "Taking herself off to the most dangerous city on the Coast. And now of all times."

"Can we send a ship after her?" Rashelin ventured.

Sirika stopped. She was struggling to control herself with deep breaths. "If those Caldunim left at dawn, they'll be halfway to Lasseny by now. They have a day's head start, but we have to do something. Yes, we'll send our fastest ship after her."

"What about notifying Duke Bassikrin that Katelin's there?" suggested Rashelin.

Sirika stared at her. "That, my dear, is the last thing we'd do. Let Bassikrin know that the next Queen of Anestra is wandering unguarded within his grasp? You think we trust the Duke that much? Never. But until we can think of something better, we'll send a scout rider in secret up the highway. I hate to say it but it may be up to that girl to get herself back here in time."

Rashelin stared back. Was there nothing more they could do to help Katelin? She was going to think of something. She had to.

Kat jerked awake, muscles rigid, slick with sweat.

The Nightmare. Again.

It was always the same. She never saw who owned the hands that reached for her, groping, clawing. No matter how hard she beat them away, however much she kicked and thrashed, they were always too many, too strong, too persistent. Sooner or later they caught her, pressed her down into mud, sand or soil; suffocated, buried alive. At least tonight's version didn't include being sealed in a coffin-like box.

Daylight broke her numbness. Was there anything she could do?

Jumping from the ship would be useless because the Coast was all cliffs and rocks. When they arrived, Lasseny harbour would be teeming, so perhaps in the crush she could give them the slip? No, Mister Leon wouldn't let his prize catch out of his sight. And she was deluding herself to think she could outrun her captors with an injured leg.

So she'd be sold at the market. She might escape from her new owner, but that could take days to plan. Time was the luxury she could least afford: it was nine days now until she had to be back in Anestra. And the penalty for a runaway slave was severe—that would forfeit her life.

Might anyone try to rescue her? Mister Leon had said it: there was no one to come after her. Nobody knew where she'd gone. Rashelin might track her movements and discover what had become of her, but not soon enough.

So was this what a rebellious young lady deserved? She'd been a selfish dreamer, desiring freedom and excitement. It had taken her from Princess to servant girl to being sold as a slave.

Outside the morning was grey with heavy rain. So Jersull had been right about that. Everything became damp and dripping. Kat couldn't get warm or dry, even with wearing her own clothes underneath the oversized slaver garments.

With a shuddering chill Kat realised that for the first time her arrows had killed someone. It had been self-defence, but she'd taken lives. Shock became loathing. Then she couldn't stop the tears of remorse and despair. Not for her victims, but for herself: what they'd done to her, what they'd made her.

They'd turned her into a killer.

She tried to harden herself to it, shrug it off, justify it. But it was done, and she was here.

When she'd had enough of self-pity, Kat blew her nose and mopped her face with a rag. She persuaded herself she could survive the voyage if only they left her alone.

The quiet of the ship was eerie, broken only by the patter of the rain. That was it. Let it stay quiet. Kat's leg hurt, and all she could find to do was to clean her bloodied trousers and boot. She ate and drank what was brought to her, and worked a splinter from her elbow.

She hated feeling helpless. Depression settled on her, as if she'd caught Jersull's permanent gloomy outlook. She had thought herself irrepressible, but this was one game that had gone all wrong. Captured by slavers: one point to them. Or more than one.

Then she couldn't stop a grim smile at a morbid thought. She ought to thank these slavers. There was no chance here of a horse to ride, but they'd given her the day's archery practice.

And she'd put up a fight before they took her.

Was this the harshness of life on the Coast? She tried to think of consolations to lift her resolve above rock bottom. No doubt she was supposed to keep her weight off an injured leg anyway. So go on, Katelin; put those feet up for the voyage. She was good at enduring: she'd had a lifetime of practice. The slavers waited on her (unbound) hand and foot. She didn't have to watch them slaver over their food—get it? And she had a private (lockable) cabin. Complete with a nice, firm, wall to wall bed.

But underneath her bravado, she still jumped at sudden noises and gnawed her nails over the ordeal at the voyage's end.

Kat blocked out the voices and ignored what she heard, but that evening someone accosted the guard outside her hold.

"Hey, Bush, stuck on guard duty?"

"Shut your mouth," the bearded slaver snarled. "You know it's not just any guard duty."

"Oh, yes. Mister Leon's special catch, that girl we took."

"The same. Mister Leon's happier than a pig in muck. Don't want no harm coming to her."

The man laughed. "No harm? Like selling her as a slave in Lasseny, you mean?"

"That's right," Bush chuckled. "Not till then. So you just move right along and forget what you were thinking."

"Here now, Bush, been meaning to ask. We attacking any more dirty great merchant ships? We lost too many on that last one. If we're not careful, it'll be our turn next."

"Didn't have you down as a coward." Then Bush lowered his voice. "But seeing as how you've asked, just so happens I do know something." Kat crawled across and pressed her ear to the door. "Before the attack, see, I overheard Mister Leon talking with the chief. Sounded to me like Mister Leon, right, was passing on orders."

"Orders? For the chief? He never took orders from no-one."

"I know. That's what I thought," Bush murmured. "But these orders, see, were to pillage the ships going in and out of Anestra, and get our hands on their gold. Supposed to be rich pickings with all the visitors for that Crowning next week."

"Sounds like normal work to me. So who gave these orders?"

"That's just it, see: the Duke."

"The Duke?" He sounded incredulous.

"Duke of Lasseny, cross my heart. Seems he's lining up allies for himself. Mister Leon, see, mentioned … Ilbassi mages … and barbarian chiefs what I didn't know … as well as us. Rumour is, right: Duke's got the Crown."

"The Crown?" It was a whisper.

"Crown of Anestra. Don't say nothing, but that Duke's planning something. And soon."

"I ain't saying nothing, Bush."

"You better not. I hear rumours going round, I'll know who's spread 'em."

"I ain't saying nothing," the man repeated, as his footsteps moved away.

It fell silent outside the door. Kat breathed again and lay down on the planks.

She was appalled that even slavers knew about her coronation, and were using it as a pillaging opportunity. But could she believe their rumours? An ambush right outside Anestra Bay was unheard of. She'd never trusted the Duke, but slavers, mages, barbarians … and then the Crown? The Duke had part of it, it seemed, but what else did he know?

Then Kat remembered her helplessness, that as a prisoner or slave she couldn't affect the fortunes of Lasseny or Anestra. That night she slept no better than the last.

The following afternoon, the slowing of the ship told Kat that it had entered Lasseny Bay. What she'd tried to forget was now too close to ignore. She hugged trembling knees to her chest, and then bit down on her fist. She tried, with limited success, to let the pain ignite the fires of anger that would cover her fear with defiance.

The ship docked, and at last Mister Leon appeared to collect her from the hold. He ordered the slaver clothes removed to reveal her closer-fitting tunic and trousers. He scrutinised her, and seemed pleased with how well she'd cleaned up.

The slaver called Bush rebound her wrists and tied her ankles to restrict her walk. He pulled her through the doorway and along a low passage, but Kat could only shuffle and limp. She made the most of the struggle to climb the ladder, for it was true that her leg was painful. But that it annoyed Mister Leon was also satisfying.

Kat emerged onto the deck, breathing hard through gritted teeth. Her eyes, ears and nose were assaulted at once by the tumult of Lasseny harbour. The bustle, the shouts and the harsh cries of gulls were deafening. Her nostrils curled at the stench of the city, which mingled with fish and the salt of the sea.

The ship was moored at the southern harbour wall, and the slavers were unloading what Kat assumed was stolen cargo. The black flag with crossed swords had been replaced with the golden weighing scales of the Lassenite merchant guild. While she waited, she spotted a name-plate, and made sure to remember: the *Sea Snake*.

Was this the moment to jump overboard or run for it? No, with bound arms and legs she wouldn't get far.

The slaver crew gathered, pointing and jeering. So Kat was relieved when at last Mister Leon ordered her off the ship. She shuffled and limped after him, prodded forward by two burly henchmen. If possible the henchmen smelt worse than the city.

They pushed through throngs of people to a sunken arena behind the harbour wall. Kat kept her muscles tense so no one would see her shaking. The arena's barriers, sandy pit and crowd of men reminded Kat of a pen for showing livestock. The henchmen dragged her in, to an uproar of shouts and whistles.

The heat and dust choked her, and a shivering sweat trickled down her back. Kat's hands stayed balled into fists, her muscles locked, her face a mask, to hide the rising tide inside her. She wouldn't give these the satisfaction of breaking her either. They wouldn't see her cry or whimper or rage or plead. She had to hide her feelings at home. She could do this. By now her defiance was strong enough.

Kat limped into place, and turned to show them all her bandaged leg and head. That would please Mister Leon.

The others for sale were middle-aged women, muscular young men, and the poor, elderly and wretched—but Kat was the only young woman there. Mister Leon wasn't the only slaver conducting business, and it became clear that he was saving her as the best until last. The other slaves went for, at most, half a dozen goldens. The traders described them as brawlers, debtors, traitors and thieves, who had forfeited their liberty for their crimes.

Kat's turn came and Mister Leon paraded her before the jubilant and hostile crowd. A growing jaw ache told Kat that she had clenched her teeth hard enough to break them. To curses from the onlookers, Mister Leon introduced her as an Anestran mercenary and spy.

So this was it: where her fate, the rest of her life, would be decided. And she had no say in it whatsoever.

Kat made a vow. She didn't know how, but one day she would get Mister Leon back for this. She promised.

The start of the auction was brisk, to the slave trader's obvious delight. A few poor hopefuls tried their luck, but were soon out-priced. The bids passed three goldens, then four and five. Kat tried to spot the bidders, but found it impossible until only three were left.

One wore the black and crimson uniform of a Lassenite army officer. Another resembled an innkeeper or merchant. Kat found herself hoping they wanted a cleaner, or a server of food and drink, and not a girl to sing or dance.

But the third man worried Kat the most. Tall and cloaked, with hooded face, he was whispering with a balding, portly man in dark blue robes.

The bidding reached six goldens, then eight and ten. Mister Leon seemed in raptures, rubbing his hands in glee. The day's record sale fuelled the crowd's excitement. Twelve goldens, and fifteen, but Kat couldn't tell whether any of the three were bluffing.

At last the officer and merchant hesitated, while the hooded man exuded nothing but confidence. He gave out a clear message: he meant to buy her whatever the cost. Who was he, to be so set on getting her? Kat's heart went cold. He must know something. About who she was. And the other man, in blue, weren't those the robes of a cleric?

The bid of twenty goldens went beyond their pocket and willingness to pay, so the other two withdrew. Mister Leon wore an expression of a lifetime of paydays having come at once. To cheers from around the arena, the slave trader declared the sale.

✳ III ✳

CLERIC

The hooded man, Kat's new master, stepped forward and counted twenty goldens into Mister Leon's greasy palm.

Her scalp prickled: those hands that counted the coins, were they dark-skinned? Her owner's face was hidden as he led her away from the slave market, and the cleric followed behind. To help her walk, the man knelt to untie her leg-bonds. He was missing two fingers from his left hand.

"Jersull!" Kat gasped.

"Quiet, my young slave," he said. She looked at him in alarm, but under his hood there was a twinkle in the Caldunim's dark eyes. Kat was speechless. It was the first time she'd seen him smile. And of all smiles it was the most welcome.

Jersull stood to untie her wrists. "Explanations in good time," he said. "First we should get back to the ship."

He grasped her hand and led her to the north end of the harbour wall. Kat spotted the *Oyster Shell* moored there, and she swept along to it on waves of relief. Jumping stars! If her leg weren't so sore, she'd have skipped along the quayside.

Jersull, Kat and the cleric boarded the ship, and the Captain met them on deck. At last Jersull drew back his hood.

"Captain Farag!" Kat exclaimed, and couldn't refrain from throwing herself at him.

"Now then, young lady." Farag's voice was stern as he extricated himself from her.

Oops. A touch too exuberant there.

He held out a hand and Jersull gave him an empty pouch.

"She cost twenty goldens." Jersull's face was grim.

The Captain stared at him. "But that's more than I gave you."

"The other twelve goldens," said Jersull, "came from Brother Armus here."

For the first time Kat turned and took in the cleric. He had a round, kindly face with sparkling blue eyes. His robes were more dusty and threadbare than any she'd seen in Anestra, and a mace was attached to his belt.

But her elation was fading at their serious faces. Were they not … setting her free?

"I'll pay you back," she said at once. "I haven't got it here, but I promise you the money as soon as we're back in Anestra."

Farag held up a hand to quieten her. He held her eye. "You have this sort of money at home?"

"Yes, I do." Then she added, "Well, my family does." No need to mention how much.

Farag nodded. "I'm a man who keeps his word, Kat. I offered you safe passage, but you had to fight to save our ship. I couldn't leave you with the slavers or whoever might buy you at the market. I accept your promise for when we return to Anestra, and you will sail back south with us in a few days' time. Until you repay my eight goldens, you are under my orders. Is that clear?"

Kat swallowed. She wasn't free. This was her new master. But despite his apparent sternness, she must have got on the right side of him. "Agreed."

She turned to the cleric, and Jersull introduced them.

"Armus, this is Kat," he said, "our passenger who boarded at Anestra. Kat, meet Brother Armus, a cleric of the Divine."

Armus held out a hand, and she took it. "Power of the Divine," she mumbled, remembering to use the appropriate greeting for a cleric.

"And her power to you," said Armus. "I met my old friend Jersull here on the harbour-side as I left the Ilbassi Shrine. He asked for my help, so I accompanied him to the slave market. Glad to be of service."

"Yes, indeed, thank you," said Kat, and chewed her lip. "I will repay you, I promise."

Armus laughed and put a reassuring hand on her shoulder. "Don't worry, young Kat. We try to avoid Anestrans becoming Lassenite slaves, and Jersull reckoned your family wealthy enough to repay us. The Temple needs reimbursement too, but I live here and won't sail to Anestra. I'll send word with Farag for you to give twelve goldens to the Temple. Until then, consider yourself in service to the Divine."

"Yes, of course." Kat risked a tentative smile. "And thank you."

Great. Now she was the property of a merchant Captain and the clerics of the Divine. She'd have to put up with being owned by strangers and given orders again for a while.

"My pleasure," said Armus. "Now, you're bandaged and limping. You're injured."

Kat took a deep breath. "Yes. I need to wash and re-dress the wounds. And I'd be grateful for food and drink too, if that's possible."

Farag smiled. "Of course. All of them." The Captain whistled for his cabin boy.

Armus said, "I'll help you to your cabin, Kat, and let's see what we can do for your wounds."

He supported Kat as she limped to the forecastle. There on her bunk, where she'd flung them two days ago, were her pack and cloak. Beside them were her fallen shortbow and dagger. She sighed with relief, moved her things and sat on the bunk.

With the sure touch of an experienced healer Armus removed her head bandage. He told her the swelling and cut were healing well. Kat took off her right boot, and he peeled away the rags. The muscles were sore, and she winced at the sharpness of the pain as he inspected the wound. Armus knelt and placed his hand over the injury, his touch firm, but gentle. He closed his eyes and bowed his head.

Kat wondered what he was murmuring. Then a tingling warmth flowed into her leg. A thrill ran up her spine and the hairs stood on the back of her neck. After a moment, Armus opened his eyes and removed his hand.

"How does it feel?" he asked.

"Better," she gasped. "The pain's gone. But it still looks the same."

He beamed and stood up. "The skin will take time to heal, but you'll walk on it better now."

"But—but what did you do?"

He held up a finger. "I thought you mentioned the power of the Divine." His eyes twinkled with a mischievous smile as he left the cabin.

Kat sat there stunned. Jumping stars again! She stretched and touched her leg. Armus had the power to heal. She wanted more of that … whatever he had. She'd heard stories of clerics with that kind of magic, so was this part of being in Divine service?

The cabin boy appeared with a tray. He was a scruffy boy, of no more than ten or twelve. He told her, "I'm Moxee. You need anythin' else, just whistle." His grin as he left revealed his missing teeth.

Kat munched the bread (no grubs), cheese and salted ham, and downed the tankard of ale. From her pack she added the last of her biscuits. After the last couple of days, it seemed like a feast.

So what should she do? Could she put the slavers and captivity behind her? Despite how this had turned out,

Mister Leon was not off the hook. Settling the score with him was postponed, not cancelled. But redeemed from the slave market: another point to her.

She whistled and Moxee reappeared. She asked him for water and cloths, and she washed.

Eight days to go. She'd return to Anestra on the *Oyster Shell,* but maybe she could ask her new masters about spending the time in Lasseny checking what she'd heard on the *Sea Snake.*

Kat went out on deck to where Jersull was supervising the hoisting of cargo. He was telling Armus about the slaver attack.

"We fought them off," Jersull said, "but they outran us northwards. They had to be heading for Lasseny, and were docked over there by the slave market. The Captain guessed Kat's fate, and sent me with all the goldens he could spare in order to buy her back."

"So they're ambushing merchant ships again to take captives to sell as slaves." Armus shook his head, and then they turned to her. "Ah, Kat. Jersull is due a night of shore leave, so he and I are going into the city. But you'll be safer if you stay on board."

Kat pulled a face. She wanted to avoid being stuck on a ship again, followed by a few more days on the homeward voyage. She turned to Jersull. "How long is it until we sail back south?"

"We plan for three days here," he replied, "to replace the men who were killed as well as to sell and buy cargo. We aim to be back in Anestra in time for the coronation."

Kat gulped again, that even a Caldunim first mate was interested in her imminent future. She tried to ignore what an event it was in the history of the Western Coast. But this timing would work well. Now, how to get herself off the ship?

"I much prefer solid ground under my feet," she said. "Can't I go with you into the city? I'll be safe enough if we stay together."

She looked to each of the middle-aged men, but they seemed uncertain. Kat tried a smile. "If I promise not to try to run off, will my new masters allow it?"

Armus smiled back. "I suppose we could take you under our wing," he said. "We have to ensure your safety, Kat, for the Captain and Temple to be repaid. But let's ask Farag if he's willing for you to come, so long as you keep with Jersull and me. I know a few Anestrans here, so we could go and try to find them."

Kat beamed. "Thank you. That would be excellent."

"Let's just add it to the list of favours you owe us," said Armus, and his cheerfulness prompted Jersull's second smile.

Captain Farag gave his consent, so while Jersull completed his duties, Kat and Armus watched the harbour. The cleric pointed across the waterfront to the Shrine of Ilbassi. It was a substantial stone building with a colonnade and courtyard in front. Its high dome reflected a dull gleam of afternoon light. Kat shivered, for the building resembled a skull, with the front windows as eye-sockets and the gates as teeth.

"I've a first task for you," said Armus, "as part of your service. I'm due back at the Shrine tomorrow for the trial of initiate Daytose. She's charged with blasphemy, with insulting the cult of Ilbassi. I was coming away from her cell when I met Jersull earlier. She's a good young woman, but it may be too much to hope that Archmage Gaitox will spare her the death sentence. I'd like you to come with me for the trial."

"Of course," said Kat, "although I'm not sure how I can help. But Armus, can I ask you about the mages? When we were ambushed outside Anestra, I saw a crimson light in the slaver chief's eyes. What does that mean?"

Armus narrowed his eyes. "A crimson light?" He shook his head and muttered, "That would be Ilbassi and his mages. But why use their magic to help slavers?"

At last Jersull was finished, and he said to Kat, "You need to be armed. Your bow is useless without arrows, so I've found an old quiver of them for you."

The arrows he handed her were no match for her Anestran ones, but had to be better than none. Kat grabbed her cloak, pack, quiver and shortbow, and said goodbye to young Moxee on deck with a ruffle of his curly black hair.

"Now then, Kat," said Captain Farag. "Until we sail south, I trust Jersull and Armus to look after my property. I expect your Goddess to hold you to your promise. How do you Anestrans call her, 'the Divine'?"

Kat nodded. "Thank you for your help, Captain. I promise by the Divine to stay with them until we return." Then she added, "And I'll try to be obedient property."

Farag smiled, and they descended from the ship.

That afternoon, Princess Rashelin decided on something. She headed through a bustling Anestra Castle towards her mother's dressing room. The largest window in this small room faced west to let in the afternoon light.

Consort Sirika was sitting at her mirror and scolding a servant girl over the mess of her hair. To Rashelin the styling was immaculate, but something still fell short of the perfection required by her mother for the evening's banquet.

"Mother, may I speak with you alone?" Rashelin smiled at the servant girl, whose anguished face glanced towards the tyrant at the dressing table. As soon as the Consort nodded, the girl couldn't leave the room fast enough.

Sirika had lined up her brushes, combs and clips in a perfect row on the table. She was touching strands into place as Rashelin said, "Let me ride to Lasseny to look for Katelin."

Sirika jerked around from the mirror. "No, you will not. It's catastrophic enough that your cousin is missing, without sending you away up the highway too."

"But it'll be days before the ship or rider return with any news," Rashelin pressed. "Is there nothing more we can do but to wait and hope that she'll reappear?"

"Nothing," Sirika stated. "We haven't the time. The ship and scout will get there and back in the next eight days, but not have time to complete a search. That girl could be anywhere. It's her responsibility to get herself back here for the coronation. We have other problems."

Rashelin scanned her mother's face. "What is it?"

Sirika scowled. "We can no longer say that the girl is unwell. The servants know it isn't true, and that she isn't here. Besides, the closer we get to the coronation, people will worry that she'll be ill for it."

Rashelin frowned and drummed her fingers on her arms. "We need a different story, another explanation. If Katelin were away, where would she go? Mannismill? And for some sort of … pre-coronation … retreat?"

Sirika pulled a face, but nodded. "She hates Mannismill, but that will have to do. And we've still got to pack up these apartments." She sniffed. "Much though I detest it."

"I'll help with that, Mother. Is there anything else I can do?"

Sirika considered her. "Yes, my dear, there is. If that girl is away, rather than unwell, then you will stand in for her at the events of the next few days—receptions, speeches, that sort of thing. Make it appear that all of this is planned."

Rashelin stared back. It was as though her mother were punishing her for Katelin's disappearance. Sirika knew how much she hated to be up front, making speeches to the whole Court. Rashelin felt that she worked best behind the scenes, talking with one or two courtiers at once. So please, no, not to be the stand-in for Katelin in the days before the coronation.

But did she have much choice? And would this help to prepare the way for Katelin to ascend to the throne?

Rashelin bit her lip, and then, "Yes, I will do that," she said.

Kat had seen from the *Oyster Shell*'s deck how the Duke's Palace dominated Lasseny. It was an opulent complex on the hill behind the port, and separated from the city by a high wall. The Duke's residence had the only greenery, tall buildings and space around it, and his black flag with a crimson star fluttered from tower and turret. Otherwise the city was slums: packed-in shacks and hovels of wood, with only a few larger buildings of brick—the markets, taverns, inns and gambling houses.

Armus and Jersull strode through the throngs and away from the harbour, with no apparent fear. Kat tried to match their confidence, but kept up the hood of her cloak. Many in Lasseny, in contrast with Anestra, bore visible arms or armour. Jersull had his scimitar, Armus his mace, and Kat's hands sought the reassurance of her dagger and shortbow.

On closer view the shacks and hovels were decrepit shelters, and the smell didn't improve with proximity. Many dwellings were propped up planks and boards of wood, held together with mud and rope. The brick buildings and shops had cracked and poorly repaired walls, with broken glass in the windows and vain attempts to seal holes in the roofs. Refuse and filth were everywhere.

"I'm staying now at the Treasure Trove," said Armus, "an inn on the desert road. We might find some of my friends there. Jersull, the last time you were here, weren't we at the

Lost Temper, up near the Palace wall? Well, it became too lively for my taste." He turned to Kat and added, "It was hard to meditate in my room with bar fights and drinking songs to all hours downstairs."

"Hey, Caldo!" A mocking shout came from a side street they'd just passed. Kat couldn't believe it: it was so long since she'd heard that racist name used to insult a Caldunim.

"Ignore it and keep walking," said Jersull.

They did so, but five ruffians chased after them. One called out, "And what's this, an Anestran holy man?" Armus said nothing.

"What's the matter, Caldo?" another jeered. "Looking for trees to swing through?" They broke into hilarious laughter. Jersull didn't react. Then one of them picked on Kat and snatched back her hood.

"Look what we have here," the ruffian said to the others. "They've got theirselves a girlfriend." An ugly, unshaven face leered at her.

"Don't you dare touch me," Kat spat at him. Her hand moved to the dagger at her belt.

"Hey, boys!" he said. "We like 'em with spirit, don't we?"

"Leave her alone," Jersull hissed, and grasped the hilt of his scimitar. Armus unclipped and fingered his mace.

"Ooh," the ruffian taunted. "Want to fight for her, eh?" Three of them drew out long knives. "Perhaps we'll take her off your hands." He gave Kat a mocking bow.

Then he grabbed at her. She ducked beneath his lunge. She flicked out her dagger and stabbed it into his thigh. Jersull swept out his scimitar and slashed at two of those with knives. Armus's mace parried a ruffian's thrust, and the force of the blow sent the knife flying across the street. Three ruffians went down, clutching leg, arm and chest.

The other two ran off down the hill. Jersull and Armus

ushered Kat away before soldiers arrived, as a larger crowd gathered at the scene.

"Well done, Kat," Armus breathed as they hurried up the hill. "A first lesson learned on self-preservation in Lasseny. Still want to come into the city?"

"We're safe enough, if we stay together," Kat replied, and Armus smiled.

Now she understood why Jersull had stayed hooded at the slave market. To avoid any further attention, she replaced the hood over her face. Oh, and another point to her.

MERCENARIES

They slowed to a trudge up the street and approached the central market. "Excuse me puffing and panting," said Armus, "but I need a gentler pace when going uphill."

"Don't worry," said Kat. "I was appreciating how much better my leg feels."

"Ah, yes. The Divine's been generous to you."

"So if you're Anestran, why do you live here?"

"I was born in Anestra and trained at the Temple," said Armus. "But for years I've worked in Lasseny and elsewhere. There's little point us clerics teaching only Anestrans, when there are those without faith in the rest of the Coast, eh, Jersull?" He said this with a teasing grin.

The southerner was quick to explain. "Brother Armus was kind enough to teach me about faith in the Divine during voyages we shared to the Caldunate." Kat smiled that Jersull managed to say this without revealing what he thought of the teaching.

The stallholders of the central market were packing away as afternoon turned to evening, and the three of them made their way south-eastwards on the road towards the desert. Armus and Jersull talked of mutual acquaintances, and Kat's gaze wandered to the buildings they passed: the Pride and Fall Tavern; a gambling house called Lucky You; and places with blacked-out windows whose purpose she didn't want to guess. She remembered the ruffians and slave market, and hurried to keep up with the men.

The sun was setting when they arrived at an inn set back from the road with a small sign: the Treasure Trove. It was a plain, brick building of two storeys, old-fashioned but well-maintained. Armus explained that the landlord, Vasimic, wanted only reputable guests, and took no one as lodger unless someone he knew introduced them.

With Armus already resident, Jersull and Kat secured rooms for themselves from the long-faced old landlord. The small bedrooms had white-plastered walls, and the basic furniture was sturdy and clean.

Kat liked it as her base for two or three nights. She removed some things from her pack and inspected her leg. She'd walked across the city on it, but it remained pain-free. In the morning Jersull would return to his ship, and she and Armus had that trial to attend at the Ilbassi Shrine. Maybe she'd learn more about the Ilbassi mages there. Should she ask her new friends about Duke Bassikrin of Lasseny?

Kat came downstairs to the common room, which had a low, beamed ceiling and the same white-plastered walls. Plain wooden tables and chairs were scattered across polished floorboards. A small log fire smouldered in the hearth and oil lamps burned on the occupied tables. A dozen people sat drinking and eating, as the evening customers came in.

Kat saw that Armus and Jersull were sitting with two strangers at a table in a corner. She appraised them as she approached.

The man looked like a mercenary: his leather jerkin revealed muscular arms, and a long sword hung from his belt. On closer view, his square-jawed face had an ugly scar across the forehead, but he made no effort to hide it with his dark brown hair. His hands were pitted and cracked, and his eyes the colour of conkers. He sat back with confidence, as though he owned the room.

The woman was barbarian, with the unmistakeable short white hair of her northern people. She looked a touch older than Kat, and was taller, more athletic. Her skimpy tunic left her long legs bare. Her grey eyes were small and narrowed, as if against a cold wind, or else in constant judgement. Either way, her expression was unreadable. A tattoo of a wolf on her shoulder made Kat think of her as a hunter who was at present astray from her pack.

As Kat joined them, Armus introduced the strangers as friends of his. The mercenary was Hedger, an Anestran and worshipper of the Divine. The barbarian woman was Sigzay.

Armus poured Kat a tankard of ale from their jug. He told her how the Treasure Trove was Vasimic's family business, with his wife as cook and his daughter to clean and serve. That way, he joked, the grasping old landlord didn't need to pay any wages. For an evening meal, he suggested the mutton stew, for although the meat might be tough, it was edible, filling and hot. They ordered five helpings of this, with bread and flagons of ale. To Kat the ale tasted bitter and strong, and when the bread came, it was grey, heavy, flat and in squares.

"So, Kat," Armus began, with twinkling eyes, "Jersull tells us you're a spoilt young lady from a rich Anestran family who has run away from home."

Kat drew a deep breath. Which explanation to give them? Best to continue with Jersull's impression. "Well, yes," she said, "I have run away from home. I suppose that my family are far from poor, but I wouldn't agree that I'm spoilt."

"What made you buy passage to Lasseny?" Jersull asked, in between chews of his bread.

What could she say? "Oh, I want to make the most out of life," said Kat, "to meet new people and see different places.

You wouldn't have me sit inside Anestra all my days, when you've sailed the seas and travelled distant lands?"

"What was it about home that made you run away?" Armus asked.

This wasn't the whole truth, but it was the simplest explanation. "My Aunt and Uncle," Kat sighed, "and the restrictions of life at home. With them, everything *has* to be done as it always has been. They've no sense of adventure, and lay down all sorts of rules on how I ought to behave. They don't understand me, or what's important to me."

"Your Aunt and Uncle?" said Jersull. "They look after you?"

"They try to," admitted Kat. "My parents and brother died in the Crown War when I was only two, so I don't remember them. My Aunt and Uncle brought me up."

Armus was nodding. "Yours are common complaints of the young against those who bring them up. But as you've found out, a sense of adventure can be dangerous, and land you in plenty of trouble."

"We're safe enough," Kat repeated, "if we stay together."

"I take your point," said Armus with a laugh. "So your sense of adventure has led you here, in pursuit of 'what's important to you'. Can we ask what that is?"

Kat hesitated. Could she trust these strangers? She wanted to, and they might be able to help her. "I love Anestra," she said, "and have learned how it was in the Old Kingdom's heyday. My last few days have shown that it isn't safe to sail the Ocean or walk the streets of Lasseny. I wish there were peace for all on this Coast, with a chance for safety, work and happiness. You can call me a dreamer, idealistic, naive … but that's how I see it, and I want to do what I can to achieve it." She took a mouthful of stew, and hoped that she hadn't sounded too childish.

"You can dream how you like, young Kat," said Armus, "and well said. I wish the Coast had more young people like you."

Sigzay spoke with the accent of her tribe. "If we correct wrongs of Coast, do not forget desert highway. Road to Anestra is full of bandits, and soon there is no safe travel between cities."

"I share your wish that things were better in Anestra, Kat," said Hedger. "Since the Crown War, Lasseny is ascendant and Anestra's in decline. I wouldn't call that a healthy state of affairs."

"How do people in Anestra view Regent Ethabos?" Armus asked Kat.

Oh dear. What could she tell them? "Well, you'll know that the Regent and Consort aren't everyone's favourite people—"

Sigzay jumped in. "I hear Regent is selfish and lazy ruler of your city. No one has hope if next war comes. Is he not in secret league with Lasseny Duke?"

Kat frowned as she chewed. She tried to think how she would describe the uneasy truce on the Coast, but Armus answered for her.

"I wouldn't say 'in league'," he said, "but it's true that over the years the Regent has appeased the Duke."

Yes, her Aunt and Uncle did all that they could to avoid another war with Lasseny, most often by allowing Duke Bassikrin to do whatever he demanded.

As they ate, Kat couldn't help watching how Hedger and Sigzay were together, their looks, smiles, touches. Sigzay had a body that men would find desirable and she wasn't shy about flaunting it; Hedger had his own charisma and impressive physique. Their affection was attractive, and Kat found her heart yearning for something like that.

Her wandering thoughts came back to the conversation.

Maybe it was time to find out what she could. "So tell me about Duke Bassikrin. What do the people of Lasseny think of him?"

"Hush," Sigzay hissed. "Keep voice down, Kat. We are in public place." They looked around, but couldn't tell if anyone had heard her. "You must know that Duke has spies."

Hedger held up a hand, and his voice was low. "Careful, Kat. If you want an answer to that one, we should continue our conversation upstairs."

The others nodded, and they finished their mutton stew in silence. With the smoke of lamp and fire, the air in the Treasure Trove common room thickened. They ordered more drinks to take with them, and heads turned as they trooped out of the common room. Kat now felt that too many eyes were following them.

They escaped up to Armus's room, as he had the largest accommodation. They sat on his bed and chairs, and Armus told Kat about the aged Duke Bassikrin.

"He's ruled Lasseny for decades," the cleric said. "In victory, defeat, prosperity and disaster his grip on power never lessens. He taxes at extortionate levels every possible source of income, all to maintain his Palace and the means of political control."

"As well as the Lassenite army," said Hedger, "he uses numerous spies. He roots out dissent from among his 'loyal' subjects, and employs bands of thugs to perform his unsavoury business."

Sigzay joined the assassination of character. "Now Duke Bassikrin trains his son, Count Bassilius, in ways of tyrant and villain. So Lasseny misrule is as Duke wishes for next generation at least."

"It's illegal here to make negative reference to the benevolent rule of the Duke," said Armus. "Unpleasant things happen to those who suggest that the Duke and his son aren't the most wise and generous of rulers."

Kat decided it was time to recount what she'd heard on the *Sea Snake*. She told them the slaver rumours: that the Duke had ordered them to pillage Anestran ships, and about his mage and barbarian allies. She didn't mention the Crown yet, as she had the beginnings of a plan about that.

After this, Hedger got up and opened the door to check that the landing was empty. Kat was startled: did the Duke employ people to listen at doors and windows, or even through walls?

Hedger sat and said, "I fear that we have to confirm all that Kat has overheard. Sigzay and I returned today from the Ironbore Hills on Lasseny's north-eastern border, and up there we noticed only a few soldiers around. Locals told us that the normal garrisons have been recalled to Lasseny city."

Armus frowned. "That weakens the Duke's border against the barbarians and the Autarch of Unta."

"Yes, it does," said Hedger. "If the Autarch, or Ravag Bloodaxe, or any barbarian chieftain, chose now to raid into Lasseny, they would find an easy time of it."

"So what is the Duke up to?" said Armus. "What can he be thinking?"

"He must have reach agreement," said Sigzay. "It is never heard of: peace treaty with Ravag, or any leader of my people."

Armus shook his head. "Even with a treaty, he wouldn't withdraw his troops. The Duke trusts no-one."

"You're right," said Hedger. "So it leaves a worrying conclusion: he needs those soldiers somewhere else. The Duke depletes his north-eastern forces, and which other way can he send them? It has to be south—and that means Anestra."

The blood drained from Kat's face and her hand flew to her mouth. "What? The Duke musters to attack Anestra? We must warn—"

"Hush, Kat," Sigzay hissed again. "We don't know that."

Kat swallowed, trying to calm her panic. She glanced at the door and window in fear of having been heard.

"Anyway," Hedger went on, "an attack may not be imminent. It'll take them a while to re-assign troops. Whatever we can learn, we've a few days' head start on their army."

"A few days?" spluttered Kat.

"Calm down," said Hedger, "and think about this, Kat. We don't have proof of an invasion, as these are only our suspicions. Soldiers move around all the time. These may be normal troop movements by the Duke, or he may have something else in mind. But it's best that we're aware and cautious."

"Beside," said Sigzay, "say is true and we rush to Anestra: who believes us, warning them? Why they listen to us, a bunch of mercenaries and report of invasions? They not let us speak to Regent or other in charge there anyway."

Kat nodded. Her Aunt and Uncle, and all of Anestra, would soon have to listen to her, but how could she mobilise her people? The Crown, she thought. But tonight she needed to think and then ask the others about it in the morning.

Now she remembered her plan before leaving Anestra to confront Duke Bassikrin over what he knew of her Crown. This was not a good idea. He sounded more inclined to imprison her than anything else.

A knock on the door was the innkeeper's daughter bringing them more ale. It took Kat some time but at last, relaxed by the chatter and ale, she found herself smiling again.

There might be a way to save Anestra. And in the meantime, she was in a Lassenite inn, in the company of a Caldunim, a cleric, a barbarian and a mercenary. Not to mention that she was in debt and service to a couple of them. What would her Aunt and Uncle think of this? Throwing a fit wouldn't begin to describe it.

That was a cheering thought. She tried to relish the freedom of this little adventure, and the new company that she'd found. Thinking of home, hadn't she missed a writing lesson? Perhaps she could make up for it now. She composed and memorised some lines of a ditty. The others noticed her distracted concentration, and persuaded her to sing it for them, to a nursery rhyme tune:

> *Oh, this fine old Lasseny city,*
> *There ain't none here to pity,*
> *We're all so swell,*
> *And there ain't no smell*
> *In fine old Lasseny city.*

> *Oh, the grand old Lasseny Duke,*
> *He won't take no rebuke;*
> *We think it funny,*
> *He wants our money,*
> *That grand old Lasseny Duke.*

> *Oh, they call me ever so pretty,*
> *But more than that—I'm witty;*
> *And all I've done*
> *Is have some fun*
> *In fine old Lasseny city.*

The others gave nervous laughs. Kat encouraged them to add further verses, but Armus conceded that none of them had her talent for spontaneous, mischievous poetry. The evening ended as Kat proposed a sarcastic toast: to the good health, and long and wise rule of the Duke and Count of Lasseny.

It was only later, as Kat tried to get to sleep, that the

chilling thoughts resurfaced. The ale had lowered her guard, and she'd been too caught up with her cleverness tonight. This wasn't Anestra. She had to be more careful about someone overhearing her.

✷ V ✷

QUEST

Last night's conspirators re-assembled for a late breakfast in Armus's room. The inn offered them watery porridge (which Kat thought too salty), more grey, heavy bread squares, and cold meats of uncertain origin. Sigzay brewed a blend of herb tea that she claimed would invigorate their morning grogginess. After a few tentative sips, Kat was amazed at how well it worked.

Before Jersull left for the *Oyster Shell*, he committed Kat to Armus's supervision. The cleric undertook to deliver her to the ship for the southbound voyage in two days' time.

It was seven days now until Kat had to be back in Anestra. She summoned her courage and tried to ignore her butterfly stomach. She wanted their help, and had to ask. With Jersull gone, all she needed to do was to cut through Armus's chatter ... and say it.

At a slight pause in the conversation, Kat drew a deep breath. "I've been thinking about what we said last night, of a possible threat to Anestra. I have two days here, and would like to ask you about doing something worthwhile for our city and Kingdom."

Armus, Hedger and Sigzay looked at each other, and then back at Kat. "Now you've intrigued us," Armus said. "You have something in mind to suggest?"

Their eyes were fixed on her. Kat felt the blood rise to her cheeks but couldn't stop now. "I've thought for a while how it doesn't look good if it comes to another war. I was hoping that those who love our city might help our Kingdom to defend itself."

"I'm sure that all of us love Anestra, as you say," said Armus. "But to shift the balance of power on the Coast sounds quite something for the four of us to accomplish. You know of some miracle to achieve this?"

There was no going back. "Yes," Kat whispered. Nerves had stolen her voice. "The Crown."

The stunned silence lasted only long enough for Kat to clear her throat. Then Sigzay burst out laughing. "The Crown? You silly girl! Not hoping much then? You want us four to find lost Anestra Crown?"

"Wait a minute, Sigzay," Armus said. "What do you mean, Kat? You think the Crown is in Lasseny?"

Kat plunged in, refusing to be put off by Sigzay's reaction. "Yes, I mean the Crown of Anestra. If anything can restore the fortunes of Anestra, then recovering the Crown would be part of it."

"Yes, it would," said Armus, "but the Crown has been sought for years. Do you know something more than the rest of us?"

"She knows nothing," Sigzay scoffed. "It is childish fantasy. If news of Crown comes to light, you think runaway girl discovers it?"

"Sigzay, let Kat speak," Armus said again. "We should keep an open mind to all possibilities. Something may be known in Anestra that hasn't reached our ears. So, young lady, what can you tell us?"

Kat turned to face Armus and Hedger. She drew a deep breath. "You know that the Crown was broken and lost fifteen years ago at the death of King Etharan in the last war with Lasseny. I didn't say it last night, but on the slaver ship I overheard that the Duke has the Crown. He can't have all of it, because one part is in the Anestran Royal Treasury. But at home I heard that Duke Bassikrin is the one person who knows what happened at the death of the King, how the Crown was broken, and where the rest of it is."

Hedger spoke up. "One part of the Crown is in the Anestran Royal Treasury? Are you sure about that?"

"Yes, I've seen it," said Kat. Then realised that they'd wonder how she'd done this, so she added, "On rare occasions they open the Treasury to visitors."

"This piece in the Treasury," said Hedger. "How big is it? What fraction of the whole?"

"About a third," said Kat. "So I want to ask you, in your travels and from your local contacts, what you've heard about the Crown. How much of it is here?"

Armus and Hedger looked at each other and shook their heads. "I think you know more than we do," said Hedger.

"So," said Kat, "two thirds of it may be in Lasseny, or some portion is elsewhere. If we find out what the Duke has, then we'll know whether we need to look anywhere else."

"That's easier to say than to do," said Armus. "Anything this precious will be behind locks and guards inside the Duke's Palace. That place is a fortress. And *he* doesn't offer tours of his treasury," he added with a grim smile.

Hedger turned to Sigzay. "Who do we know who works inside the Palace?"

She didn't answer him. "This is pointless discussion," Sigzay said. "Never will you discover what fraction is inside Palace, or get to see it. Perhaps you think to break into fortress and steal it? Or to knock on Duke's door and ask very nice for your Crown back as generous goodwill gesture?"

"I don't know what we might try," said Kat. "That's why I'm asking for your help and information. Because we need to do something. The coronation is soon, and Anestra needs every possible part and power of the Crown."

"You're right," said Armus. "Young Princess Katelin becomes Queen. So much depends on her, and she needs all the help we can give her." Kat swallowed hard at the way Armus talked about her. If only he knew who sat before him ...

Armus turned to Hedger. "A quest to restore the lost and broken Crown. What do you say to that, Brother Hedger, to helping our new, young Queen?"

Hedger had a faraway look. Kat found herself praying that he'd go for it and join her in this. Perhaps the best she could achieve in a couple of days was to mobilise others in the quest for her Crown.

The light in Hedger's eyes broke into a smile. "Well, I'm not one to turn down a challenge ... or a handsome reward. Does our well-filled Anestran Treasury still offer that generous bounty for the Crown? Or is our only reward the Kingdom's future and glory?"

"The reward still stands," said Kat. "One thousand goldens, if that motivates you to seek this."

"I won't say if reward or the good of Anestra is first in my thoughts," said Hedger. "But we ought to know the whole picture. I'm sorry, Sigzay, but I'm more with Kat than with you on this. We should find out what we can, and not sit here and say that nothing can be done."

Yes! Thank him!

"Fine," Sigzay said. The barbarian's face was one big scowl at being outnumbered in the discussion. "You try what you like, but Crown is superstition and nonsense. Some say it has magic but I believe not at all."

"The Crown," spluttered Armus in indignation, "is not superstition or nonsense! I know some call it magic, but it's our ancient, sacred relic. It shines with Divine glory for the ruler of Anestra, and even the smallest part gives unrivalled spiritual power."

"That's right." Hedger was on the edge of his seat. "And it's such a potent symbol. As well as the powers, the people believe in the Crown. Remember the saying: with a Crowned King, the city will never fall. So Kat's right. There's nothing better to unite and inspire our people than the Crown."

"So how long you got?" said Sigzay. "How long to this Crowning of your new, young Queen? How quick you need to find anything?"

Kat wasn't about to volunteer that she'd been counting the days.

Armus looked to be calculating. "It must be about a week."

Kat nodded. "I realise that this might take time, so the sooner we begin, the better. What's our first move?" She smiled at Armus. "If my master agrees, on our way to the Ilbassi Shrine, can we look at this impregnable fortress of the Duke of Lasseny's Palace?"

Captain Norbil of the Lassenite army strode across the Palace grounds towards the Duke's Hall. Poplars and cedars cast welcome shade, and the lawns and bushes had been trimmed into bizarre patterns and shapes. Exotic flowers clustered in every corner. Norbil found inspecting the gardens an excellent means of distraction. Better than dwelling on nerves or dread ... or how his report would displease his lord.

His boots echoed in the bare entrance corridor, and he drew a deep breath before the Hall's lacquered doors. He checked the straightness of his uniform, and smoothed down his hair and moustache. He nodded to the wardens, who opened the doors, and he marched in.

His eyes took time to adjust from the sunshine outside.

The bricked-up windows robbed the Hall of daylight, and gloomy lamps hung from chains that ran the length of the roof. Crimson velvet curtains darkened the space further, and the air had a whiff of staleness. Norbil started across the floorboards that were painted in stripes and swirls in dizzying patterns from side to side and corner to corner, and navigated past the large black rugs and animal skins.

He approached Lasseny's other marvel: the ancient Duke Bassikrin, perched on a lime green throne. He was still alive then. Still keeping going through strength of will and a thirst for power, determined to endure until at last his son replaced him.

The Duke's unblinking, calculating black eyes drew him in. The face was stern and wrinkled, amid untidy grey hair and straggling beard. The lord of Lasseny would be tall if he stood, but these days it was only the armour that held his decrepit body upright. He never sat back in his throne, or looked comfortable or relaxed. He stroked a large white ferret that lay curled on a cushion in his lap.

The Duke's masterful son, Count Bassilius, stood to one side of the throne. The Count was heavily built, with a handsome face and well-trimmed hair and beard. He regarded the Captain with the same unblinking black eyes as his father. A huddle of messengers and spies fidgeted in the corner of the Hall.

"Report," barked the Duke, with no hint in his voice of the weakening that comes with age.

Captain Norbil saluted and cleared his throat. "My lord," he began, "the monks … would tell us nothing—"

"Nothing?" roared the Duke. "You mean they didn't say a word, or they said they didn't have it, or they didn't say they had it?"

Norbil swallowed, struggling to grasp the question's

alternatives. "They wouldn't confirm or deny anything, my lord. They … didn't say they had it," he decided on at last.

"But what about you, Captain? Do you think they have it?"

Norbil scrambled through the possible answers. He settled on, "I think … they c-could have it, my lord."

"Excellent!" said the Duke. "They won't tell us they have it, and they won't give it to us. So what should we do then, Captain?"

"We should … take it from them, my lord?"

"I should think so!" Duke Bassikrin waved Captain Norbil away and he stepped aside with relief. The old despot stroked his ferret while all waited for his decision and instruction.

"Bassilius," he said at last.

"Yes, Father?"

"Take a battalion and go to our friends the monks again. Search the place, and bring back whatever of our little prize you can find."

"And the monks?" said Count Bassilius. "What if they object?"

"Well, let me see." The Duke creased his face to reveal stained, broken teeth. It could have been a smile. "Remind me, my son, what we do for withholding information and resisting my orders?"

Bassilius grinned. He gave a sudden twitch, an involuntary flexing of the neck. "Execution?"

"Indeed. Set off at once. The days press upon us until that wretched girl's Crowning. It's time to put our plans into motion."

"And the slave traders?"

"Ah yes, the slavers," said the Duke. He clicked his fingers. The ferret raised its head, and a messenger hurried forward.

"Go to the harbour and speak to that slave trader. Pass on the order that the time has come. He'll know what to do."

Kat, Armus, Hedger and Sigzay walked in the late morning sunshine from the Treasure Trove to the centre of Lasseny. Armus had agreed to go to the Shrine of Ilbassi by way of the Duke's Palace. Kat guessed that Sigzay had come along to say 'I told you so' when she conceded the impossibility of breaking into the fortress.

They approached the Palace walls and Kat's heart sank. She'd seen the place before, but never with an eye to infiltrating it. Even her climbing skills were no match for this. The blocks of stone were set so that no toe or finger-holds remained. The topmost parapet overhung the sheer walls, so the climb would be perilous even with a rope. And before reaching the wall, there was the tiny inconvenience of a deep, muddy ditch.

Then Kat saw the gatehouse. The checkpoints, barricades, gates, drawbridge and portcullis bristled with soldiers in black and crimson uniforms. Kat took a guess: did the Duke prize his security and privacy? So maybe their best chance for information was to bribe someone known to Hedger and Sigzay who worked inside.

Sigzay's smugness was annoying and predictable. But Hedger indicated that the Palace gatehouse was no place in which to loiter. Before they could feign nonchalance and saunter away, an officer called out, "You four, stop where you are!"

They stopped and the officer approached, a squad of soldiers behind him. "What do you think you're doing here?"

Armus smiled. "We're sorry to have bothered you, sir. My friends wanted to see the Duke's magnificent Palace. I hope that isn't a problem."

The officer's eyes narrowed. "You're Anestrans, aren't you?" Armus's cleric robes had given that much away. "I should arrest you as spies and take you in to be questioned."

Oh no. That would get them inside the Palace, but Kat couldn't let herself be questioned. Someone would recognise her. She edged away.

"You could do that, sir," said Armus, "but I ought to inform you that I'm due for an appointment soon with Archmage Gaitox at the Shrine. If you detain us, you need to send word to the Archmage to explain why I'm delayed." Armus's smile now hid a touch of steel. You tell him, master.

From the Palace there came a sudden braying of horns. The officer looked as startled as they were. Had the alert sounded because of them? Should they run for it? But no mass of guards approached. And there was cheering at the gatehouse.

The officer became curt. "I've more important things to do. Clear off, and don't let me catch you here again."

They started away, Kat's relief mixed with morbid fascination. Over her shoulder, she couldn't ignore the increasing commotion behind them. The guards raised the portcullis, lowered the drawbridge and opened the series of gates. Someone was coming out. Armus and Hedger confirmed the banners of the bodyguards, but Kat knew them as well: Count Bassilius.

Kat's stomach clenched. They tried to move aside, but leaving the scene was impossible. At the call of the horns, Lassenites were gathering from every hovel and alleyway. For their lord-in-waiting, they lined the road and cheered in wild excitement.

Kat stood amazed at this apparent devotion for the Count: waving, shouting, whistling; the banging of pans and implements—all with the greatest volume and gusto. Anyone would think the Duke's agents were there to note any lack of enthusiasm in greeting his son. She peered around. Was that ... true?

The procession approached. Hedger bawled in her ear, "What do you think of the welcome for their rulers?" Kat shook her head and drew up her hood.

Hedger could pass for a devoted Lassenite; he cheered and whooped with the best of them. But Armus stuck out in his cleric robes, and Sigzay and Kat wouldn't join in. Sigzay folded her arms and Kat hid behind Hedger.

Behind the lines of banners, trumpeters and bodyguards, Count Bassilius rode a grey stallion and acknowledged the adulation of the crowd.

Kat stared from under her hood as the Count's eyes rested on Armus and Sigzay, and then on Hedger. Bassilius scowled. That the cleric was Anestran, and Sigzay barbarian, was clear. But did the Count recognise Hedger's distinctive scarred forehead, or see the insolence and derision in the mercenary's eyes? Kat couldn't have been more desperate for them all to show no disrespect.

Bassilius rode on to more adoring subjects.

That had been close. The crowd moved on and began to disperse, so Hedger stopped his phoney devotion. He turned and saw Kat standing behind him. She drew back her hood, smiled and stepped away.

Hedger had noticed her hidden close behind him in the crowd. And there was something in the way that he looked at her.

✶ VI ✶

ARCHMAGE

Hedger frowned. "They're more twitchy than usual around here," he said. "We should follow Count Bassilius. See where he's going and what he's doing."

Armus nodded. "I agree, but Kat and I are due at the Shrine. Can the two of you do that?"

"Yes, Sigzay and I will follow him. If he goes to the main army barracks then we'll discover what's happening there."

"Do be careful," said Armus. "If our suspicions are correct, then they won't like Anestrans snooping around."

"Don't worry, Brother, we'll be discreet," said Hedger. "Remember that I'm well known here; few would dare to trouble us. Have fun with the mages—not my favourite people at the best of times."

"I'm sure we will," said Armus, with a grim smile. "Can we meet on the waterfront later, outside the Shrine?"

Hedger nodded and set off with Sigzay, as Armus and Kat left for the Shrine.

It couldn't have been easier to follow Count Bassilius. They could have closed their eyes and followed the trumpets and cheering.

As they went, Hedger glanced at Sigzay. "What do you make of young Kat?"

He could feel the sharpness back from her. "She is foolish dreamer," Sigzay said. "Scrawny. Ugly."

Hedger grinned. "Only compared to some. Yes, idealistic

and naive, but I don't hold that against her. I think she's hiding something."

"Hiding what?"

"I'm not sure. She could be a spy for the Duke, perhaps, but they said she arrived here on a slaver ship. I think it strange that a slave should know about the Crown of Anestra."

"You say we not trust her?"

"More that we should listen and watch. I guess she's no more than a wayward daughter of an Anestran noble family."

Sigzay snorted. "Then she deserves slavers catching her."

"But she has courage, and the luck of the Divine that it turned out as it did."

As Hedger had suspected, the procession wound its way to the southwest of the city, and to Lasseny's main army barracks. The crowds parted to allow the Count, his bodyguards and entourage to enter through the compound gates, and then they began to disperse.

Hedger and Sigzay stopped a short distance away. A rough wooden fence separated them from a dusty square of ground that served as an exercise yard. The square had a ramshackle collection of buildings on three sides, but they'd never seen it so busy.

Swarms of Lassenite soldiers milled around the carts and wagons that half filled the yard. They were loading them with sacks and crates from storehouses. A steady stream of empty vehicles was entering the compound, and then driving off full towards the desert gate.

Hedger felt a chill of realising dread. His fears had become true, but he had to hide them. "Time to confirm what's going on," he murmured. "I see someone we know."

He started towards the compound gates, and approached a muscular, grizzled man supervising the passage of the vehicles. He had a shaven, misshaped head, and his bare arms and face were riddled with scars.

"Hedger the Sword!" the man cried, on catching sight of them. He abandoned to others the supervision of the carts, and clasped forearms with Hedger.

Hedger smiled at the mercenary nickname they'd given him, originating as a joke on his name, that he lived by the 'edge of the sword'.

"Sergeant Xaftab," Hedger replied. "It's good to see your ugly face still attached to your neck."

Xaftab's grin was indeed ugly. He turned to Sigzay. "And the charming, terrifying Sigzay. You still keeping this young man in order?"

"You ask what is impossible, Sergeant X," said Sigzay.

Xaftab moved to shake hands, but lunged to grab her wrist. Sigzay was quicker, evaded his grasp and jerked her knee into his stomach. Xaftab doubled over, but held her leg. They crashed sideways to the ground.

Hedger stepped back and folded his arms to watch. He chuckled: no matter how often they repeated this contest, it always ended the same way.

They rolled and scuffled in the dust until Sigzay twisted and emerged on top, her shin across Xaftab's throat.

"Submit," the Sergeant gasped. They got up, dusting themselves down. "Good to see you're staying sharp, my girl," Xaftab said, rubbing his stomach and neck. "Won't go so easy on you next time."

Sigzay scoffed, and Hedger said, "If I were you, Sergeant X, I'd wrestle with someone else. That's if you value your bones and joints staying intact."

He motioned them a few steps towards the fence. He nodded towards the compound, and murmured, "I see you're keeping busy. Something we should know about?"

Xaftab narrowed his eyes, but smiled. "You should come with us, my friends. Plenty of work for such as you. And the Duke's paying more than usual."

Hedger raised an eyebrow. "Depends on where you're going."

Xaftab gave a knowing nod. "Can't give details," he sniffed. "But we start from the desert gate and highway."

"You remember I'm Anestran born?" said Hedger. "You ask for my sword against my countrymen?"

"Ah, now," Xaftab said, "that amounts to choosing to win or to lose. But I'd rather have the two of you beside me than against."

Hedger and Sigzay exchanged a look. "We'll consider it," said Hedger.

Xaftab stepped backwards. "Choose with haste," he said. "We leave tomorrow." The Sergeant turned and lumbered toward the carts at the gate.

Armus and Kat threaded their way through the stalls of the central market and started down the hill towards the harbour.

Kat noticed a mixture of responses from the Lassenites towards Brother Armus. Some glared at his robes that identified him as Anestran and a cleric of the Divine. But others nodded, stepped aside for him, greeted him with respect. Maybe these knew of his work and power as a healer, which had earned him the beginnings of affection. Kat decided that she liked him too: a man with more important things on his mind than appearances, with his shabby, frayed robes.

The buildings became more derelict as they descended the hill, and they could hear the uproar of the harbour. Kat's nose had grown used to the city's rich fragrance, as she began to smell fish and the sea.

"You told me to come with you for this trial," Kat said as they walked, "but I'm not sure how I can help."

"Of course you can help," said Armus. His smile was all encouragement. "During the proceedings you can offer secret prayer to the Divine for us."

Kat gulped. How could she offer prayer for them? She wouldn't know what to say. And no prayers of hers were adequate to assist clerics through a blasphemy trial. But could she refuse her master?

"Um … all right," she said. She was in Divine service, and this was his job. He was exercising that annoying habit of clerics: trying to stretch her faith.

"Perhaps I ought to warn you," said Armus. "You may feel a touch unwell as a result. Ilbassi doesn't like us praying to anyone else, especially the Divine, in his Shrine."

This was sounding better and better. "A touch unwell? What do you mean? Such as?"

"Oh, a bit dizzy or sick, slight headache, that sort of thing."

Kat swallowed. 'Not looking forward to this' was an understatement. She asked, "Armus, is there anything else I should know? For instance, is it true that the cult of Ilbassi practises animal sacrifice?"

"Yes, I'm afraid so," said the cleric. "They offer human blood too—not much, but always some. There's life and power in blood, you see, and when they shed and offer it to Ilbassi, it strengthens him."

Kat's cheeks went cold and she tried to swallow away the disagreeable taste in her mouth. But it remained.

They arrived at the waterfront, and Kat surveyed the ships. The slaver vessel, the *Sea Snake*, was preparing to depart. Kat resisted the urge to launch an immediate attack. She'd better not, since she'd only an Armus—and not an army—beside her. Her mouth twitched at the private joke.

And there was the *Oyster Shell* docked by the harbour wall. Two days now until they set sail.

Armus led her to the Shrine of Ilbassi, and its crimson star atop the dome caught the midday sun. Kat hesitated: the building still resembled a skull, and she was entering by the teeth.

The Shrine guards stopped them at the forecourt gates. Armus explained that they'd come for the trial of initiate Daytose and that Kat was his assistant. The guards confiscated their weapons and Kat's hooded cloak, and admitted them to the shady colonnade.

They waited, and Armus hummed to himself. Perhaps it was a sung prayer or chant. The acolytes and mages of Ilbassi stalked past—all bald heads and flowing crimson garments. The trimmings and adornments seemed to be reserved for the full mages. Everyone glared at his robes, but the cleric seemed unperturbed.

Kat wished they hadn't taken her things; she felt naked and nervous without them. She shivered and tried to lighten her mood with a wry observation: did everything here in Lasseny have to be crimson and black, as it served for all robes, uniforms, banners and flags?

A guard summoned them for the start of the trial. Armus murmured to Kat, "It's best if you say nothing," and she nodded, relieved. Then he added, with twinkling eyes, "Except, of course, in secret from your heart to the Divine."

What had she let herself in for? All right. If she had to.

Divine, please help them.

But at once a dizzy, sick headache began.

They entered a wide, circular chamber, with bone-white stone pillars supporting a gallery. Sunlight streamed through high windows beneath the vaulted dome, and dust hung in the air like lazy flies under the trees in summer. The only furniture was a stone throne in front of the far wall. It wasn't subtle: without corner, furniture, hood or cloak, there was no hiding from Ilbassi.

Mages and acolytes filled the perimeter, and there were whispers and movement in the gallery. Kat's hackles rose at the large stain in the centre of the floor, the colour of dried blood.

On the throne sat Archmage Gaitox, a gold star adorning the front of his robes. His hypnotic blue eyes drew in Kat's gaze. He held a hidden power ... that was bewitching ... but with too much of the predator about him.

Two Lassenite soldiers brought through a side door a thick-set young woman with light brown hair and dark blue robes. She strained against bound wrists and stared about her. Armus walked across and spoke with her.

Kat wanted to give her a reassuring smile, but the initiate didn't look her way. And she was supposed to be praying. Should she keep thinking: Divine, please help them? But the more she prayed, the sicker and dizzier she felt, and her headache was beginning to thump.

The Archmage raised a hand and all fell silent. A mage whispered in his ear, and then stepped back. Gaitox's resonant voice filled the chamber.

"Initiate Daytose, you are a follower of the Divine. Know that your Goddess has no authority here. You have come before me, and I am the emissary of Ilbassi himself. He is the god of truth and justice, so you must answer all questions with honesty." The Archmage flicked his hand. A crimson light descended from the dome and engulfed the young initiate. Daytose was struck rigid.

Armus stepped forward. "Archmage Gaitox, I am Brother Armus, cleric of the Divine, and spokesman defender for initiate Daytose."

"I know who you are," Gaitox said, in an unimpressed tone.

Armus must have recognised the enchantments, for he said, "The initiate admits her guilt, so there's no need to impose the Hold or Truth Spells on her."

"That is for me to decide," said the Archmage.

Kat went colder at the thought of a Truth Spell. She wanted her secrets to stay hidden, thank you. What she might be asked … and have to tell …

"Initiate Daytose," Gaitox was saying, "in the name of Ilbassi, do you accept that you are guilty of blasphemy?"

"I admit my guilt, sir," said Daytose, and swallowed hard. Only her face could move.

"Tell us what you said that was blasphemous."

Daytose struggled for a moment, but then spoke out. "I said that those who worship Ilbassi are fools." Armus winced, but Daytose continued. "The only true deity is the Divine of Anestra, the all-powerful, and ruler of Ilbassi. Lassenites should seek the Divine and join her favoured people of Anestra." Armus sighed, and a grumble ran around the chamber. The Archmage raised his hand and silence resumed.

"I see," said the Archmage, and the corners of his mouth curled. He was toying with her as he counted the charges on his fingers. "So you're foolish enough to abandon Ilbassi, you speak grave blasphemy, and also treason against the Duke?"

"Yes, sir."

"And these criminal statements: were they in a private conversation? How many people heard you?"

"It wasn't in private," said Daytose. "I was in the central market, sir, and I was shouting. I'd guess a few hundred heard me." Armus groaned. It had to be worse than he'd thought. Kat tried to keep praying … but the sickness was worsening.

The Archmage flicked a finger and the crimson light ceased. Daytose crumpled.

"Spokesman defender," said Gaitox, and Armus stepped forward. "Your initiate is guilty of blasphemy and treason, and is hereby convicted of both. Have you anything to say before I sentence her?"

How could Armus appeal to this tyrant's better nature, when the Archmage might not have one?

"Archmage Gaitox," said Armus, "Daytose is young and inexperienced. You might compare her zeal to that of your newest acolytes. We plead that you and Ilbassi show mercy and compassion, to forgive an over-enthusiastic woman."

"Mercy? Compassion? Forgiveness?" Gaitox scoffed. "You forget, cleric, that it is not your weak, all-forgiving Divine who judges your initiate. Your 'Great Mother of us all'." The sneer from around the chamber matched the derision in his voice. "Ilbassi is rigorous in justice, exacting in punishment. Your initiate deserves death, but now or later matters little. You Anestrans and Divine worshippers will die soon enough. If not death now, what sentence should I pass on her, cleric?"

Armus looked stunned. An option besides death was left open. "Um … banishment from Lasseny, of course. And a fine on the Temple, as apology for her insults to the Duke and this Shrine?"

The Archmage considered, his gaze flickering between Armus and a squirming Daytose.

It was the moment of decision. Kat had to pray as hard as she could. Divine, help them now. Her stomach churned and her head felt about to split open.

And then the Archmage noticed her.

His face hardened as he glared at her. An icy finger ran down Kat's spine. Somehow he'd sensed her prayer.

Kat reeled as some power or enchantment came out of him … but she struggled to resist.

Her vision clouded: a white light enveloped her, while Gaitox was bathed in crimson. The space between them sparked and crackled. Their eyes locked and wrestled, but Kat had set her will and refused to be intimidated.

Oh, no. She wouldn't crumple. Let the bully try it: his Ilbassi against her Divine.

Kat braced herself for a bitter fight.

The Archmage flinched and looked away first. To her amazement, the contest had lasted only a few moments.

Kat's vision cleared. She slumped and wanted to vomit.

The chamber was tense, waiting. Had no one else seen that?

If he was shaken, the Archmage gave no sign. Gaitox said: "The fine will be large. Fifty goldens, delivered within ten days, and banishment. Or else death. Which will it be, spokesman defender?"

That fine was excessive! But Kat guessed the Temple could afford it. Besides, what price for a young woman's life?

"The fine and banishment, Archmage," Armus said at once. They couldn't let him change his mind now.

"Very well. Take her away." The Archmage dismissed them. Kat walked out, her nausea and headache beginning to subside.

The guards granted Armus a minute with Daytose in her cell, while Kat recovered in the colonnade. So she and Daytose had escaped these jaws of death. Archmage: no points; Katelin: one.

She was relieved when Armus joined her. He was holding a scroll, and they retrieved their weapons and cloak at the forecourt gates.

Hedger and Sigzay were waiting on the waterfront. Hedger moved close and murmured, "Our suspicions are confirmed. We should speak of this back at the inn."

Kat heaved a breath to control her panic, but she was almost reeling too much to take it in.

Armus said, "I need to send this scroll to Anestra to ask for delivery of the fine. We can visit the worship room by the market on our way to the Treasure Trove."

The cleric walked with Kat, and he seemed concerned to distract her thoughts. "Daytose is one young woman who is grateful for her life, and she and I thank you for your prayers."

"I'm not sure my prayer was that effective," said Kat, "but I tried. And yes, the Shrine gave me a headache, and made me dizzy and sick."

Armus turned to her. "Oh, I'm sorry. I hope it wasn't too bad."

"It was awful. What was it, then?"

"I call it Ilbassi's sick jealousy," he said. "He uses illness against those who annoy him."

Kat frowned. "At one point I was in a fight with the Archmage. It was like a spiritual battle between the Divine and Ilbassi, with him and me in the middle of it."

Armus stopped and stared at her. "I wondered how Daytose escaped death. Divine power must flow through you without us realising it."

Kat walked on and Armus followed. What did he mean by that? Was it good to channel Divine power, then?

"I noticed something else," said Armus. "Kat, did you hear the Archmage say: 'you Anestrans and Divine worshippers will die soon enough'?"

"Yes, he said that," said Kat. "I took it as a normal insult and threat."

"After Hedger's report," said Armus, "we have to believe that he means it."

Sigzay wanted to buy from the market more bolts for her crossbow, and more arrows for Kat, so Hedger went with her to get them. Armus and Kat ventured up a side alley, into the back of a building, to the worship room of the Divine. It was empty except for a young man in dark blue robes sitting at a desk, reading. He looked up from the volume of The Tome, and Kat met his bright blue eyes. He had a freckled face, curly ginger hair, and she guessed him to be about her age.

"Initiate Prento," Armus said, and the young man rose to meet them. His lanky legs meant he towered over them.

"This is Kat," Armus said, and she looked up at Prento. The initiate took her hand, bowed low and kissed it. "My Lady Kat," he said, "I'm honoured."

Kat felt annoyed at the flush rising in her cheeks. He'd called her 'my lady'!

"I must interrupt your studies for a while, young man," Armus was saying. "The Archmage spared Daytose's life, I'm relieved to say. But the Temple needs to pay a fine within the next ten days."

Prento nodded. He tapped his chin with a sly smile. "So let me think. In a race to Anestra between you and me, Brother, who do you think would win?" Kat let out an involuntary giggle at the thought of such a contest.

"That's not fair," said Armus with a laugh. "You have longer legs. So here's the Archmage's judgement." He handed over the scroll. "Please give it to the Under Father himself. The sooner you leave, the better, and be careful on that desert highway."

Prento held his arms wide. "Be careful on the highway? What do you mean? This is me, remember."

Kat stopped herself from grinning as Prento smiled at her. "A pleasure to have met you, my Lady Kat," he said, and bowed low with a flourish.

Kat curtsied. "Likewise, my Lord Prento, sir."

Prento closed The Tome and left for his lodgings. But he

took one last look over his shoulder at Kat. Oh, she shouldn't have watched him go as well.

Armus and Kat rejoined Hedger and Sigzay outside. They weaved their way past the insistent calls of the market stall vendors and set off down the desert road.

While the others talked, Kat found herself thinking about Prento. It felt strange to meet a boy her age who didn't know who she was. She had little chance of seeing him again, though, which was a shame, because he was funny. And friendly. Maybe he was too studious and devout to be interested in girls. Mind you, he'd kissed her hand, and looked back as he'd left. But lanky, freckled, curly and ginger? 'My Lord Prento and Lady Kat' indeed!

The afternoon had become warm, and they walked in the shade of the buildings. Now it was Sigzay's skimpy clothing, and not Kat, that caused male heads to turn. She might envy Sigzay's longer legs and fuller figure, but sometimes she preferred to pass unnoticed.

Kat tried to focus. Hedger and Sigzay's suspicions were confirmed. So any quest for the Crown would have to wait, since the fragment was unreachable inside the Duke's Palace. The more urgent task was to warn Anestra of imminent Lassenite attack. The quickest way to do that was by sailing south, even if it were two days before the *Oyster Shell* left.

But as they neared the Treasure Trove, Sigzay hissed, "Don't look round. Into inn quick. Someone follow us."

☆ VII ☆

CHASE

Kat's muscles tensed, but she resisted the urge to look behind. They hurried inside to the refuge of the inn.

Before they could speak, the landlord, Vasimic, intercepted them. His face was thunder. What was going on? They'd been out for a few hours and his opinion of them was ruined.

"Two minutes," Vasimic announced. "That's how long you four have got. The Duke's men were here, reporting your 'inadequate respect for Count Bassilius today'. I won't have trouble in my place, so you will settle your bills and leave."

They paid up and grabbed their things, while Sigzay watched the street. Kat was adjusting her quiver and pack as they set off away from the inn. She was trembling.

"Let's head out of the city," said Hedger. "Sigzay, tell us about the Duke's spies."

"One follow us since market," she said. "Another watch the inn. One still follow us. The other hurry down this desert road."

Kat hadn't noticed any of that.

"So one keeps us in sight while the other gets help to tackle us," said Hedger. "We should change direction, as if heading for somewhere in the city. Hide our intentions."

They turned right into an alley, down towards the harbour, and quickened their pace.

"Great," said Sigzay, glaring at Kat. "Now see who get us in trouble."

"Hold on," said Armus. "Don't blame Kat. None of us has

adequate respect for the Count, as far as they're concerned. And this was coming sooner or later. The Duke considers all Anestrans to be spies and wants us out of his city."

"What can we do?" Kat said. "The *Oyster Shell*? Could we go back to the harbour and escape from the city by ship?"

Hedger shook his head. "The way to the harbour takes us past the main barracks. And the *Oyster Shell* isn't yet ready to depart, so we'd get Jersull and his crewmates into trouble. We'll have to escape into the desert on foot."

"Now, Kat," said Armus, "I realise that Farag and Jersull are expecting you. They might think you've given me the slip and become a runaway slave. There's nothing we can do about that now, but they can't complain if you stay with me, as agreed with Jersull."

Kat hadn't thought about what the Caldunim might think. It was more that her planned route back to Anestra was blocked. As they hurried through side streets, Kat's insides were churning. How long would it take her to walk home from here? But she had to escape from Lasseny first.

"Hedger, what did you mean by 'tackle us'?" said Kat. Her voice quavered. "Kill us?"

"Not straight away," said Sigzay. "They escort to Palace for questions by Duke. He wants to know who prisoners are, and all they know, before torture and death."

The blood drained from Kat's face. Was that supposed to reassure her? She gripped Armus's arm. "We mustn't get captured," she hissed. "It would be catastrophic."

Oh. They all heard that.

"All right," said Hedger. "Sigzay may have exaggerated, but I agree that we need to evade capture."

Their erratic course took them through squares and behind buildings, but glances confirmed that their pursuer still kept them in sight.

"They stop us at desert gate," said Sigzay. "That quickest escape route from Treasure Trove to make for Anestra."

"You may be right," said Hedger, "but we've little choice in leaving the city from here. Let's see who waits for us at the gate."

They peered around the last building at the end of an alley. A wide space stretched before them to the city wall, which was not high on the inside, and at intervals stone steps led up to it. A few guards patrolled along the top.

Parked along the inside of the wall was a line of wagons and carts, their drivers chatting in small groups. Hedger nodded towards them, and turned to Armus and Kat.

"These are the supply wagons for the invasion of Anestra," he breathed. "They leave down the desert highway tomorrow."

Kat stared. Then gulped. Before her lay the beginnings of the conquest of her people. Hedger had said their suspicions were confirmed, but so soon? And so much? She had the urge to sabotage the carts, but couldn't think how. Hedger was speaking again, so she tore her mind away from her fears and back to the present. She had to get herself out of the city instead. Concentrate, Kat.

"No way out there," said Hedger. He indicated to their left, to the desert gate and the road down which they would have come. The way had been barricaded, and the guardhouses overflowed with soldiers and thugs. "There's no fighting our way through them," he went on. "Let's skirt to the right, behind the cover of buildings, to a clearer stretch of the wall. We should get our weapons ready."

They retreated and took a course through side streets parallel with the wall. Their tracker followed their route. How could they reach the wall unnoticed?

Hedger loosened his sword, pulled a rope from his pack and knotted a loop in the end. Armus unclipped his mace.

Sigzay had a short sword, a crossbow and bolts, and Kat readied her shortbow and arrows. The curve of the wall took them out of sight of the desert gate.

"The sooner we make our move the better," said Hedger. "Without alerting all those at the gate that we're further along the wall."

"I never thought I'd end up fighting my way out of this city," said Armus. "After all I've done for these Lassenites."

"Yes, it's time to take our leave of their hospitality," said Hedger. "First we must silence the one who follows us. Missile weapons ready?" Kat and Sigzay nodded. He said, "On the count of three: one, two, three!"

They whirled round and loosed an arrow and bolt at the spy. He was caught in the open, collapsed in the alley and lay still.

"So far, so good!" exclaimed Kat.

"We're not out yet," Hedger reminded her. "Now we stroll up to the wall. No rousing suspicion by running."

Here the guards on the wall were sparse. The four of them concealed their weapons under their cloaks and left the cover of the buildings. They meandered towards the line of wagons and the nearest steps. It was all Kat could do not to break into a sprint.

Before they were halfway to the wall, the frantic blowing of a high-pitched horn erupted from the alleyway behind them.

The spy wasn't dead.

They abandoned concealment and ran for the cover of the wagons. Kat and Sigzay fired arrow and bolt at the closest guards.

The spy's warning horn was joined by those of soldiers on the wall. On all sides, guards drew swords and ran to prevent their escape.

They piled between two wagons and made for the steps. Hedger's long sword was out and he took the steps three at a time. With unstoppable strokes he cleared the first of the guards. Armus's mace was ready close behind, for any that evaded Hedger's sword. Sigzay and Kat shot another missile as they mounted the steps.

The motley army from the desert gate appeared on their left. Thugs, ruffians, soldiers and guards raced to catch them, both inside and on top of the wall. Hedger looped the rope over a battlement and threw the rest of it down the sheer drop outside.

"Down the rope, quick!" he shouted. "Armus first, then Kat."

Hedger swung his sword to fend off the guards, and Sigzay and Kat gained the top of the wall. Armus rolled himself over the parapet and clambered down the rope. Once he was halfway down, Kat followed him over. It was a long drop.

"Hurry up!" yelled Sigzay. "They come!"

Armus fell from the end of the rope to the dusty ground below. He readied his mace, and called up, "I'll need some help here in a minute."

Kat looked up. Of course, one sergeant had to be smart enough to have thought about outside the wall. Most of the soldiers were above her, but one Lassenite squad hurried along the base of the wall towards where Armus stood.

Kat had descended far enough to let herself fall to the ground. Her balance regained, she fired an arrow at the advancing soldiers. Hedger and Sigzay abandoned their position and scrambled over the battlement. Hedger grabbed the rope on the way, and half slid, half fell down the wall. He landed in a heap beside Kat.

Sigzay halted near the top, and cut the rope with her short sword. She skittered down the stonework until a spear glanced off her arm. It dislodged her hold, and she too fell to the bottom. Hedger staggered to his feet beside where her body lay sprawled in the dust.

Kat's arrows had picked off a couple of soldiers, but ten of them still approached. Hedger shook his rope-burned hands. Sigzay struggled upright, winded and dazed. Spears thudded around them and a heavy stone landed on Kat's foot.

Ouch! "Let's go!" she shouted.

Kat hobbled after Armus to get out of range of the wall. Hedger and Sigzay stumbled after her. The soldiers were closing, the odds in their favour. Were their orders to capture or to kill?

She had to disable their leader. She identified the sergeant and let off a last, short range arrow. He crumpled, clutching his stomach. Sigzay shot a bolt, and then they backed off before engaging hand to hand. Hedger and Armus readied themselves for a last stand.

The Lassenites flung their spears. One struck a glancing blow to Hedger's leg, but no others found their mark. The remnant of the squad wavered.

Kat could almost see the calculating in their eyes. Their sergeant had fallen, and their prey was armed and evading them. With each of them that fell to bolt and arrow, the odds were approaching even.

Hedger roared at the faltering Lassenites. With chilling anger, and confident menace, he twirled his long sword and swaggered towards them. Armus went with him. Sigzay and Kat loaded further missiles. The morale of the soldiers broke and they fled for the city gate.

An arrow whistled nearby. So the Lassenite archers had made it to the wall, or had feared hitting their own until now. But their arrows fell wide and short.

"Come on!" shouted Hedger. He set off at a jog away from

the city. He called over his shoulder, "We've scared off pursuit for now. But it may give us only a few minutes."

Kat broke into a limping run. Sigzay and Armus followed at a trot.

Kat scanned the land before them: a dusty plain stretched to the Coastal Range mountains. "Where can we go?" she said. "Is there somewhere to hide?"

"It's barren," panted Armus. His red face glistened with sweat. "The only cover ... might be the mountains."

"There are canyons," said Sigzay, coming up beside them.

Kat glanced behind. "They're not coming after us."

"We've a head start ..." puffed Armus, "... but we must keep up our pace. We can't assume they'll think us ... not worth following."

The afternoon sun was bright and warm, and the heat and exertion made them all sweat. Kat's mind was filled with running on a painful foot.

At long last the foothills loomed before them. There was no sign of pursuit as they reached a canyon's shady entrance.

Armus collapsed on a rock and heaved for breath. They stooped to drink and splashed their faces in the cool stream that trickled out of the canyon. Kat slumped to the ground, pulled off her boot and massaged her foot. It was the other leg from the knife wound, but it would bruise.

They bandaged the gashes on Sigzay's arm and Hedger's leg. Armus recovered his breath enough to pray and lay hands on Hedger and Kat. Sigzay declined his healing touch. "Is nothing," she said. "Only scratch."

Kat found herself staring through the rocky canyon floor. She struggled to focus on anything. The air was hot, dizzy, stifling. She closed her eyes, heaved some breaths.

What was she supposed to do now? They'd been chased

from Lasseny, and she couldn't sail south on the *Oyster Shell*. So, foiling all her plans: one point to them; escaping capture: one point to her.

At last she straightened her back and asked, "Do we hide for a while in this canyon, or press on south?"

"I see little benefit in hiding," said Hedger. "I'd say go on south. We should keep off the road, as that's the way the Lassenite army will go. But we can skirt and follow the foothills, and shelter in the canyons when necessary."

"I agree," said Armus. "If we're heading for Anestra, then let's leave Lasseny some miles behind. They may not send soldiers after us, but we ought to be on our guard."

"So weapons ready and go south by foothills till night?" said Sigzay. The others nodded. "I hope we are not run all the way. I need steady walk. Am winded and sore from fall."

"Me too," said Hedger. "We should pace ourselves and recover, in case we need to run and fight again."

"Oh, walking please, please," begged Armus.

They took a last drink from the stream and adjusted their packs. As they emerged from the canyon, they watched for movement on their left, where the highway to Anestra snaked this side of the Great Salt Lake. As they walked, the sun sank towards the high ridges on their right, and lengthened the cooling shadow of the mountains across the four walkers.

The banquet was in full flow.

Around Princess Rashelin, Anestra's Hall of the Court hummed with the murmur of politeness. Silver cutlery clinked against china plates, and the fires in the hearths cracked and hissed. The vaulted, timber ceiling was lost in the shadows of the candlelight that flickered across the walls' banners of silver and blue.

The guests seemed to be enjoying themselves, chatting with excitement about the forthcoming coronation.

If only they knew.

At top table, Rashelin could do little more than push the food around her plate and stare into the tablecloth.

"The duck is good, don't you think?"

Rashelin stirred. Her mother had turned to her, with the intention of breaking her trance. Rashelin forced a smile, and nodded. She made herself place a small piece of duck on her fork.

"Thank you for your speech of welcome to the guests, my dear," Consort Sirika said. "You did that well, I thought."

Rashelin shook her head as she chewed. She'd been nervous, rushed her words, but at least it was over for tonight.

Then Sirika murmured, "You're worried about Katelin, aren't you?"

Rashelin looked at her mother. Maybe it was the candlelight, but this evening her face seemed softer, her eyes gentler. Still stern and commanding, but more the caring mother of when Rashelin had been little.

"Yes, I am," she sighed.

"We all are, Rashelin." Sirika's voice was warm with affection. "These are dangerous times, and so much depends upon the wisdom of her decisions."

Around top table the others were engrossed in their conversations, so Rashelin took the chance for a private talk. "I wish there were more we could do to help."

"We are helping. We're holding everything together. That's no small contribution to the history of the Kingdom in a time of Regency."

"Yes, I know. But I mean to help Katelin, to encourage and support her."

Sirika's humph was as derisory as usual. "It's hard to

help someone who doesn't wish to be helped, you know." She stabbed her knife into the duck, and fat flowed out into the gravy.

Rashelin sipped her wine. Did she dare to challenge her mother over what lay at the heart of the future of the Kingdom? "Mother, I've never understood why you and Katelin don't get on. We're in the same Family. We all want what's best for Anestra. Why can't we work together towards that common goal?"

Sirika laid down her cutlery, reached a hand onto Rashelin's arm. Instead of an outburst, there came a smile.

"My dear, sweet Rashelin. You have such a kind and gentle heart. That's your greatest strength, you know. You forgive, you reconcile, you bring people together. The Divine knows how much we need people like you in the Court and the Kingdom. But when we're called to rule, we lose the luxury of being everyone's friend. We have decisions to make. We choose between alternatives, to follow what we believe to be best. Some disagree with us and would choose a different path, so we bear the burden of being unpopular."

Rashelin clasped her hands. "I think I understand that. You and Katelin choose different paths for the future of the Kingdom. But for the sake of the Divine, can't we all submit ourselves to the Life Weaver's guiding?"

Sirika smiled. "Your faith in the Divine does you credit, my dear. You've always been so devout. But the Divine doesn't do everything for us, you know. She trusts us to think for ourselves, to decide, to speak, to act. She's entrusted to our Family the rule of this Kingdom. So we need to be strong, resilient, and sometimes even ruthless. We must counter all threats to the stability and wellbeing of the Kingdom, and that includes the selfish whims of that cousin of yours. That's why the Divine put steel in our blood."

Rashelin shivered. She didn't like anyone being as ruthless as steel, but understood what her mother meant.

On Sirika's other side, Regent Ethabos gave out a loud guffaw at some joke. Heads across the Hall turned their way, and then resumed their talking and eating.

Rashelin made a further appeal to her mother. "I hate it when you and Katelin fight. She has a good heart, you know."

Sirika's eyebrows rose and her grip on Rashelin's arm became painful. "A good heart—even if she has one—is not all that's needed. Is that what sent her off to Lasseny? Always seeking adventure, and her freedom? Is that why she demeans the majesty of the Queen by mixing with commoners whenever she can? She must have wisdom, and sound judgement too, and that comes through experience. That's what we'll give her, even after she's Crowned, whether she wants it or not."

"Won't you listen to her point of view once she's Queen? Won't you have to take into account her choices and decisions?"

Sirika took up her cutlery, and returned to sawing and dissecting her duck. "You are right that this is a time of change. So it's important to have the firm hand of experience on the helm. The thought of subjecting our Kingdom to the whims and fancies of that rebellious girl's heart? That, my dear, is a risk that your father and I are not willing to take."

✳ VIII ✳

CANYON

It had been a while since Kat had been in canyon country. South of Lasseny Bay, a line of hills rose into the Coastal Range's jagged peaks that towered over the Western Ocean. On these eastern slopes, tumbling streams carved gorges through the foothills, as though a giant knife had cut slices out of sandstone cake. The streams ran on to oases on the desert floor and then lost themselves in the Great Salt Lake. Only in the canyons, and along the trickling watercourses, were there any ribbons of green, where yucca and mesquite bushes clung to life, with junipers on the loftier slopes. Kat remembered to scan the rocky ground for the local inhabitants: scorpions, lizards, spiders and snakes.

The four walked in silence, each lost in their own thoughts. The air was cooler in the mountain shadow, while on their left the desert plain shimmered in the afternoon sun. Before the daylight faded, their steady pace covered a dozen miles southwards. Lasseny disappeared behind them without any sign of pursuit. They were too busy preparing to invade, Kat thought, to worry about escaping mercenaries.

At dusk they entered a canyon, and Kat dropped her pack in exhaustion. They washed and drank at the stream, but denied themselves the comfort of fire for fear of attracting attention. In case they needed an escape route, Sigzay scouted the way out of the back of the gorge.

They munched bread in the dark and arranged turns on watch: Armus first, then Sigzay, then Hedger, and Kat before dawn. Each claimed a patch of rough ground to sleep on. The chirrup of insects and the calls of the night were their desert lullaby.

When Hedger woke her, Kat shivered in the cold night air. Tired though she was, her sleep had been fitful. Hedger lay down, leaving Kat in waking solitude.

A chill flowed down from the mountains at night, and the rock was even harder than the planks of the slave traders' hold. Kat sat huddled in her thin blanket and cloak, her breath condensing in clouds in front of her.

There was no moon, and the stars glittered overhead. It was so clear, and they were so bright, that Kat wished she'd taken the trouble to learn all their patterns and names. She wondered if it were true: that the heavens were spanned by an enormous black sheet, pierced with unnumbered pinpricks. They said that if you could press your eye to the sky, then you'd see the Divine beyond. And that the stars twinkled when the White Goddess moved behind the holes.

Kat filled her lungs. The air smelled fresher now that they'd forsaken the dubious fragrance of Lasseny. Could she ever feel at home in this vast and silent wilderness?

A scorpion hunted its way down the opposite side of the gorge. Time crept by with the same slow pace. At last the pale light of pre-dawn grew at the canyon entrance. Kat willed the sun to rise, as she needed the warming beams.

She stood, stretched and yawned. Then she padded to the mouth of the gorge to watch the desert sunrise. Delicate purples and pinks stained the distant high clouds as the sky turned the colour of pearl. It was as though the dawn knew that she was beautiful, and was blushing at being watched.

A tired smile creased Kat's face. The same sun rose on the city of Anestra, but she doubted that it ever looked this wonderful. Yes, this was one benefit of running away: to be here in the wild. To be alone, unknown, no assumptions, expectations or responsibility. To have the freedom of the others not knowing who she was. To have a free and peaceful spirit.

Kat jumped at a movement in the corner of her eye. Sigzay stood next to her.

"Sorry to startle," Sigzay murmured. "I move quiet, and do without thinking. I not disturb you enjoy sunrise."

"Stunning, isn't it?" whispered Kat. They stood in silence. In time the edge of the sun's fiery disc appeared, and Kat pretended that already she felt its warmth.

"Are the other two awake?" she said.

"They stirring."

"I don't suppose there's much for breakfast, except for grey bread squares and water."

"Think not," said Sigzay. "Maybe fruit or leaf to chew, or hunt animal for meat. Depend if you enjoy taste of lizard."

Kat pulled a face. "Did you get much sleep?"

"Sleep good. I turn soft in city bed, but put barbarian into wilds, and sleep good. You sleep?"

"I feel as though I've not slept at all, but I must have done. My bones were cold."

Sigzay smiled. "Also northern strength—I not feel cold like you from south. But, Kat, you shoot good. So maybe there blood of barbarian in you."

Kat laughed. "Well, thank you. But, no, I think not."

If only Sigzay knew.

"Now you cold," said Sigzay, "but sun will beat us all morning. We move while sun low."

"I need that warming sun. And breakfast too before we set off."

Turning their backs on the sunrise, Kat and Sigzay re-entered the gorge as the dawn stretched her golden fingers across the land.

Armus was stowing a blanket in his pack, and Hedger was splashing his face at the stream.

"Will be hot," Sigzay announced, "so we must start walk soon. And need find food, as Lasseny bread runs out today."

"And good morning to you," said Armus, closing his pack. "I agree with going early, but after some breakfast and talking first. We should discuss what we're aiming for now."

Hedger wiped his face on his forearm. "Assuming we've escaped from the Lassenites, do we head back to Anestra?" He got out four of the bread squares and passed them round.

"We cannot seek your broken Anestra Crown," Sigzay said. "Part in Lasseny, part in Anestra, and know no more. So nothing we can do." Kat heard a note of triumph in her voice.

Armus sat on a rock and said, "What we plan now depends on something else. I think that Kat has some explaining to do."

She became aware that the three of them looked at her. She blurted out, "What are you talking about?"

"You haven't been honest with us, Kat," said Armus. "There's more to you than you've told us."

Oh no. Kat didn't like where this was going. And her cheeks were heating up. She'd just relished being unknown, and now this threatened to spoil it. But she couldn't think what to say to stop or distract them, so bit a large mouthful of bread instead.

"We know that you come from Anestra," Armus went on, "and you admitted your family's well off. Your hands and face are pampered, not weathered or cracked. So you're not used to roughing it in the wilds. You can fire a bow, but I don't think you learned that by hunting for food. You're from some noble family, aren't you?"

Kat continued to chew. She didn't want to listen to this conversation. To distract herself, she bundled up her blanket and tried to stuff it in her pack. She wasn't going to tell them. She wasn't.

Armus continued. "Jersull told me how you arranged passage from Anestra. All hooded and cloaked, you boarded in the dark before dawn. No one was to know of your secret escape, and then a handsome price paid to the Captain. And at the Shrine of Ilbassi, Divine power flows to daunt the Archmage himself. So who are you, Kat?"

The blanket and pack were refusing to co-operate. Could Armus drop this please?

When Kat didn't answer, Sigzay spoke up. "Yesterday, we are chase from Lasseny, and you say, 'We must not captured, that catastrophic'. I understand you adolescent fear of torture, but you fear something more. And you know all about broken Anestra Crown, and what in Royal Treasury."

There came a pause and Kat finished her mouthful. Hedger stepped across, took her blanket, folded it, smiled and stowed it in her pack. He hadn't spoken yet; maybe he was saving himself with some killer persuasion.

Kat leaned against the canyon wall and took another bite. She folded her arms. All their unanswered questions of the last two days had tumbled out at once. Why were they so curious? Could she get them to drop this line of questioning? Or could she refuse to answer? She wished the wall of rock would open for her to hide in.

Kat swallowed and filled the awkward silence with the best defence she could muster. "Have you finished? I haven't asked about who you are, or where you come from either. I thought we're allowed to retain some mystery. We all have secrets, and things we'd prefer to forget." Her words came out sharper than she intended.

Hedger broke his silence. "You're right, Kat. You don't have to say anything you don't want to. You can stay mysterious if you wish." He held her eyes for a moment. "But there may be things you could tell us. You're among friends here, if recent friends. We're loyal to Anestra, and agreed to seek the broken Crown with you. If there's some danger we don't know about, then maybe you should say it. It'll help us to decide which paths to take."

Somehow Hedger had started the crumbling of her defences. He'd sensed the debate going on behind her eyes. If she told them, would it spoil everything? And which story should she give them … or did it have to be the truth? Sigzay began to speak, but Hedger raised a hand to stop her.

Kat glanced at each of them, and then back at the ground, tight-lipped. If they knew, what would they do? They'd insist on escorting her back to Anestra, which was where she needed to go anyway.

Hedger moved beside her. He said, "Can you help me with something, Kat, that happened yesterday morning? You remember Bassilius riding by outside the Lasseny Palace?" Kat nodded. "We'd mentioned him, and here was your chance to see him. But you hid behind me with hooded face—a dangerous move with the Duke's men around. So you didn't admire the handsome Count, but that wasn't it, was it? You didn't want him to see you."

Kat's stubbornness softened further before his warm, conker eyes. Yes, these were friends, and loyal to Anestra. If they knew and understood her situation, maybe they could help her. And the canyon wall hadn't opened to rescue her either.

She unfolded her arms and let them drop. She drew a deep breath and hoped she wouldn't regret this. She murmured, "No, I couldn't let him see me."

"Why not?" chorused Armus and Sigzay.

"Because he'd recognise me."

"Recognise you?" Sigzay sneered. "You sure?"

"Yes, I'm sure," Kat breathed. "He'd recognise me at once."

"Why is that?" Hedger probed.

Kat turned back to Hedger's eyes. "Because he wants to marry me."

Sigzay burst out laughing, snorting with incredulity. Hedger stared at Kat. Then he smiled.

"You silly little girl!" Sigzay managed at last. She wiped back tears of disbelief and laughter. "You think you irresistible pretty, but doesn't mean everyone wants marry you. Especially Lasseny Count!"

"Shut up, Sigzay," Kat snapped. The irritation at the ridicule overflowed at last. "You understand nothing." Her tone of voice made them all shut up. "Of course Count Bassilius wants to marry me. He's asked me so himself."

They stared at her, mouths half open. Kat rubbed her face, composed herself, and softened her voice.

"I told you that my name is Kat," she said. "That's true, but it's a nickname, a shortened form. My full name is ... Katelin."

There was silence.

Then Armus mumbled, as if his brain worked to connect things together. "Katelin ...? As in ...?"

"Yes," said Kat. She lifted her head. "As in Her Royal Highness, the Princess Katelin of Anestra and the Western Coast. Heiress to the throne of the Old Kingdom. At your service," she added, with a mock curtsey and a resigned smile.

Sigzay threw up her arms in disgust and stalked a few paces away. Armus stared at Kat, and then said, "You're not."

She shrugged. "I am."

Hedger had a boyish grin plastered across his face. "Well said, Your Highness. Thank you for trusting us. That will make things easier now."

"Easier?" snorted Sigzay. "Easier, now we say 'Your

Majesty' before speaking and 'Your Royal Highness' at every step?"

"Don't be stupid." Kat's sharp tone returned. "I've been 'Kat' so far, and that's what I'll be from now on. No mention of this must be made to anyone else."

"But ..." Armus said, "... the whole Western Coast is preparing for your coronation, and you're stuck out here? You're the most powerful person in the entire Kingdom."

"Not yet," said Kat. "The story of my life so far: not yet. I'm always 'in waiting', or 'designate', or 'the future Queen.' I have no power at all right now."

"But ..." Armus spluttered, "... you were for sale at the Lasseny slave market! And back there ... you could have been captured ... or killed!"

"Yes, that was close, wasn't it?" Kat grinned. But none of the others were smiling. "Anyway. Now you can see how grateful I am that you and Farag bought me. And we could all have been captured or killed, but I've nothing worse than a stabbed leg and a bruised foot."

"Such casual disregard for your personal safety," said Hedger. Kat was surprised by the angry tremor in his voice. "I think we have to insist that the three of us become your bodyguards and protectors, Kat, until we deliver you to Anestra."

Kat was about to protest that she could look after herself. Then she remembered that a few times in recent days she'd needed the help of her friends.

"Yes, um ... Kat," said Armus. "Your safety must now become our first concern." Sigzay rolled her eyes at this, but didn't say anything.

Kat sighed, feeling restrictions on her freedom approaching. And it seemed as though they'd have to get used to still calling her 'Kat'.

"After all," Hedger went on, "your slavery, capture or death would be catastrophic for Anestra. You carry everyone's hopes for the future rule of our Kingdom."

Kat grimaced. "Please spare me the lectures I've heard all my life about how important I am. There are others in the line of succession—my Uncle and cousins—who would welcome the chance to seat their behinds on the royal throne of Anestra. That's why Bassilius wants to marry me: not for my 'irresistible prettiness', but for access to power in Anestra."

Hedger's tone softened. "He seeks a marriage alliance between Lasseny and Anestra. I understand. He sees you as the way to gain control of the Coast, if you'll have him."

"Don't worry," said Kat with a laugh, "that's *never* going to happen."

"Don't be so sure," said Armus. "You may think you can refuse him, but in diplomacy and war, distasteful things can happen. What if the Duke attacks Anestra, and he defeats and conquers you? What if it's a term of the surrender, that you marry his son: what then?"

"I'll give my life to defend Anestra," said Kat. "He can marry my dead body."

"Let's hope it doesn't come to that," murmured Armus.

"Anyway," said Kat, "now you know why my escape from Anestra had to be secret, and why I didn't want to be captured in Lasseny." She planted her hands on her hips. "Any more questions?"

"Yes," said Hedger, "just one. How long have we got, Kat?"

"What do you mean, how long?" said Kat. "Until what?" Couldn't Hedger leave this? She didn't like to think how close it was.

"Your eighteenth birthday," said Hedger.

"It's in … um … six days' time," Kat whispered.

"Six days' time." Hedger nodded.

"What?" said Sigzay. "What happen when she eighteen?"

"Tell them, Kat," he insisted.

It was as though she recited an official statement, long rehearsed. "When I turn eighteen—in six days' time—I come of age. I cease to be a child, a ward of the Court, and become an adult. The Regency of the Kingdom, which has lasted for fifteen years since I was two years old, comes to an end. The rule of Anestra passes from my Uncle, the Regent, to me, and I become Queen. My eighteenth birthday is my coronation day."

Sigzay nodded, a curious look in her eyes. "So silly little girl becomes Queen of Western Coast." She held out a hand. "I must be honoured to know you … Kat."

It didn't sound like the ridicule was over. But Kat took her hand. "And you too, Sigzay," she said.

Armus stood up. "I don't know what to say. Power of the Divine?"

"And her power to you," said Kat with a laugh. She gave him a warm embrace.

Hedger was gazing at her. "Princess Katelin," he breathed. "So it is you." He shook his head, but couldn't hide his grin. "Let me get this straight. Ten days before you ascend the throne and are Crowned Queen of Anestra, you abscond from the city. You're captured by slavers and bought by Armus and Jersull at the Lasseny slave market. You meet us, and we embark on some heroic quest to retrieve that sacred relic, your lost and broken Crown. We escape from the clutches of the Duke, and now—while the whole Western Coast prepares for your coronation—here we are, in a desert canyon. And we have six days in which to escort you home, safe and sound. Is that about right?"

Although his tone was light, Hedger seemed more serious about her situation than she was.

Kat beamed. "Something like that!"

Hedger reached across and embraced her too. "You amaze me, Princess," he whispered.

"Thank you," she whispered back.

✳ IX ✳

DESTINY

I guess we've spent long enough talking, and we wanted an early start," Armus reminded them. "If we keep a steady pace and avoid detours and delays, it's a four or five day walk to Anestra. Did you realise the timing would be this tight?"

Kat shook her head. "I thought I'd sail back on the *Oyster Shell* in a couple of days, and be there in plenty of time."

Armus drew a deep breath. "Well, that route's closed to you. So if we're to reach Anestra in time for your coronation, we'd better get started."

"Someone fill bottles," said Sigzay, "and I see what to eat up here." She headed further into the gorge.

They finished their bread, drank their fill from the stream and Hedger replenished the bottles. Sigzay returned carrying two leafy branches and a large, freshly killed lizard. "See what I find," she said.

"Ugh," said Kat. "But if that's lunch, we'll be hungry and grateful by then."

Sigzay stowed her prize lizard, they hoisted their packs and set off. At the mouth of the canyon they turned right and southwards on a faint, beaten path. The early sun was warm on their faces. Sigzay gave Hedger a branch to hold (an edible type of ironwood, Kat learned), while she picked the leaves off the other and stuffed them in a pouch on her belt.

Armus and Kat walked together in front. The cleric had found a battered, wide-brimmed hat in his pack. Kat didn't have the heart to say how comical he looked, but it did keep the sun off his balding head.

"I'm sorry that none of us recognised you, Kat," he said. "We've been away from Anestra so long that we don't even know our own Royal Family."

Kat smiled. "Don't worry. My Aunt and Uncle have hidden me away in Anestra Castle all my life. 'To protect me,' they say. I suppose that everyone on the Coast has heard of me, but no one sees me except at a distance. Only those in the Castle know my face."

"I can't tell you how excited I am," said Armus, "you being … who you are. It explains a lot."

"Explains what?"

"How can I put it? Since we met two days ago, it's felt like the Divine has watched us. That we were *meant* to meet and travel together."

"And you've never felt like this before?" Too late Kat realised that might not be appropriate to say to a cleric.

Armus didn't seem to mind. "I've known the presence of the Divine before, in worship and teaching, but this is different. Not every prayer for healing is granted, believe me. Her eyes are upon us, to guide, protect and empower us. The Divine wanted us to escape from Lasseny, and for you—seeing who you are—not to be captured. She has a plan for you and for Anestra. She may even help you to find the Crown. It's invigorating."

"You believe in fate or destiny then? That the Divine has things she wants us to do?"

"She doesn't control us, if that's what you mean," said Armus. "People call it fate, or destiny, or the Divine will, but we all have the freedom to choose. There isn't a single path, set in stone, for each of us to take. We seek the

Divine, or we ignore her. If we learn what she wishes, we can decide to follow her or not. She treats us as growing children, and allows us to choose, even if it means we reject her."

"But what about me as a Princess," complained Kat, "and about to become Queen? Isn't that my destiny? I didn't ask to end up first in line for a throne, so where's my freedom of choice in that?"

Armus thought for a moment, and Kat's boots crunched on a patch of gravel. "None of us chooses when or where we're born, our parents or family. We're born where we are and make the most of it. We're the children of carpenters, blacksmiths, farmers, soldiers—or Kings and Queens. We choose a profession, and aim for the best we can be."

"But I didn't choose the profession of Queen," said Kat. "I become one in six days' time, whether I want it or not."

"Children of farmers or blacksmiths might wish they had different families, but that's not how it is. Most would say, with your background, that you have more opportunities than anyone."

"It doesn't feel like that." Kat couldn't hide her gloom. "I'll have to be responsible for everything, and with so much expected of me. And everyone—my Aunt and Uncle most of all—will try to get me to do what they want."

"I can only imagine," said Armus. He looked at her sideways as they walked. "It doesn't sound as though you're looking forward to being Queen. Is that right?"

"I know it sounds ungrateful, when I've been born a Princess." She paused. Perhaps she'd said too much. But if anyone could help with her fears, then Armus might be the one to do it. She squinted at him, and the rising sun caught her eye. "To tell you the truth: for years now I've dreaded becoming Queen."

Armus raised his eyebrows. "I'm sorry, Kat," he said. "Living your life with dread is hard to bear. There may not be easy answers, but I'll give that some thought."

They walked on in silence, and Kat looked ahead over the rocky plain. At least she'd managed to express her fears to someone.

Then Armus said, "What about me? Do you think it's an easy life as a cleric? Do I have to be responsible, and is there much expected of me?"

Kat thought about that. "No, I don't think it's easy being a cleric. You're expected to be perfect: always loving, patient, kind, ready to share your wisdom. But didn't you choose to be a cleric, and sign yourself up for this life?"

"Only to a certain extent," Armus chuckled. "I didn't grow up wanting to be a cleric, if that's what you mean, but then the Divine called me. My choice was to follow that calling. We could say that she calls you to be Queen of Anestra, and you have to decide what to do with that call."

Kat stared at her boots in dejection. "You could have chosen to deny your call, but I've got no choice at all."

"Of course you have choices." His voice was gentle. "Even today, I could resign as a cleric and try my hand as a farmer instead. A few days ago you abandoned being a Princess, to become an adventurer for a while. But to resign as a cleric—or to abdicate a throne—is a drastic decision. Some choices are irreversible and we have to live with the consequences."

"No, I could never abdicate," Kat said, "no matter how much I hate becoming Queen. If I did, it would hand the Kingdom over to Uncle Ethabos and Aunt Sirika for good. Apart from how I feel about them, that would be disastrous for the future of Anestra. I love the Kingdom too much to let that happen."

"Ah, yes, I see," said Armus. "The Regent and Consort would banish you, as an abdicated Princess, from Anestra too. Your choices affect many more people than only yourself." Armus took off his hat, wiped his sweaty forehead on his sleeve, and jammed the hat back on. "I believe the Divine's calling is good. She saw I might be a useful cleric and that I'd be productive and fulfilled. So I reckon the Divine sees in you the abilities and temperament to be an excellent ruler of our people."

Kat sighed. "I hope so. One of my fears is that I'm not suited to these duties, but too restless, blunt and impulsive. I'd want to change everything. I hate being told what to do, or have things expected of me. They assume things about me, and I hate that. I want the freedom to make all my own choices, to live my own life and do what I like. Why can't I be my own person?" She kicked a stray pebble along the path. "But you're saying that if you resign, or if I did abdicate, we'd be unfulfilled for the rest of our lives."

"I can't speak for you," said Armus. "I only know my own calling and abilities. You know your heart and conscience, and how the Divine speaks to you. We have to accept the things chosen for us: our parents and family, our time and place of birth. But consider this: the call of the Divine can alter with time—from one thing at one stage in our lives, and then change to something else later."

Kat turned to him. "So I might be a Princess one day, an adventurer the next, Queen next week, who knows what after that—and all according to Divine calling?"

"Of course," Armus smiled. "Sounds exciting, doesn't it? Who knows what choices I might face today?"

"Is it all right to rebel against my destiny, then?" asked Kat.

"Well, you can try," said Armus with a laugh. "Perhaps

it's more a question of discovering what your destiny is. Yes, go on. You rebel all you like, and let's see what destiny does about it."

Kat grinned. That was a freeing thought. "You are wise, Brother," she said. "I hope I can learn to live with an attitude like yours."

They walked in silence for some minutes, and the air was warming up. Then Kat said, "So, um … master … I owe you and the Temple twelve goldens. Until I repay that from the Royal Treasury, am I still in service to the Divine?"

Armus laughed again. "Yes, Princess. Always. But I think we can grant you a little leeway. After all, the clerics know where to go to collect on your debt. But don't you know how the Anestran Royal Family has something of a … unique … place in Divine service? Weren't you taught about the Divine as you grew up in Anestra Castle?"

"Well, yes," said Kat. "My Aunt and Uncle insisted that I learn all the history and traditions of Anestra, the Old Kingdom, the Temple, the Divine, and so on. But nothing like this. Nothing about how the Divine might affect me in my life or my choices."

"That's a shame," said Armus. "Only I've remembered something else. I heard it in my training at the Temple, and never gave it much thought until now. You know how you told me of your fight with the Archmage in the Shrine of Ilbassi?"

Kat nodded. "I've never felt anything like it."

"They say that Divine power runs through the Anestran Royal Family; that she chose your ancestors for the rule of the Kingdom. That explains how you stood up to the Archmage. It's because of who you are."

Kat stared at the cleric. She'd always known her destiny to be Queen of Anestra. Armus describing her as the channel of Divine power in the world only made her feel even more responsible. She trudged on in silence.

This Divine had better help her with everything then.

Captain Norbil waited. That was the thing with guard duty, and what he was paid for: waiting. At least it wasn't some lowly door or gate that he guarded. No, he stood beside Duke Bassikrin's lime green throne.

The old man looked to be in a doze, his hand resting on the sleeping ferret in his lap. He wasn't, of course, but played this trick to see if his soldiers relaxed their guard. Captain Norbil had achieved his position through one thing: staying attentive.

Norbil heard footsteps in the entrance corridor, and the Duke's eyes snapped open. Bassikrin glanced Norbil's way, but the Captain was as alert as ever.

The double entrance doors swung open and Archmage Gaitox swept in. He approached the throne and inclined his head.

"My lord Duke," he said. "We are ready."

"Excellent, my good Archmage," said the Duke. He drew a deep breath. "I have waited long years for this. Those fools Ethabos and Sirika have always been pliable to my wishes. Now we will teach their niece the same lesson."

"She will surrender to us, my lord," said Gaitox. "I have no doubt."

Duke Bassikrin regarded him. "No, she won't. You don't know the stubbornness of that girl. She refuses everything. But no matter. That's the point of armies and mages, eh?"

The Duke almost smiled. It was rare for Norbil to see his master in such a good mood.

The Archmage smiled back. "And we have our surprises ready for those wretched Divine-worshippers."

"Good, good," said the Duke. "You can tell me about those on the way."

"So we have six days now in which to get there."

"Yes, I'll be glad when authority transfers from Ethabos and Sirika to that girl. Those devious schemers would try to negotiate a compromise. That served me well through the Regency, while I bided my time and strengthened my forces. But time runs out for me, my friend. I have no time for deals or compromises now. I will conquer Anestra, so that when my rule passes to Bassilius those self-righteous whiners are under his boots."

"But this girl, this Princess Katelin, you said that she refuses everything. That she'll never surrender."

"I'm counting on it." The Duke grinned. He was in a good mood. "I intend to land on that urchin with unstoppable force before she has time to think. We can rely on her not to listen to anyone's advice, and with forced marches we may even be in time to spoil her big day. She's refused me too often, so now I will crush her. I'll make her marry my boy, and their children will rule this Coast. And when she refuses my terms—well, it's been too long since our men had a good fight. They'll be delighted to smash the life out of those 'children of the Divine', and gorge themselves on her loot."

Bassikrin raised an arm to Norbil. The Captain lifted the ferret to the floor and assisted his dear old master to rise from the throne. The Duke took a long look around his Palace Hall. Behind them, the ferret crept back onto the throne and curled up.

The Duke tottered on Norbil's arm towards the entrance doors, Archmage Gaitox allowing him to lead the way. "We will meet Bassilius on the highway. He won't have reached the monks yet, but he can deliver the prize to me on the way. Then we will have the power of their Goddess too."

The Archmage nodded. "We'll force those misguided fools to worship Ilbassi instead, and our god will be supreme. Then he will reward us who serve him well."

Captain Norbil found himself relishing this outcome too. His masters would have all power: both spiritual and political. The Archmage would control the Temple of the Divine in Anestra, and Lasseny's Shrine of Ilbassi. The Duke would control the Coast, from Anestra's Castle as well as from his own Palace. It would be good for his masters, for Lasseny and for Captain Norbil too.

At the doors, he wanted to mark the moment. So Norbil said, "Ilbassi go with you, my lords, and give you the victory."

Bassikrin and Gaitox turned, and seemed to notice the Captain for the first time. For a stomach-freezing moment, Norbil thought he'd spoken out of turn.

Then the Duke half smiled again. "Thank you, Captain. You will keep order in the city until I return. Although that should be easier since we're taking the troublemakers with us. And don't forget to feed the ferret."

Captain Norbil gave a crisp salute. The Duke and Archmage left the Palace Hall to follow the forces that had set off from the desert gate.

The four walkers paused by the trail where stunted trees provided some shade. Armus took off his hat and fanned himself. They drank from their bottles, and Sigzay handed them ironwood leaves to chew. These tasted bitter but they surrendered their juice.

The sun became hotter as it climbed into a clear blue sky. Hedger and Armus walked in front, and Kat kept pace with Sigzay now, who seemed to lag behind on purpose.

With the men out of earshot, Sigzay asked her, "You like Hedger, do you?"

"Do I like him? Yes, he seems a good man."

"And think he likes you?"

Where was this heading? "Um, I don't know. He's friendly and helpful."

"And think this Princess and Queen help you."

"Helps me? I don't know what you mean."

Sigzay stopped, her finger pointing, but her voice was calm, controlled. "I tell you, Kat: Hedger and me friends for long time. He rescue me when captive and save my life. I bound to him, and he devoted to me. I think you not innocent as you appears. I warn you not get in pretty little head to interest in him."

"You warn me?" Kat held up her hands. "No, wait. You listen to me, Sigzay. What's between you and Hedger is none of my business, but I'd never try to break up your friendship. I like him as a friend, and that's all. He's far too taken with you to give me a second glance. And he doesn't interest me in that way."

Sigzay's eyebrows shot up. "He doesn't?"

"No. So you needn't worry about me." Kat resumed walking. "Anyway, Hedger doesn't strike me as the sort to be impressed by titles, position or wealth."

Sigzay matched her pace. "Good. Glad that clear."

They walked in silence. But Kat had hoped to count Sigzay as a friend. So she said, "But don't you dare get in the way between me and Brother Armus …"

Sigzay stopped, aghast. Kat couldn't hide the teasing smile that twitched her mouth. They collapsed into laughter.

Their uncontrollable mirth caused Hedger and Armus to turn around to see what was so hilarious. The girls, of course, told them nothing.

At midday they took refuge from the sun's prickling heat under the rocky wall of a canyon, and quenched their thirst from a stream. Sigzay lit a fire with dry grass and dead branches to roast her desert monitor lizard.

Armus sat and closed his eyes to meditate, so Hedger and Kat explored the canyon for anything more to eat. The steep gorge rose between the two foothills, and the stream tinkled through waterfalls and pools. They spotted mountain gazelles perched on the canyon walls, grazing on outcrops of green.

Kat nocked an arrow to her shortbow, as Hedger waited and watched. She took aim at the nearest gazelle, and sweat trickled down behind her ear. Was that from the sun, or knowing that Hedger watched her? She loosed the arrow, and flushed with pride as it sank into the creature's flank. The gazelles scattered and the wounded prey fell to the canyon floor. Hedger was on it, sword in hand, and released the animal from pain.

They returned to the fire in triumph. The lizard was cooking, and Sigzay set to skinning roast gazelle for lunch. Kat glowed as Hedger praised her skill, and admitted that she'd excelled with targets as a girl. At times, she'd even been allowed to train with the Royal Archers. "I'm sure Aunt and Uncle only allowed it in the hope of instilling me with discipline and obedience," she added.

They rested through the heat of the day, until Sigzay woke them with the roasted meat. She handed them each a leaf with two lumps of meat.

"A test," she said. "See who tells lizard from gazelle."

Kat inspected the meat, but couldn't distinguish them. She bit and chewed, and the others did the same. Was the lizard darker and tougher than the gazelle? They all guessed, and Hedger and Kat were correct. To grins all round, Kat declared her roast gazelle to be the best she'd ever tasted.

Before they set off, Kat went to bathe in a pool she'd seen

up the canyon. She stripped off and eased into the cool water. The sky was bright through the mesquite trees, and the canyon around her was still.

It was bliss: to wash away the sweat and dust. And who needed doubts or fears anyway?

The sound of footsteps interrupted her daydreams. She scrambled to cover her underwater nakedness as Hedger came into view.

He gave a lopsided smile. "We're preparing to go. When you're ready … my lady."

He disappeared. As she dried herself and dressed, Kat found that she was grinning. She couldn't decide between outrage and amusement. He'd seen her naked shoulder!

WILDERNESS

S upper is served, milady."

"Thank you, I'm coming." Princess Rashelin rose from where she knelt beside a bookcase.

The library was a mess. Books, papers, crates and packing cases littered the patterned carpets. Many of the oak bookshelves were empty, but some were still full. Rashelin sighed, and then followed the servant girl to the dining room. She'd hoped that helping her parents to pack up the royal apartments would distract her from other matters weighing on her mind. But it hadn't.

Regent Ethabos and Consort Sirika were already sitting at the long, mahogany dining table. Rashelin crossed the plush carpets to her place and pulled in the upholstered chair. Walker, the butler, filled her glass with white wine, and topped up her father's. Her mother was having only water.

"The packing in the library is going well." Rashelin tried to sound cheerful. "I think we've as many crates in there as we'll need."

Ethabos was spreading thick butter on a small loaf.

Sirika said, "Thank you, my dear. Your father and I are grateful for your help, but you know that we object to being ousted from this apartment at all."

Oh dear, Rashelin thought. Mother was in a bad mood. They'd been over this so many times. She sipped her wine and said, "Perhaps you could go down to Mannismill for the summer. You'd be with the boys, and you enjoy the fresh air of the countryside in the south."

"That's not the point," Sirika said. "We resent being evicted from our rooms for the sake of that useless cousin of yours."

Rashelin decided not to start another family argument by standing up for Katelin again.

The soup course arrived. Ethabos had devoured half his loaf and now started on his large bowl of clam and herb soup. Rashelin took some spoonfuls and a bite of bread. Sirika dipped at her soup and indulged her usual obsession: tidying the butter dish after her husband's assault upon it.

Once the servants had vacated the room, Rashelin said, "The story that Katelin is on retreat at Mannismill seems to be holding so far."

Ethabos grunted. Sirika said, "You know that we're fed up with making excuses for that girl. But what can we do? People are asking questions, and what would they think if they knew the truth?"

Rashelin had some soup. She hesitated to upset her parents by continuing the conversation, but there were things she wanted to know.

"I was wondering," she said at last, "what happens with the coronation if Katelin doesn't return in time?"

As expected, her parents stopped and stared at her. Ethabos's mouth was full, so Sirika said through her teeth, "My dear, that girl *must* be back in time. The coronation *has* to run according to tradition and reflect well on us. That's all there is to it. Do you think she'll have forgotten what day it is?"

"No, I'm sure that Katelin is well aware of the days," said Rashelin. "But what if she's been detained in Lasseny, or delayed along the way?"

Ethabos finished a mouthful and spluttered, "If she hadn't run off in the first place, then none of this would arise."

"But she has gone," said Rashelin. "Do we delay until she returns?"

Sirika glared at her. "Don't you know how long we've been preparing this coronation? Don't you realise how many distinguished guests are coming, and how the eyes of the whole Coast will be on us? Can't you see what an utter catastrophe it would be if something went as wrong as that? Do we delay indeed!"

"I know we've worked hard to arrange everything, but if she isn't here … what can we do?"

Sirika sniffed. "Well, one can't hold a coronation without the Queen." The words seemed bitter on her tongue.

"What if she's held prisoner by the Duke?" Rashelin asked. "Does the Regency continue until she's Crowned?"

Her parents looked at each other, and Ethabos returned to demolishing his bread and soup. Sirika's tone was acid. "We understand that your cousin becomes the legal Queen on her eighteenth birthday, whether Crowned or not. If Bassikrin has her, then we would need to negotiate her release."

Rashelin nodded and took a spoonful of soup. "The Duke and Count declined their invitations to the coronation, didn't they?"

"Yes, they did," grumbled Sirika. "They're as furious with that girl as we are. Refusing the marriage alliance! I'll never understand how your cousin can be so selfish as to reject what is in the best interests of the Kingdom."

Rashelin thought it best not to start that argument again. Was Katelin's preference irrelevant in choosing whom she would marry? They ate in silence.

Then Sirika went on, "Still, we can hope to remedy that

after the coronation. The marriage to Bassilius will add further pressure on that girl to do as she's told." Ethabos was nodding.

"Katelin has never got on with Bassilius," Rashelin said, "and she doesn't respond well to being told what to do. I can't see that improving once she's Queen."

Sirika's words were sharp. "Becoming Queen doesn't stop her from being our niece, you know. That girl owes us. We've given her the last sixteen years of our lives. The least we have the right to expect is that she'll do what we say."

"Katelin will want to make her own decisions, though. I can't see her turning into a meek figurehead or puppet, when she could be a Queen with the power and authority to rule for the good of the Kingdom."

Sirika snorted. "That girl doesn't know the first thing about running the Kingdom, or what's good for it. She'll be useless at it. So we'll continue to tell her what to do, and then she'll do it. The last thing Anestra needs is that foolish girl getting it into her head to change everything and upset everyone."

Rashelin sighed. She hated conflicts, especially within the Family, and too many of them were approaching. She sipped her wine, but had lost her appetite for the soup. The herbs were leaving a bitter taste.

There was one last thing she had to ask. "What if something worse has happened … and Katelin has been killed?"

Her parents looked at each other again. For a second, Rashelin glimpsed a transformation in her mother's face. Sirika had let slip a smile, before she'd concealed it.

"As tragic as that would be," Sirika said, "at least it would solve some of our problems. Your father would become King, and you'd be next in the line of succession."

Rashelin was appalled. She'd gone cold at her mother's smile. This was Katelin's life!

Then the servants re-entered the room.

They continued south until darkness fell and for a few miles further under starlight. The night air was still and cool, and Kat's eyes adjusted to a wilderness bathed in silvery grey. She reminded herself to savour each hour and moment of freedom.

The next day, high clouds made the sun hazy and the walking more comfortable. They were making good progress. But that following night, as they looked for somewhere to camp, Sigzay stopped them in their tracks.

Everyone strained to listen: voices ahead. They crept forward in the darkness, and the sounds changed to coarse banter and raucous singing.

They retreated and held a whispered conference.

"Bandits," Sigzay hissed. "They hide and attack highway travellers. We destroy them." Kat was startled by the fierceness in the barbarian's voice.

Armus held up a hand. "Wait a minute. Rather than fighting, can't we avoid them? The four of us can't take on a whole horde, and we have more urgent matters than ridding the Coast of bandits." He motioned at Kat.

Hedger nodded. "We should find out their numbers and if they have lookouts. Then slip past them in the dark. Sigzay, could you spy on them from above?"

Sigzay glared at him, then climbed straight up the rock wall beside them onto the canyon rim. Kat judged it not a bad ascent.

They waited for the barbarian to return from above the bandit camp. Sigzay took long enough for something to have happened.

At last, unhurried, she crept back to them.

"Fourteen bandits," she whispered. "Two guard canyon mouth and all have weapons, not ready. They in middle of eat and drink. Have campfire and torches. We see them, they not see us. Also, have prisoner: young man in blue robes."

Kat's insides clenched. She and Armus looked at each other in alarm. "Is he tall, with curly ginger hair?" she asked.

"Think yes," said Sigzay.

"Initiate Prento," said Armus. "He came this way from Lasseny. We have to rescue him."

The others nodded. No more avoidance, they had to attack. But Kat noticed her heart had begun to thump. So she'd meet him again, with even the chance to rescue him. And Prento didn't know her true identity.

Kat climbed after Sigzay up the rock wall to the rim, while Hedger and Armus stayed at canyon floor level. Her eyes were accustomed to starlight, and Kat made out the silhouette of Sigzay against the flicker of torches and fire. She peered at the bandits below.

Sigzay launched their attack with crossbow bolts into unsuspecting figures away from the fire. Kat followed up with her arrows. It was too easy, like shooting deer cooped in a pen.

The bandits shouted and scattered. As planned, Sigzay and Kat were invisible to them, black figures against background stars. Answering arrows whistled past them, until Kat picked off those with bows.

Some bandits hid against the wall at Kat and Sigzay's feet, while a couple fled up the gorge. A group ran for the canyon mouth, where shouts and the clash of arms told Kat that Hedger and Armus had entered the fray.

Sigzay and Kat fired at any bandit that showed a target. The cries and ring of steel from their left continued until

Hedger and Armus appeared. Two bandits threw down their weapons in surrender.

Kat saw Hedger approach the fire, bloodied sword drawn. A bandit on the ground swung a leg. Kat gasped as she'd thought him dead. He kicked Hedger's feet from under him, and the mercenary crashed to the ground. The bandit grabbed a sword and was up and on him.

Kat scrambled to nock another arrow. Hedger and the bandit rolled on the ground, too close to the fire, wrestling over the sword. She couldn't risk hitting Hedger.

The bandit pulled his arm free and lifted the sword.

Kat fired.

The arrow thudded into the bandit's back. He slumped across the prone and helpless Hedger, the sword missing his head by an inch. Hedger rolled the bandit off him and scrambled to his feet. But the battle was over.

Kat and Sigzay descended to the canyon floor. Hedger and Sigzay disarmed and tied up the injured and surrendering bandits. Armus and Kat went to the prisoner, who lay huddled in a rocky cleft.

Kat's dagger released Initiate Prento's bonds. "Ah, my noble Lord Prento, sir," she said. "Would you like your humble servants to get you out of trouble?"

"My Lady Kat," he exclaimed. "And Brother Armus, come to rescue me, excellent. I was about to put my escape plan into action, but seeing as you're here ..."

"Your escape plan?" Armus rolled his eyes. "What happened to you?"

"I was running down the highway early this morning," said Prento, "and saw these people ahead. I should have been less trusting, but I was too close before I realised what they were. They caught me and brought me here."

"You were lucky not to be killed on the spot," said Kat, as she gave him some water.

"Not at all." Prento beamed. "Who'd want to kill me? I had no coins or valuables, so they asked what I was doing. I told them about delivering the scroll to the Temple. That set off a debate: how to make me continue to Anestra, then ambush the goldens on my return. They hadn't concluded anything when you turned up. Why are you this far from Lasseny?"

"We outstayed our welcome in that city," said Armus, "and were chased from it two days ago. We're on our way to Anestra, and came across your little band of robbers while looking for a place for the night. You'd better join us."

"Thank you," said Prento. He frowned. "Daytose needs my swift return to Lasseny, so I'd better run ahead in the morning. If I can take food, drink and the copy of the judgement, I'll set off at first light by myself." He grinned. "Will you survive on your own without me?"

Armus and Kat glanced at each other and shook their heads. Kat liked Prento's self-confidence, but couldn't decide if it was an act, boyish naivety, or faith that the Divine would look after him.

Kat bandaged a gash on Armus's arm. Hedger searched the bodies and campsite for food and valuables, and found Prento's scroll. Sigzay retrieved undamaged bolts and arrows, because she and Kat were running out of missiles.

The five of them moved on from the scene of battle, leaving the surviving bandits to fend for themselves. They walked in silence for fear of being heard, so Kat had no chance to talk with Prento.

They chose a corner inside a small gorge, lay down with no fire, and kept watch in turn. Kat couldn't sleep and felt ridiculous. Oh, yes: rescued Prento from bandits, another point to her. Why couldn't she ignore that some boy lay a few feet away? It wasn't him at all, of course, but the battle that had churned her up. Right. Relax.

Or perhaps it was him. But she wanted him as a friend, nothing more. Friendship would be good. Yes, that would be nice.

They rose at daybreak and gave Prento some provisions. Kat wanted to talk to him before he left, so she went to sit with him as he munched on a hunk of dried gazelle meat. She couldn't think what to say, and so ventured on the subject that was always on her heart: what people did with their lives.

"So, your lordship, why did you become an initiate?"

"Divine calling," Prento replied, his mouth full.

"As simple as that? Brother Armus said something similar."

Prento nodded. "What about you? What do you do?"

Kat leaned back, resting on her hands. The rays of the rising sun caught her eyes. "I suppose I'm a rich girl who doesn't know what to do with herself."

"Rich or poor only governs how many choices you get," said Prento. "What are you good at?"

Kat shrugged; then indicated the gazelle meat. "Shooting a bow?"

Prento smiled. "Ah, the hunting profession. Or maybe the army, the Royal Archers."

Kat let the sun warm her face. "I used to think that being out here held all the answers. In the wilderness, to be free, living off your wits, an adventurer or mercenary, like Hedger and Sigzay."

"But … you don't think this now?" Prento said when Kat had paused.

She sat up, leaning forward again. She wound a blade of grass around a finger. "I don't know what to think any more."

Kat felt his eyes on her. "What does your heart tell you?"

he said. "You should find what you love and follow that."

"Is that what you've done?"

"Yes, I love the Divine more than anything."

Kat tried a smile. "So then, if I fall in love, that will give me some answers?"

Prento regarded her, held her eye. He then gave a pretend serious intake of breath. "My Lady Kat, falling in love is a wild and risky path to take. It can lead you in many dangerous directions."

He got up, and offered Kat his hand to help her up too. She took it. A warmth twitched his mouth and eyes. "I hope that you find the love of your heart, my lady."

Kat gathered her courage, reached up and embraced him. As a friend. She hoped he got that message. "The speed of the Divine for the rest of your way, your lordship," she said.

"Thank you again, my lady," he said. He bent low and kissed her hand. "Now you're sure you'll be safe, and don't need directions?" She aimed a playful slap at him. He said, "I guess I'll have left Anestra by the time you get there."

"I suppose so," Kat said. She shrugged, but then held his gaze. "We may see each other again somewhere."

He nodded and smiled. Yes, the message had been received.

With a cheerful wave of his hand to the others, Prento set off at a loping run. He disappeared around an outcrop of rock into the growing light of the desert morning.

Kat heaved a sigh and rejoined the others.

The four of them walked on through a hot, tiring and uneventful day.

Kat had too many hours in which to ponder, and at first she thought about Prento. She smiled at how he called her 'his lady', but didn't know that she was his Princess. How much would her royalty help or hinder a friendship with him?

She'd always been wary of the intentions of men and

boys, the sons of nobles who angled for a match. Some, like Count Bassilius, wanted power, wealth and reputation. She hoped that Prento would be different, a friend not interested in her royalty and riches.

Later in the day, the prospect of returning home loomed ever larger. Kat had left Anestra with thoughts of the Crown, but she'd discovered almost nothing. Now the quest for these new friends was to get her to her coronation on time. If she hadn't run away, she'd have saved them all this trouble.

But they'd discovered the invasion threat from Lasseny. What could she do about that? Was she was any closer to saving the Kingdom from conquest? And only four days now until she became Queen.

Her homeward steps became more reluctant and despondent. So when she lay down that night, she wasn't surprised when The Nightmare of clutching hands returned.

"Tell me you thinking."

Hedger stirred from staring at the distant, darkened horizon. When Sigzay had woken him for the midnight change of watch, she'd stayed up with him. Instead of lying down where Kat and Armus slept, she'd sat beside him, hugging her knees.

Hedger leaned his head back against the canyon wall. Their voices were low so as not to disturb the others. "I was thinking," he murmured, "that when we get to Anestra we could buy enough food to have a feast."

Sigzay rested her head on her arms and smiled. "My cooking not good?" she teased.

He reached an arm across her shoulders and squeezed. "You know I love your cooking, but out here we have to conserve what we find. We eat enough to keep us going, but never overfull. I'm looking forward to stuffing myself to the brim." As if to reinforce the point, his stomach rumbled.

Sigzay gave him a gentle elbow. "Sounds good." They nestled together and returned their gazes to where the distant stars met the desert. The night insects had subdued their chirrup, and her warmth was enticing.

Sigzay spoke again. "Since we leave Lasseny, you seem distant, quiet. You troubled. Tell me."

Hedger smiled. Her grey eyes and white hair glinted in the starlight. It was sufficient to remind him why he'd fallen for her. Her directness was both endearing and uncomfortable, for how honest could he be? "You know me too well, my wolf," he said. "I can't hide much from you, can I?"

Sigzay shook her head and waited.

Hedger interlocked fingers with her and sighed. "I'm worried about Anestra. The threat from the Duke is real. And now we're caught up in it, because we've the Queen of Anestra right here. Who can say whether Kat is up to the challenge? We need to help her."

"We are help her. We get her safe to Anestra, and in time for Crown."

"It's what happens afterwards that worries me," said Hedger. "What if the Coast descends into war? Lasseny won't be safe for Anestrans then."

"Leave them to it. Go elsewhere. We cannot fight war for them."

Hedger touched Sigzay's arm, and she looked into his eyes. "I can't leave them to it. Anestra matters to me. It's my home, my city, my people. If they're at war, then I have to help. And now that Kat's here, I want to help her too."

"What about Kat?" Sigzay's voice became sharper. "She matter to you? You feel for her?"

Hedger hesitated. He had to say this with the utmost care. For Kat meant more to him than Sigzay could know. "She's my Queen. Or she soon will be. I owe her my loyalty, my allegiance. If she asks for my help, or asks me for anything, then I should do it. So, yes, she matters to me. But not in the way I think you meant."

"She not my Queen," Sigzay muttered. She fell silent. In the darkness it was even harder than usual to read her face. At last she said, "So we reach Anestra, you want stay for while?"

"Yes, I think we should—"

"I don't."

She pulled away and stood up. "I go sleep." She stalked off into the darkness.

Hedger moved to follow, then stopped. He watched her curl up, separate from Kat and Armus. He breathed out, long and slow.

For the rest of his watch he alternated between a vacant stare at that faraway point of horizon, and gazing at the huddled, vulnerable form of his young Queen-to-be.

The next morning, the highway from Lasseny to Anestra drew closer to their line of foothills, but they agreed to stay off it. Their path was not much rougher than the road and had the benefit of secrecy. For the highway had movement along it: horsemen, carts, individuals and groups.

The ground had changed from sand and rock to dry, stony earth. Flies buzzed about their heads, and scrubland rodents darted for cover in tufts of grass that grew beside the track.

Kat walked with Hedger. Sigzay shouldn't be jealous now, should she?

"So how did you and Sigzay meet?" Kat asked, after a while. "She said you saved her life when she was a captive. And that she's bound to you, or something."

"That's right," Hedger said. "I rescued her from a feud between the barbarian tribes that had condemned her to death. So according to their custom, her life belongs to me. Not that I'm complaining, you understand. She has the best eyes and ears I know."

"Only eyes and ears?"

Hedger grinned. "Well, she can cook too." They laughed. "No, I have to say that as friends go, she's the best. I couldn't be without her. She calls herself 'my wolf'."

Someone's life bound to yours. How would that be? Yes, that was the sort of devotion Kat wanted.

Hedger broke their silence. "Kat, I'm sorry we didn't get anywhere with your quest for the Crown. It was courageous of you to suggest it."

"I was thinking last night how foolish I've been," said Kat. "We've found out nothing, and all I've done is to cause you trouble."

"Don't be hard on yourself," said Hedger. "Your intentions were good, and you shouldn't worry about troubling us wanderers. We take all this in our stride."

"That's kind of you to say," she said. "I'd hoped to help Anestra, but now I've made it difficult even to attend my own coronation."

"But you have helped Anestra. When we arrive, we can warn of the Lassenite threat. At least you're in a position to do something about that."

"Don't remind me," said Kat. "Yes, we've discovered that the Duke is invading, but that's different from defeating his army. I'm not a general or good at battle tactics, so how can I help to defend the city?"

"You'll be surprised," said Hedger, "the difference it makes to a soldier—to fight for their Queen, and not a Regent they despise."

Kat hadn't thought of that. But would it make enough of a difference? She batted away a persistent fly. "We know that

Lasseny's army is stronger, so my first days as Queen will see Anestra defeated. Instead of us ruling the Coast from our Castle, as in the Old Kingdom days, we'll be subjects of the Duke. He'll be the overlord, we'll be the vassals, and—as Armus has said—I'll be forced to marry Count Bassilius. I'll have failed as Queen, and the ruin of Anestra will be at my hands."

"Whatever happens, Kat, it won't be your fault," said Hedger. "If Lasseny conquers Anestra, the blame is the Regent's. He hasn't strengthened our army, or sought to contain the threat from the Duke. But I understand now. You hoped for the Crown to secure Anestra's freedom: to inspire us, and that Divine power would tip the balance in the coming war."

"Finding and restoring the Crown was always my childhood dream," said Kat. "I can't change the Regent's mistakes, or avoid becoming Queen, but at least I could seek for the Crown. To recover a fragment, or restore it to completion, would make all the difference for Anestra. But none of that will happen now, and my hope has been in vain."

After a silence, Hedger said, "Can I suggest something, Kat? You'll have to forgive that I'm a simple man who deals with only one thing at a time. How about if we worry first about your timely return to Anestra, and then get you through your coronation, and then deal with facing the Lassenites? Each problem in turn."

Kat nodded. "Yes, that sounds better, manageable. One thing at a time." She paused to look at him. "But to tell you the truth, I am dreading becoming Queen."

Hedger's frown wrinkled his scarred forehead. "Dreading it?"

Kat sighed. Should she tell him everything? It had been a relief to admit her fears to Armus, and she was desperate for help from anyone. Maybe it was easier to tell a relative stranger than a friend. Kat didn't know why, but she felt she could trust Hedger, that he would understand.

But she hadn't told Armus the true depth of her fears. For the first time ever, could she explain the terror that sometimes afflicted her?

She kicked some stones as they walked along. "I've always been a free spirit: rebellious, wilful, impulsive, running from home and wanting my own way."

"I can see that," said Hedger, "and I feel the same. My freedom's the most important thing to me, and that's why Sigzay and I chose this life. We're masters of our own destinies: we go where we wish, and do what we choose."

"Yes, I envy you that," said Kat. For a moment, Hedger looked ashamed of what he'd said.

"But once I'm Queen," she went on, "I'll have to sit in the Court all day in my robes and finery. I'll listen to nobles and officials whine their complaints about precedence and ceremony. And they expect me to restore the glory of Anestra. How am I supposed to recover all the lands that once belonged to the Old Kingdom?"

Hedger's look was sympathetic, but he gave her no answer.

She pressed on. "Being Queen has so many restrictions and duties, and they tell me I'll be useless at it." Her words were coming in a rush, and tears stung her eyes. "It stifles me, the burden of all that's expected. And every day, every decision, will be a fight with my Aunt and Uncle. I'm ... frightened. Sometimes it scares me witless, and I don't know if I have the strength for it. It fills me with a panic, like ... like a fear of being buried alive. It's a nightmare, only one where I can't wake up. My life as I know it ends on my birthday, when the burden of ruling a Kingdom is added to my years of being bullied. It becomes an ornate and comfortable prison. Or a war, a battleground." Her voice cracked. "Or a grave." She shuddered a breath.

Hedger had stopped, staring at her. Even the flies seemed silent. "Oh, Kat," he said, and placed a cracked and pitted hand on her shoulder. She risked looking up at him.

His conker eyes had filled with tears, and he said, "No, I couldn't face that either." He swallowed hard, cleared his throat. "I'd choose freedom and the wilderness any day."

Hedger walked on, his head down. Kat trembled in the silence, and followed him. She breathed hard to slow her pounding heart.

He agreed with her. She expected him to tell her off for running away ... but he'd have done the same.

And he felt for her. That much was clear. Maybe he couldn't help her, but at least she'd explained her dread. He didn't seem to think she'd made a fool of herself. It felt like a growing friendship between them, and more brotherly than how she viewed Prento.

But now there was no way to avoid it: the nearer they came to Anestra—every hour, every mile—that terror was daunting her again.

✳ XI ✳

ENCOUNTERS

When a large canyon opened on their right, the four walkers escaped from the midday sun. They sheltered along the southern rock wall, ate, and drank from the stream. Hedger, Sigzay and Kat dozed in the shade while Armus kept watch.

The air was warm and still. Armus tried hard to resist the nodding of his head. He wasn't used to long walks, wilderness discomforts or short nights of sleep. But he struggled on as lookout to allow the others to rest. From time to time he closed his eyes to meditate for a moment.

The next thing he knew was an urgent shout from Sigzay. "Up! Awake!"

His chin jerked from his chest. He blinked, wiped some dribble. Sigzay was up and the others were stirring.

"Awake! Run!" Sigzay screamed.

Armus tried to grasp what was happening. Sigzay grabbed Kat and pulled her to her feet. The two girls left everything and fled up the canyon.

Only now did Armus register the sound of tramping feet. He whirled around. Black and crimson uniforms were at the mouth of the canyon.

Armus fumbled for his weapon. But the Lassenite soldiers had spotted him, and more followed behind. He was too slow and late to flee. Hedger was beside him now, but they couldn't fight so many. Armus stood, dropped his mace and raised open hands in surrender.

The Lassenites were a hundred strong, a dozen of them on horseback. They surrounded and disarmed Armus and Hedger.

"My lord," called the Lassenite officer. "We've found a couple of brigands in the canyon."

To Armus's utter dismay, the contingent was led by none other than Count Bassilius.

The Count rode up and dismounted. He surveyed the two of them, and then the weapons and packs. There was a flicker of recognition as Bassilius met Hedger's eyes.

"Send a squad up the canyon to find the other two," said Bassilius. "Let the men have water and rest. I'll deal with these two myself."

The Lassenites drank from the stream and collapsed in the shade, while ten of them marched up the canyon after Sigzay and Kat. The officer gathered their packs and weapons, heaping them against the rock wall.

At Bassilius's order, four soldiers pushed Armus and Hedger to the ground and tied their ankles and wrists. The Count regarded them from his perch on a shady rock nearby. A soldier brought him water, and he drank it all.

Armus berated himself as lookout. He deserved whatever now befell him, but what trouble had he brought on Hedger, Sigzay and Kat? His cleric's vows required him not to lie, so his answers needed to be careful.

Bassilius said, "Who are you?"

"My name is Armus and this is Hedger."

"And the other two?" When Armus hesitated, Bassilius repeated, "The other two—who ran off—who are they? Don't pretend that you're carrying two packs each."

"Their names are Sigzay and Kat," said Armus.

"What are you doing here?"

"We're travelling from Lasseny to Anestra."

"Why do you skulk in canyons instead of using the highway?"

Armus tried a smile. "Like yourselves, we find the road too sun-baked. We need some shade in the midst of the day, and to drink from the streams."

Bassilius looked unconvinced. "What were you doing in Lasseny?"

Oh dear. Clerics of the Divine were only tolerated, as the Duke reckoned them Anestran spies. Armus said, "We are mercenaries."

Bassilius scoffed. "He looks like a mercenary," he jabbed a finger towards Hedger, "but you wear the robes of a cleric."

"As well as being a mercenary," said Armus, "I also serve as a cleric of the Divine."

"I knew it." Bassilius congratulated himself, and his face twitched in agreement. "You're all Anestrans then?"

"Sigzay is barbarian, but the rest of us are Anestran," said Armus.

"I saw some of you near the Palace a few days ago." The finger jabbed at Hedger again. "What were you doing there?"

"Our friend Kat had arrived in Lasseny," said Armus. "She asked to see your magnificent Palace and we took her to see it. We were lucky enough to see you come out and ride past."

"And you are spies." It was a statement, not a question.

"No, we're not spies," said Armus. "We've done honest work in Lasseny, and kept ourselves out of trouble in your fine city."

"If you're not spies, why did the other two run off as we arrived?"

Armus couldn't think of an excuse, and Hedger spoke up. "Perhaps to avoid being tied up and questioned for no good reason?"

Hedger's tone made Bassilius jump to his feet. "I will tie

up, question and execute whom I wish," he barked at him. "Even if you're honest men—which I doubt—and not spies, then by your own admission, you are mercenaries. So you're brigands and robbers, hiding in canyons to waylay highway travellers." He paused and calmed a little. "I'm told that four 'mercenaries' fought their way out of the city near the desert gate a few days ago. Was that you?"

"What's the matter, Bassilius?" Hedger snapped. "Wish you had an Ilbassi mage with a Truth Spell? Don't worry, I'll tell you the truth. Yes, that was us."

Armus rolled his eyes but said nothing. What was Hedger doing?

"You insolent wretch." Bassilius shoved Hedger to the ground and stood with a boot on his chest. "So you are hiding something. I'll avenge on you the injuries and deaths of each of my men."

"You left us little choice." Hedger's voice was calm. "Law-abiding citizens have no place under your father's oppression."

Armus winced as Bassilius's boot squelched into Hedger's stomach. Hedger folded in half, retching, writhing. The Count spat on his prostrate form and roared, "I should drag you straight back to Lasseny for my father to deal with. But I'm on an urgent and important mission, so you can wait till my task is completed. Then you'll wish you never crossed me." Bassilius stalked away and sat in a shady spot by himself.

Hedger was gasping for breath, his face pressed hard into the rock. There was nothing Armus could do to help him. At last, Hedger struggled to a sitting position, rubbed his midriff with a bound arm and laid back his head. Armus met his eyes, but they said nothing. No water or food was offered, and the ropes chafed their ankles and wrists.

Armus tried to understand what Hedger had done.

Antagonising the Count had been a bad idea, but had it made any difference? Bassilius would never have let them go, because they were Anestran mercenaries.

But maybe Hedger had been clever with the questions, although at his own expense. He'd provoked Bassilius's temper into violence. The awkward questions had ended before unguarded answers betrayed their secrets. So had Hedger had the insight and courage to save Kat?

And what about the girls? To avoid any danger of Bassilius seeing Kat, Sigzay should take her straight to Anestra. Yet would Sigzay's love for Hedger make her linger here, or even worse, attempt a rescue?

The Count had said he was on an urgent and important mission. Anestra was three days away from Crowning their new Queen, so was that his urgency? A hundred Lassenites posed no threat to the city, but were strong enough to ensure that something was accomplished. What could that be?

Sigzay and Kat lay still and flat on the ledge. They had stumbled, then sprinted up the gorge, and achieved a minute's head start on the searching Lassenite soldiers. At the head of the canyon, they'd scaled the rock face on their left in a rapid ascent to the ledges and rim above.

Their pursuers hadn't tried to be stealthy, and they heard them before they appeared. Sigzay and Kat threw themselves down on a wide ledge and froze.

Ten Lassenites tramped up the canyon, convincing each other of the hopelessness of catching fugitives on a mountainside. They discussed a hot and difficult climb, and the danger of enemies throwing rocks from above. They agreed to sit and wait, and then pretend that they'd conducted a thorough search.

A venomous brown canyon snake slithered onto the

ledge. It flicked a black tongue towards Sigzay and Kat. They budged not a muscle.

The snake slid nearer, drawing its zigzag body across the smooth rock. Kat debated the greater danger: snake venom, or being seen by the Lassenites?

She rotated her eyes to Sigzay. "Don't move," the barbarian mouthed.

The tension in Kat's muscles grew painful, and she willed both snake and Lassenites to lose interest. Each moment seemed like hours, and the snake seemed to taste her sweat. It stretched its mouth, revealing glistening fangs.

At last the Lassenites gathered themselves and marched off down the canyon to report their lack of success. The snake was distracted by the movement below. It slithered away and Sigzay and Kat breathed again.

They climbed out of the gorge and over the rim to the top of the Coastal Range foothill. The mountain peaks soared jagged and forbidding behind them, and they were high enough to see over the plain. A breeze stirred the grass and made the sun more bearable than in the hazy desert below. They sat and recovered their breath.

"Good afternoon," Sigzay said, with obvious irritation. "Not wake-up call we expect. I not like Armus as lookout."

"He must have fallen asleep," said Kat. "I don't blame him; we're all exhausted."

"We should be more alert," Sigzay said. "So Lassenites capture other two, and will question before do worse to them."

"What have we got with us?" said Kat. "I've only what I'm wearing, which includes my dagger. But we've no packs, no shortbow or arrows, no crossbow or bolts."

"I have short sword," said Sigzay. "Time for wits and skill to survive."

Kat knew they were vulnerable without their bows or packs.

And how much did she trust Sigzay as her sole bodyguard and protector? She asked, "What shall we do about Armus and Hedger?"

"What can do?" said Sigzay. "You not think that we, short sword and dagger, tackle so many?"

"I agree it doesn't sound good. But we can't abandon them."

"You think of rescue," Sigzay said, incredulous. "I normal with you in that, as my Hedger caught down there. But Kat, I remind who you are."

"I know," Kat snapped. "It gets in the way of everything. I can never do what I want because of who I am." She felt tears coming, but blinked them away. She pulled up blades of grass and threw them aside.

"Also remind," said Sigzay, "you be Crowned in three days, and we still day or two walk to Anestra. Kat, you need get back to—"

"You think I don't know that?" She heaved a breath. "But it doesn't feel right to leave them. I need to think about this. Can we walk somewhere, or get on our way while I think?"

"Of course," Sigzay said. "Now soldiers give up search, we go along rim and see what they do. We track crowd of them, but they not spot two up here. We aim south and east, leave canyons and foothill, head for Anestra."

Kat nodded, but hadn't registered what Sigzay had said. They stood and walked off, Kat already lost in thought. Why did everything have to go wrong? Why was it all so difficult for her?

Their steps were wary, careful not to disturb stones. They spied the Lassenites resting in the shade below. Kat stopped short of the rim, while Sigzay ventured forward to check on Armus and Hedger. Kat was supposed to be thinking, working this out, but she couldn't even find the beginning of a plan.

Sigzay returned, and they retreated out of earshot. "Hundred Lassenites," she whispered. "Tie up boys as prisoner. Pile weapons and packs in corner—but have worse news."

"What could be worse?"

"Is Bassilius down there."

Kat groaned.

"I recognise him talk to Armus and Hedger," Sigzay said. "Guards wear his badge. But what he and men doing here?"

"He makes it more dangerous to attempt a rescue," said Kat. "If he sees or captures me, he'll know what a precious prisoner he's caught."

"Exact," said Sigzay. "Still think of rescue?"

"Why isn't it another Captain down there?" Kat fumed. "Why does it have to be Bassilius?"

There was silence between them.

Kat had had enough. That was it. She couldn't stand this anymore. If all of this was her destiny, then she wasn't having it.

She refused.

"You hear that, Divine?" Kat hissed. "I refuse. You can sort out your own destinies."

Sigzay frowned. "What you say?"

Kat was too angry to answer. She clenched her teeth, chewed her lip, bit her cheek. Anything to stop the tears of self-pity. Sigzay said something about food, but Kat wasn't listening.

Everything was going wrong. She should be able to control herself, but she was at a loss.

She gave up.

This was one game she didn't want to play anymore. She could run away from Anestra altogether, and never go back.

When Kat said no more, Sigzay got up and walked off.

Kat sat alone on the hilltop.

She was too restless to stay seated, and got up to gaze at the wide, desert plain in front of her. It shimmered in the dusty heat, with hazy mirages of movement on the road. On either side of her, the foothills rolled like billowing waves, cut through by the streams that tumbled from the heights behind.

Kat turned to look at the peaks. The eastern side of the Coastal Range towered above her, the ridges and summits swathed in cloud and dusted with snow. A week ago she'd sailed north on the other side of those mountains in the hold of the slaver ship. The moist prevailing winds crashed into the granite barrier and drenched that seaward side, where waterfalls cascaded from the cliffs.

Kat looked to the north, but Lasseny was more leagues away than sight could reach. What was that? In the distance—a blur? She shielded and narrowed her eyes. Of dust rising ... or smoke ... or a whole mass of people moving?

The Lassenite army.

Kat stared. And shivered. She knew it in her head. But this was different. To see them coming.

It was as though they marched on her alone. They were coming to get her. To capture, crush and kill her. The hands that clawed, to catch, bury, suffocate. The Waking Nightmare.

This was her destiny. And it was without hope.

She couldn't watch. Or think about it. She hated the despair, and tore her eyes away.

With relief, and reluctance, she turned to her right.

Towards Anestra. Her home.

Southwards the mountain range lowered to high hills, and the inland skies were cloudier. The landscape was greener, as the moist sea breezes watered the fertile ground. Soon they'd come to the outlying farmsteads and cattle stations, the first vineyards, olive and citrus groves of Anestra.

Did she have to abandon her friends and head straight for the city to ensure her safe and timely arrival?

It might sound like perfect sense, but Kat wasn't comfortable with that choice. There had to be more than just saving herself, but the turmoil in her heart prevented clear thinking. And there was only Sigzay to ask for advice.

Kat jumped with fright.

Someone was there!

They were watching her. She was sure.

She whirled around, thinking Sigzay—or someone—had come up behind her.

But there was no one in sight.

She wasn't imagining it. Someone was there. She could feel them. A presence. Something ... or someone ... was invisible.

She stared around, panicked. No, she wasn't going mad. She wasn't.

Katelin.

She reeled to hear it, clear in her head. She wanted to scream, but her throat was parchment. She could only croak, "Who is it?"

A word formed in her mind, a whisper, a name. The pit of her stomach dropped. She ought to kneel or fall flat on her face. But her feet were rooted to the spot.

Divine.

Tears stung her eyes. Anger and frustration surged to the surface. She wanted to run but her muscles had locked. She assailed the presence with a lifetime of rage. If only she could move, she would batter the air, flail her arms, throw herself with all her might.

It's not fair, it's not fair, *it's not fair*!

But the more Kat raged, the more the presence held,

enveloped her. Thoughts and feelings streamed into her mind and heart.

The presence didn't threaten, but comforted. Calmness and tranquillity were on offer. And a strength sufficient to support her in bearing all burdens.

But Kat wasn't ready for them yet.

The Divine accepted her feelings. She didn't have to be alone. The Divine would help and walk with her if she wished.

Kat closed her eyes, breathed in and out. That should have quelled the trembling inside. But it didn't.

She'd just refused the Divine, hadn't she? And her hopeless destiny. And thought about running away for good.

What was going to happen now?

A patient silence.

At last, Kat murmured, "Divine?"

The dam broke and the tears flooded down her face.

There was no sound except for the whisper of the breeze through the grass. She wasn't talking to herself, for she knew that the presence listened. "It's not fair," she sobbed. "I never wanted to be Queen."

I know, Katelin. But trust me.

"But ... but the Lassenites are coming. And it's all down to me."

No. It isn't.

Kat tried to be calm, to trust. To think. It wasn't all down to her?

She whispered, "So ... what should I do next?"

She listened.

Gentle words entered her mind: *Dear Katelin. What do you feel you should do? What do you want to do? My child, trust your heart.*

Kat drew a deep breath ... but the presence had gone. The Divine departed as she had come: sudden, mysterious.

Kat collapsed to the grass. She stared at the sky in bewildered awe and exhaustion.

Time itself stopped as she lay there.

Then her mind began to ignite, until everything inside her was ablaze at the encounter.

Jumping stars! She couldn't just have met ... the Divine. Was that the presence of the ... of the White Goddess? The Life-Weaver herself?

Why had the Divine come to her now?

Because all her life she'd blamed the Divine for her destiny, hadn't she?

And she had to be clear about what she should do.

✷ XII ✷

DECISIONS

Princess Rashelin crossed the Hall of the Court.

The banqueting tables were still there, ready for the evening feasts. Ministers and officials sat and worked at them, or talked in the side aisles. Nobles and courtiers inclined their heads to her as she passed.

Rashelin had been summoned to the Council Chamber, and this was rare enough to cause her concern. Her parents were careful and strict about who was allowed to attend. Maybe there was a stalemate: the rest of the Council disagreeing with the Regent and Consort, and they could only decide an important matter through an outsider's casting vote.

Regent Ethabos chaired the meetings, and of the Royal Family, only Consort Sirika was present by right. The Council had invited Rashelin to attend a few times over the years, but as no more than an observer, and for the discussion of ceremonial matters.

In recent months, Katelin had insisted on being present, against the Regent's and Consort's wishes. She'd gained the Council's permission, but only with the compromise that she could attend and listen, but that as a child she had no right to speak. Rashelin remembered Katelin's fury at this, but she'd persuaded her cousin to bide her time. If she could be patient, everything would change with the coronation.

Rashelin reached the far end of the Hall, and nodded to the guard at the Council Chamber doors. These were opened for her, and the conversation within ceased.

It was an oak-panelled room, warm with oil lamps. A dozen chairs surrounded a polished, oval table, all but one of them occupied. Regent Ethabos presided, Consort Sirika at his side, with the oval completed by the heads of the great noble families of the Kingdom.

"Your Highnesses, Ladies, Lords," Rashelin said to the silence, and curtsied.

"Ah, yes, my dear," rumbled her father. "Please sit."

Rashelin did so, but noticed that all the faces were grave. What had happened? It could only be bad news.

Although Ethabos was in the chair, all eyes turned now to Consort Sirika.

"Rashelin, dear," her mother began, "the Council have asked for your opinion and vote. I remind you that nothing of this may be mentioned outside this room. In particular, no news must reach the ordinary people for fear of causing a panic. Late this morning, our scout rider returned down the desert highway with a disturbing report. A large army of Lassenites is marching south toward us."

Rashelin gave an involuntary gasp. She looked around the table for signs of distress, but the ladies and lords remained impassive. They had heard this news already, of course, and mastered their surprise. Rashelin caught the eye of General Bolas, who stroked his walrus moustache as he watched her. He gave a slow nod.

"As you would expect," Consort Sirika continued, "we're seeking to confirm the size and nature of the force. At their present rate of approach, they might reach the city gates in a few days."

Rashelin found her voice. "But why? Why would Duke Bassikrin send an army?"

Those around the table exchanged glances. This must be what they'd discussed. Or argued about. Rashelin noticed a tension in the room now from an unresolved debate. Or from a shouting match.

It was General Bolas who answered her. "The Council have concluded that the Duke of Lasseny wishes to make a show of strength. The army would seem more than a guard of honour, or a sign of respect to our new Queen. It appears to be more of an invasion force, a means of conquest. Duke Bassikrin wishes to enforce our agreement to his terms."

"That is one interpretation only, General," Sirika countered.

So the Consort and the General were on opposite sides in this argument.

"We need to discover the Duke's intentions," Rashelin's mother went on, "and negotiate an avoidance of bloodshed. There are peaceful ways to forestall an invasion, or conquest, as you insist on describing it."

"They'll be here in a few days?" Rashelin asked. "What about the coronation?"

Sirika nodded. "Given the army's current location, unless they force their marches, they are unlikely to reach us in time. The Council have agreed that we will not change our plans because of rumours, fears or intimidation. The coronation will go ahead as arranged. Nothing and no one will stop it from proceeding."

Except for Katelin's absence, came Rashelin's grim thought.

"Needless to say," General Bolas added, "we're mustering our army to the highest alert. But our lords and their retinues are gathering already for the coronation, and no soldier is on leave. However, there is a limit to what we can do in a few days, after fifteen years of neglect."

Rashelin winced at the criticism of her parents, and Sirika's eyes flashed. Through clenched teeth, the Consort hissed, "You may ask your question, General."

Bolas inclined his head, and turned to face her. "Princess Rashelin, you may sense that the Council is divided over our response to this threat. Some favour continued negotiation with the Duke, whilst others of us feel that Anestra should stand up against her enemies. If she weren't away on her pre-coronation retreat at Mannismill, we would ask for our Princess Katelin's thoughts on this matter. As you know her heart and mind better than any of us, what do you think she would do?"

So that was it. The Council was asking her to be Katelin's spokesperson. The stalemate was the response to the Lassenite threat: General Bolas and the rest of the Council on one side, her parents on the other. Members of the Council might guess that Katelin would choose to stand up to the Duke rather than to continue to appease him. Rashelin's parents would expect their daughter always to side with them, but did she have the courage to oppose them?

Rashelin looked around the table. The tensions were there; they had made their arguments for war, or for peace. They were deadlocked, and her casting vote would break their stalemate.

She placed her hands on the polished surface of the Council table. The silence was absolute. For a moment she traced the grain of the wood with her finger.

Rashelin decided not to focus on second-guessing the politics of the Council. They had asked her a question about Katelin, not to decide the fate of the Western Coast.

What would Katelin do? Rashelin knew her cousin well enough to answer that at once, but how could she say it without infuriating her parents?

She cleared her throat, and felt her words weighed down by the life or death of the Kingdom. "What would Queen Katelin do?" Her voice sounded small, but she made the point of elevating her cousin from Princess to Queen. She avoided looking at her parents, but gazed into the table instead.

"Queen Katelin would resist. She has no time for bullies or intimidation. She stands up to them, opposes them, fights them, as the only way to stop them." Rashelin glanced at the thunderous faces of her parents. It was almost as though she spoke about them, rather than about the Duke. "If Duke Bassikrin is bringing an army, then Queen Katelin would want all Anestra to join her in fighting for our freedom."

From the corner of her eye, Rashelin saw General Bolas lean back in his chair.

When Sigzay returned, Kat sat up. The barbarian had found juniper berries on bushes round the canyon head. These, and ironwood leaves from her pouch, she gave to Kat.

They chewed and Sigzay said, "So you think and find answer?"

"Yes," said Kat. "I've made a decision." She thought she wouldn't mention the presence, as she wasn't sure Sigzay would understand. Or the sight of the Lassenite army, as that would weaken her argument.

"We get you safe to Anestra."

"We should rescue Armus and Hedger first."

Sigzay stared at her. "Lassenites are coming."

Of course. Sigzay's sharp eyes had seen them too. "They're not here yet," Kat replied. "We still have time."

"I see. What make you this decision?"

"Up here," said Kat, "we're in the midst of the Western Coast, where cities and Kingdoms hang in the balance. I thought it was up to me to decide its fate. But I'm too small to rule the destiny of all this." She waved her arm across the panorama in front of them.

"So?" said Sigzay, after Kat had paused.

"So I've remembered," Kat went on, "to take one problem at a time, and try to do what's right with it. The right thing now is not to abandon our friends, but to try to save them. Armus rescued me at the slave market, and I should do the same for him. I can trust the Divine to look after the rest, the bigger things."

Sigzay rolled her eyes, and then shook her head. "I try, but I never understand you three: Hedger, Armus and now you. This 'trust the Divine' thing. You make strange decisions, no logic. I point it out, and you say: 'Divine guides', or 'Divine calls me to do'. I not get it."

Despite herself, Kat smiled. "One day, Sigzay, I hope you will. But for now it's not about me, or Princess, or Queen or anything else, but about helping our friends. I'm comfortable with that, and if you are too, then we should plan our rescue." She stood up.

"So we not start for Anestra? We lose time and wait for chance to rescue?"

"That's right."

Sigzay got up too. "As you wish, Your Majesty. I in no hurry to be anywhere."

Kat scanned her face. She heard the mockery, but Sigzay's face was unreadable.

They crept towards the canyon rim to watch the Lassenites below. Kat had never felt so settled about anything before. If the Divine had guided her heart, then she was following it. Perhaps she was learning how to make important and difficult decisions. And to trust her heart.

The late afternoon sun sank towards the mountains and the breeze was still warm. Kat watched Bassilius with distaste, so full of himself.

The Lassenite officer roused the soldiers and they took a final drink from the stream. Count Bassilius, his bodyguards and most of the troops set off for the highway. Eight men remained to guard Armus and Hedger.

Look at that!

They backed out of earshot. Sigzay smiled and whispered, "This Divine of yours: I like that odds go from two and hundred, to two and eight. We wait for dark to rescue boys."

Kat beamed and nodded.

The eight Lassenites lit a campfire, and argued over the lots drawn for guard duty. One went to the canyon mouth to watch the highway and plain, while the others ate by the fire.

At last six of the soldiers lay down for sleep. One sat watching Armus and Hedger as the fiery embers dwindled to a sullen glow.

Overhead the stars were bright and the moon was new. In the semi-darkness Sigzay and Kat retraced their steps and descended in silence to the canyon floor. Sigzay led the way with her short sword and Kat padded behind, gripping her dagger. The Divine better be right about this.

Sigzay peered around an outcrop. The soldier on watch was sideways to them, absorbed in polishing his broad sword.

Sigzay glided across the canyon floor, as quiet as a shadow. Kat could see her only because she knew where she was. Kat held her breath.

Sigzay lowered herself behind the lookout. In one swift movement she clamped a hand to his mouth and struck his head with her short sword pommel. She caught his weapon before it clattered to the ground, then laid out his unconscious form.

Kat's eyes popped. Such ruthless efficiency was both appalling and impressive. A soldier shifted in his sleep and Sigzay froze. He settled again, and Sigzay crept past the campfire. Kat breathed through her mouth, and hoped that no one could hear the thump of her heart. The other poor lookout would meet the same vicious expertise.

Sigzay reappeared and moved to the sleeping soldiers. Kat tiptoed towards Hedger. Her dagger severed his ankle bonds and he was alert in an instant. Hedger held out his wrists and Kat sawed them free.

Sigzay was executing knockout blows and disarming the oblivious Lassenites. Hedger stepped across and picked up the sword of the first unconscious lookout.

Kat crept to Armus, to cut the rope at his feet, but her touch disturbed the sleeping cleric. He mumbled, tried to stretch, then said, "What?" His movement scraped the dagger hilt on the rock.

The loudness startled them and the Lassenites began to wake. Sigzay leapt and pinned one of them to the ground. Hedger lunged for another, who sat up and reached for his sword.

"Surrender!" Hedger barked. The point of his broad sword hovered at the soldier's throat. The man stiffened. But the remaining soldiers were awake.

Sigzay's pommel robbed the pinned soldier of consciousness. She booted a rising Lassenite in the stomach and leapt to wrestle another. The soldier at Hedger's feet gave a yell of betrayal, knocked the sword point away and grabbed his own weapon.

"Stop!" Hedger shouted. He parried the Lassenite's sword and kicked his wrist. The weapon clattered against the canyon wall. Hedger pushed him to the ground with a boot on his chest. "Surrender!" he shouted again, and the Lassenites took a moment to stop struggling. Of the seven soldiers in the canyon, four were unconscious, two pinned down, and the last writhed and cradled his stomach.

Kat had freed Armus's legs and they stood up. She severed his wrist bonds.

"Surrender?" Sigzay hissed. "What you thinking?"

Hedger said nothing.

"What we do with them?" Sigzay said.

Hedger frowned. "We can't kill them. We should bind and leave them here."

"What?" Sigzay snorted. "Bassilius finds and rescue? Which side you on?"

"They can tell us what Bassilius is doing here," Hedger snapped back.

"We ain't telling you nothing," spat the soldier pinned by Sigzay, before she silenced him with her pommel.

"Stop it!" Hedger shouted at her. "We can't beat information out of them. You need to learn again that your short sword isn't the answer to everything. Our quarrel is with Bassilius, so we'll find out what he's doing some other way." Sigzay glared at him but didn't reply.

Kat kept out of their argument, but thought she sided with Hedger. An icy silence fell between Hedger and Sigzay as they disarmed the Lassenites and tied them up. Kat and Armus busied themselves with retrieving their packs and weapons.

They left the Lassenites as they'd fallen and exited the gorge. They passed the sprawled body of the lookout, a final example of Sigzay's handiwork.

Kat's heart was racing: the rescue was accomplished. Something she'd decided and attempted had succeeded. Lassenites: no points; Katelin: one.

They hurried south towards Anestra along the line of foothills. But on their left, some miles to the east, a red glow and flicker of fire lit up the night sky.

Rashelin kept turning over in bed. It was no good. She couldn't sleep knowing someone was upset with her. Although it was very late, she had to get up and talk to her mother. She scoured the darkened Castle and royal apartments until she found Sirika in the sewing room.

The oil lamps cast their flickering light around Sirika's chair and across the needlework on her desk. She gave no more than a brief glance as Rashelin came in.

Rashelin padded across and slumped into the chair opposite her. Sirika was a picture of concentration as she threaded her needle through the fabric.

"How can you work on that at a time like this?" Rashelin breathed.

Sirika didn't look up. "It calms me, my dear. Helps me to think."

There was silence, until Rashelin sighed. "Mother, I'm sorry that I upset you. At the Council meeting."

Sirika paused in her work, and her steely eyes regarded Rashelin. "There's no need to apologise when you speak the truth. Bolas asked you a question, and you answered to the best of your knowledge. Because you're right. That cousin of yours will resist Duke Bassikrin. She'll want to fight, and drag the whole Western Coast into war. It's not your fault that she chooses to bring grief to every family in Anestra."

Rashelin swallowed. "But, Mother, the Duke marches on us with an army. What else can we do?"

"We can negotiate, my dear. It takes those with experience, such as your father and me, to realise that we don't have to fight to resolve our disagreements. We can talk. There is diplomacy and compromise. We can maintain peace without bloodshed."

"But Duke Bassikrin is a bully. He demands more and more from us. There comes a time when we must stand up against him."

Sirika laid down her needle, placed her work to the side.

"Stand up against him? My dear, sweet girl. You are too young to remember the Crown War as we do. You haven't seen conflict, or battle, or when the chaos of war comes to your doorstep. You haven't known the bitterness of grief that sweeps a city when so many of her sons and daughters have fallen. When everyone has lost someone." Sirika looked away, her grey eyes unfocused. "There is blood, and weeping, and agony and screaming, and pain beyond all describing. Limbs are severed, heads smashed in, young bodies pierced through. You and I are not in the midst of it, where the violence is unimaginable, where each one struggles for their life." She shook herself, and her gaze returned to Rashelin's face. "No, my daughter, we must avoid war at all costs."

"What did the Council decide to do when Duke Bassikrin arrives?"

Sirika sniffed. "The Council concluded that our new Queen should meet him. That's if she's even back here by then. But your father and I will instruct her to agree to his terms."

"Don't we have the strength to resist him?" Rashelin's voice was small.

Sirika sighed. "No. The scout reports that all Lasseny is emptied. The Duke brings not only his whole army, but allies too, and his backstreet thugs. Anestra has no force that could resist such an invasion."

"We should have prepared for this."

Sirika squared her shoulders. "What would you have us do? Spend all of Anestra's resources these last fifteen years on the army? Turn the whole city into a war camp? There are other things in life, my dear, besides marching and fighting and battles. The glory of Anestra is her culture. We have fine treasures and architecture, music, art, learning, poetry, a noble history, fine food—should we abandon all of these to become a military machine?"

"No, I suppose not," Rashelin admitted. "If you can persuade Katelin to surrender to Bassikrin when he arrives, is that it? We've no other plan?"

Sirika forced a smile. "Well, he won't be able to keep his army here for long. Our new Queen will agree to the Duke's demands until he sends his forces back home. Then we can negotiate with a stronger hand, without a sword at our throats."

"But, Mother," Rashelin spluttered, "that is negotiating in bad faith. You're asking Katelin to agree to something and then to break her word."

"And what do you think Duke Bassikrin has done?" Sirika countered. Her eyes flashed. "Marching on Anestra is treason. He is a subject of the throne and Crown of Anestra, and he comes here with his whole army. He is a man without honour, more greedy and power-hungry than we could ever have envisaged."

Rashelin stared. "And yet you would surrender to him? Make new deals and compromises with him? Force Katelin to marry Count Bassilius?"

Sirika's voice was calm, measured. "It is always sound tactics to seek to ally yourself with the strongest power around. That is what we have done. At least the Anestran royal line will continue through that girl. That's assuming she's still alive and ever gets back here."

"But he's betrayed us, threatened us, he's invading us. How can we ever trust him?"

"And what if we fight, and then lose? Answer me that. How is that any better? Then we'd still have to accept Duke Bassikrin's terms, but many will have died for nothing. No, my dear, we must always avoid fighting and bloodshed, because it's too much of a gamble, and the cost is always too high."

Sirika turned back to her needlework, signalling the end

of the conversation. But her voice softened. "Go to sleep, Rashelin. It's not your fault. I don't deny that our situation is weaker than we would like. But what else can we do? Bring war to Anestra? I think not. And you'd better pray that nothing fatal has befallen that girl, otherwise it will be you who marries Count Bassilius."

Rashelin went cold, but could think of nothing more to say. Silence fell between them. Sirika worked with her needle, and Rashelin got up. Her voice quavered as she spoke. "I will pray to the Divine, then," she said, and left.

✴ XIII ✴

FIRE

They huddled behind a rocky outcrop for the rest of the night, but Kat struggled to sleep. Where could it be that burned? At first light, the fiery glow became a plume of smoke to the east. The early rays of the rising sun picked it out as an ominous smudge against the high cloud.

They discussed the position, direction and distance, and Armus guessed the fire to be the monastery at the oasis of Timajet. Kat felt sick.

"The monastery lies east of the highway," said Hedger. "That's not on our route to Anestra."

"We should investigate," said Kat. Armus nodded with vigour.

Sigzay rolled her eyes again. "How often we say this, Kat? We get you safe to Anestra. And at once. Princess."

"It's two days to my birthday," said Kat. "We have time."

"If this was caused by Bassilius's men," said Hedger, "then they might still be at Timajet. We can't risk them seeing us."

"So we need to be careful," said Kat, "and make sure the Lassenites are no longer there. If we can help the monks, then we must. Listen. None of you are in a rush to reach Anestra. If I'm willing to delay my arrival, then why can't all of you accept that?"

Hedger stared at her and then nodded. Sigzay muttered something about reckless, foolish decisions.

Kat wondered if the rescue of Armus and Hedger had

made her bold and rash. Or was this another of those 'trust her heart' things?

The monastery lay two hours' walk away. As daylight grew they hurried forward and scanned the road for movement. Smoke began to catch in Kat's throat.

"Down!" Sigzay hissed.

They flung themselves to the ground. They crawled into a dip of bare earth and dry grass, and Kat peered eastwards. A mile away there was movement among the trees beyond the road. A troop of horsemen rode up the lane from Timajet and turned northwards on the highway. Even Kat could tell it was Bassilius and his bodyguards … and they were in a hurry. The riders pulled ahead and foot soldiers lagged behind.

Kat cowered in the hollow. She felt stupid for holding her breath—so far away from them. When the last straggling soldier disappeared behind a rise to the north, they moved towards the road.

"I count eighty-three," said Sigzay. How had she done that? Best eyes and ears. "So they take casualties or some still at Timajet. Be cautious and weapons ready." She loaded her crossbow and Kat nocked an arrow. Gripping her shortbow helped with the shakes.

They ran across the gravel and beaten earth of the highway and into the lane to Timajet. The nearer they got to the palm trees of the oasis, there could be no mistake: the monastery was ablaze.

No … it couldn't be …

They began to see bodies. Monks in their plain grey robes had been stabbed, hacked, burned and decapitated, falling by the roadside as they'd fled. Kat tried not to stare at the twisted, disfigured corpses, but couldn't tear her gaze away. She stepped around the blood, but her bile was rising.

All of this. Last night. At this peaceful site. While Kat and

Sigzay had rescued their friends, Bassilius and his soldiers had slaughtered and burned.

They heard voices. Two Lassenite soldiers appeared, hurrying away from the monastery. One was showing the other a silver candlestick.

"Stop where you are!" Hedger ordered. The Lassenites dropped the candlestick, drew swords and rushed at them. Kat's arrow and Sigzay's bolt felled them at close range.

One soldier was dead with a bolt in his head. The other clutched the arrow in his chest. Hedger's sword tip trembled at his throat.

"Lassenite," Hedger hissed. "How many of you are still in the monastery?" Kat had never heard such rage in his voice.

The soldier struggled to breathe or focus. "What are you doing here?"

"Answer me," Hedger ordered. "How many still here?"

"Plenty." The soldier spat at him. "You Anestran scum have had it."

Hedger spoke through clenched teeth. "Why are you so far behind Bassilius and the others?"

The soldier retched and choked. "We make sure ... everyone's dead," he croaked. He convulsed and breathed no more.

With reverence, Armus picked up the candlestick to carry back into the monastery. But beyond the fallen entrance arch, devastation assaulted them.

Wooden structures had collapsed and still burned. The Lassenites had set fire to fabric, thatch and other combustibles. They had scorched, battered and knocked down walls of brick and stone. Roofs had caved in. Palm trees and bushes flickered with flame. Ash floated down from the heavy pall of smoke that hung in the air.

Kat was forced to cough ... but her breathing was shallow.

She covered her nose and mouth against the stench, but couldn't swallow away an acrid taste.

They edged into the courtyard. Armus choked with rage. The bodies of monks lay strewn across the blackened cloisters and the grey-coated grass. There was neither sight nor sound of life. The smoke caught Kat's eyes and tears streamed down her face. She stopped, numb and heartbroken, amidst the ruin.

The poor monks hadn't stood a chance.

"Look here," said Hedger. At his feet lay a bodyguard of the Count of Lasseny, battered to death with staves and clubs. The Lassenites had made no attempt to remove their dead ... or hide their guilt.

"Someone there," Sigzay breathed.

They ran across the courtyard and entered the chapel. It too was in ruins, open to the sky, every window smashed. The roof timbers lay in smouldering bonfires with the charred remains of prayer desks, benches and stools. The Lassenites had looted the reliquaries, safe boxes and cupboards, strewing the contents across the floor. They had bludgeoned the altar to rubble. All was black and covered in ash.

Voices came from a side room vestry and, without thinking, Kat ran to the doorway. Two Lassenites appeared, dragging an old monk. Before Kat could react, one soldier grabbed and twisted her, clamping her arms to her sides. Her shortbow fell and a broad sword scraped her neck.

"Back off and drop your weapons," the soldier ordered. "Or we kill them." The other Lassenite had the old monk in a similar grip.

A desperate silence.

Sigzay and Armus stepped back but kept their weapons poised. Hedger was tauter than a bowstring, on the balls of his feet, knuckles white on his sword hilt.

Kat cleared her throat. "You harm us, and you won't leave

here alive. Release us, or my friends will kill you." Had she managed to keep the panic from her voice?

There was a pause. The blade at her throat was sharp and cold, and the breath in her ear was putrid.

Kat let the soldiers weigh up the relative strengths; then made herself speak again. "Rather than anyone being killed, I suggest we make an agreement."

"What?" Sigzay hissed. "You not going to—"

"Shut up!" Kat shrieked. Why couldn't Sigzay let her handle this? It was her life that was at stake. Then, over her shoulder, "If you let the monk and me go unharmed, then we'll let you escape with your lives."

Sigzay snorted. The others stared at Kat. Hedger edged forward, his face an agony of indecision.

"How can we trust you not to shoot us as we go?" said the Lassenite who held her.

"My friends are blocking your only way out of this chapel," said Kat. "They'll allow you past to the door. You release the monk and me, and then I suggest you run for it. If we're unharmed, I give you my word that we will not chase you. Anything else and I promise that we will kill you." The soldier hesitated, so she added, "Otherwise this is where you die."

The Lassenites looked at each other. "Agreed. Let us past." They shuffled forward, and the sword edge bumped Kat's throat. Armus retreated to one side, Hedger and Sigzay to the other. The soldiers neared the ruined chapel door.

"Release us," said Kat. Sigzay stepped forward, her crossbow trained on them.

The soldiers threw Kat and the monk to the floor and ran. Sigzay started after them at once, but Hedger grabbed her arm.

"No!" shouted Kat. "Let them go!"

"You let them escape!" Sigzay's eyes were wild as she thrashed to get free of Hedger.

"Yes, we are," Hedger insisted. "Kat gave her word."

"They find Bassilius and tell him of us," yelled Sigzay.

Kat started to get up. "When Bassilius reaches the canyon, he'll know what's happened, that we overcame his men and rescued you."

Hedger was at her side, helping her. "Are you all right?" he choked.

Kat drew her arm out of his grasp. "Yes, I'm fine." She brushed herself down. Why was he so concerned for her, all of a sudden? Oh, yes, bodyguard and protector.

Kat stared at her bow on the floor, fallen where the soldier had grabbed her. Her hand went to her throat; she could still feel the blade. She could have been killed. Despite what she'd said to Hedger, she wasn't fine, but she'd managed to control her fear. And she'd taken charge of the situation, hadn't she?

"Even so," Armus was saying, "I'm shocked. All this murder and destruction, and you let two of the butchers escape."

Kat sighed, and looked at the monk. "I couldn't think how else to save our lives. Those two aren't to blame as much as those who ordered this massacre. There's been too much death here already."

There was silence, until Hedger said, "I understand."

The old monk spoke from the floor. "Yes, thank you for saving my life. Who are you?"

Armus hurried forward and knelt beside the old man. "We are friends. I am Brother Armus, a fellow cleric. This is Kat, Hedger and Sigzay. We've escaped from Lasseny and are heading for Anestra. We saw the smoke and came as soon as we could. But don't I recognise you? Aren't you the Abbot?"

"My name is Ruis," said the old man, "and I am the Abbot." He surveyed the chapel. "Or I was. Is anyone else alive?"

Armus shook his head. "Not that we've found. How did you escape being killed?"

"Pretending to be dead," said Ruis. "Then those two found me. They were going to kill me on my own altar." He stared at the wreckage around him. "Have they destroyed everything?"

Armus nodded, and helped the Abbot up. Ruis brushed dust and ash from his plain grey robes, but he moved as though stiff and aching. He had a short, wiry body, and his bony face had close-cropped hair and blue-grey eyes. He coughed at the smoke.

"Sigzay and I will check the rest of the complex," said Hedger, "while the two of you look after the Abbot." He and Sigzay left the chapel.

Ruis said, "I ought to collect a few things before we leave."

Armus and Kat followed Abbot Ruis to the vestry, where the furniture and hangings had also been smashed, ripped and burned. They moved a pile of debris to reach a floor safe, from which the Abbot took a bundle of parchments and a small metal box.

"The records of the monastery," he explained. "And a few personal things." He tucked them in a pocket and they left the chapel.

Ruis sat on a stone bench in the courtyard and drank some water. Kat's heart ached as the old man noted each dead monk. They waited for Hedger and Sigzay, who reported no other Lassenites or survivors.

"A lifetime of work ruined," said Ruis, "and all the brothers gone. It's true that the Divine takes to her those whom she loves, and leaves behind those with work still to do." He sighed. "They came after dark. I hid in the vestry all night, but heard everything. I never thought I'd experience such hell. I waited and hoped that they'd gone, but a few were left to finish the slaughter. They've destroyed so much."

"But why?" said Armus. "Why did they do this? There can't have been much wealth here."

"No, we are a poor brotherhood," said the Abbot. "Or we were. We gave hospitality and charity, and worked for our sustenance. Why did they do this?"

He thought for a minute and they waited. Ruis looked at the ground and muttered, "Now that they've destroyed this place, I suppose that I can tell you. The Lassenites will announce what they've found soon enough."

He looked up. "Timajet guarded a secret. The Duke of Lasseny's spies discovered it … or he worked it out himself. He sent a Captain here, but I wouldn't tell him anything. So the Duke sent his son to ransack the place and slaughter those who resisted. What were they after? They searched until they found it, and it could only have been one thing. They were after the Crown."

✳ XIV ✳

HIGHWAY

The others all turned towards Kat.

Her hand flew to her mouth. "The Crown!" she gasped.

"Yes, the Crown of Anestra," murmured Ruis. "We had a part of it in a reliquary behind the altar, but that's now empty and smashed."

"No!" whispered Kat. Both her voice and heart had stopped working, and she swayed on her legs. The hand that steadied her was Armus's.

She leaned on him, and the flames crackled around them. Part of a nearby building fell with a crash.

A Crown fragment had been here. And she'd lost it. They were too late, and this had all been in vain. Bassilius had taken it back to the Lassenite army.

Their eyes were still on her so Kat held back her tears. Anger stirred deep inside, but it couldn't yet break through the layers of despair. She needed to get away from this place of death. She rubbed her face, and said, "We must leave."

Abbot Ruis stood up. "I need to report to the Temple and arrange for the burial of the brothers. My pace may be slower than yours, but I'd be grateful for company on the road to Anestra."

"Of course," said Armus. "We're honoured to escort you, Abbot."

Ruis and Armus stood together and prayed for the departed, and then they all left.

They took the lane back to the highway and turned south. There was no sign of the Lassenites. Their heads were down and they walked at the pace of the Abbot. No one spoke for a long time.

Kat kept gulping down breaths. What had she done? Could she have done or decided otherwise, or been able to prevent this? Had she somehow caused the Lassenites to do it? She should feel furious, or sad, or guilty, or something, but there was nothing. Her mind was seared with defeat and ruin and death.

A drizzle began from the morning's clouded sky. The highway became muddier and the gravel crunched beneath their feet. They started to pass the lanes, woods and fields of the country estates that filled the land between Timajet and Anestra.

Kat found that Armus walked next to her. His presence was comforting, protective, fatherly, and at last she was able to speak. But the words that came out were bitter. "What do you think now of the Divine will and purpose?"

Armus blew out his cheeks and the sparkle had gone from his eyes. "I don't know," he said. "It all seemed so hopeful a few days ago. But I can't see how this helps ... our quest."

"Do you think Abbot Ruis knows much about the Crown? Without saying who I am, could you ask him to tell us about it?" She couldn't face anyone else knowing how important the Crown was to her.

Armus nodded, and they slowed to where Ruis walked in silence with Hedger and Sigzay.

"Abbot Ruis," said Armus, "can you tell us about the Crown?"

Ruis sighed. "How much do you know and what do you wish to learn? Since we had the Crown fragment at Timajet, I've researched it with particular interest. Where should I begin?"

Armus said, "Perhaps with how the Crown was broken, and how one part came to be at Timajet?"

"Yes, I can tell you that," said Ruis. "I was there when it all happened."

Kat stared at him in amazement. Wasn't Duke Bassikrin the only one who knew? But here was a man who enjoyed astounding an audience.

"It was fifteen years ago," Ruis began, "during what we now call the Crown War. Duke Bassikrin arranged a parley with King Etharan at Timajet. Both men arrived with larger forces than agreed, so the talks never stood a chance. The Duke had further troops nearby with orders for an ambush. I witnessed the striking of the first blow. The Duke swung his staff at the head of the King and the Crown flew into a wall. The bodyguards charged and chaos broke out. The King died in the first assault."

The casual mention of her father's murder sent a twinge through Kat's heart. Hedger made the connection also, for Kat saw him swallow as he caught her eye.

"Both sides fought for the Crown," continued Ruis. "It was hacked and crushed, and ended that day in pieces large and small. An Anestran soldier took one large piece and escaped over the wall during the fighting. He hid it until after the war and then gave it to the Anestran Treasury. Duke Bassikrin took the other large part to keep in his Palace in Lasseny. The Timajet monks could only hide and flee. The Duke moved on to assault Anestra city, and we returned to the monastery, to carnage and destruction. We buried the King in the chapel, and gathered with care every last fragment of the Crown."

Kat remembered now. She'd gone there as a girl to see her father's resting place. Once this was over, she'd return to the monastery and visit his grave in the ruins of Timajet chapel.

"They must have been tiny," said Armus, "those fragments of the Crown. Did your monks reconstruct it?"

Ruis smiled. "No, we didn't need to. The Crown is a sacred relic and repairs itself. We positioned the fragments in place, and before our eyes the Crown fused together. No human craftsman could repair each detail of writing and design, and leave no mark. It was as though that part had never been broken."

"When the Crown War was over," said Armus, "you didn't return your part to Anestra. Why not keep it with the other piece in the Treasury?"

"Indeed I thought about that," said Ruis. "Long and hard. I liked having the relic at Timajet, of course, but to be honest with you, Brother, I didn't trust the Regent and Consort. The Coast was in turmoil, and their men came to search at Timajet for the Crown. I told them the truth: that only the tiniest of fragments had been left. Then came the rumours of their secret league with Lasseny. So I bided my time. Their reputation didn't improve, and I considered it safer with clerics than with them. At least we understand the artefact's power."

No, Kat didn't trust the Regent and Consort either. But if the Abbot had sent his part to Anestra, they'd have two thirds of the Crown in the Treasury by now.

"Safer with clerics?" said Armus. "I suppose it's unfair to ask what you think of that decision now."

Abbot Ruis heaved a sigh. "Yes, after last night, I accept that my choice has come with a terrible cost, if Bassikrin now has more of the Crown than we do."

"Will two thirds of it be more powerful than one?" asked Armus.

Ruis nodded. "Very much so. The Divine bestows her power where she wills, but she always works through the Crown. Two parts will at least double its power."

"Duke Bassikrin is no Divine worshipper," said Armus. "How will he use the power of the Crown?"

Ruis frowned. "That's hard to say. Like many others, the Duke considers the Crown a magic item, that it bestows spiritual power on the wearer. But what will the mages of Ilbassi do with it? I know about the Crown, but I'm no expert on Ilbassi, his mages or spells. And the Duke will be pleased to keep the Crown away from Anestra's Royal Family, who receive its unrivalled power."

Armus's shoulders had slumped. "So the Duke has most of the Crown, and he's bold enough to attack Anestra. We no longer have the courage or strength to resist him."

Abbot Ruis didn't look as defeated as Kat thought he should. "I'm surprised at you, Brother," said the Abbot. "Don't you have faith in the Divine?"

Kat grumbled to herself. What was it with these clerics and faith? In the midst of disaster they always resorted to it. Was their faith supposed to make everything all right?

"Of course I have faith," spluttered Armus. "But it's hard to see the Divine's purpose being served when our hope is gone and our Kingdom's about to be ruined."

"Believe me," said Ruis, "it only seems that way. Fear and despair are not the ways of courage and faith. The Divine is loving and good, and is generous in providing for us."

"How can you say that?" Kat blurted out. "The brothers are dead, your monastery's burned down and your whole life's work is ruined. I'm sorry, Abbot, but I'm not convinced by your 'courage and faith'."

The Abbot's voice was sharp. "Don't think for a moment, young lady, that I take the ruin at Timajet as a trivial matter." He controlled himself, and his tone became serious but gentle. "I believe with all my heart in what I just said, more than you can know."

Kat felt the rebuke. But doubted she'd ever have his sort of faith in the Divine. If she'd just met the White Goddess, shouldn't their path, and the outcome, be clearer?

A word from Sigzay interrupted them: a cart had turned onto the highway behind them. They walked on through the drizzle, but the pair of donkeys clopped nearer.

They waved for the farmer to stop, but he seemed reluctant to do so. He only halted at the pleading of Abbot Ruis, in his shabby, muddy robes.

"Whadda ya want, old man?" said the farmer.

"Sorry to delay you," said the Abbot. "I'm from the monastery at Timajet, and we've been attacked. You may have seen the smoke."

"I seen it."

"We're hoping you could help us with a lift towards Anestra."

"My cart ain't fit for passengers."

"We don't expect any comfort," said Ruis. "Just to get along the road."

"We're willing to pay for your help," said Kat. She fished a silvered out of her belt pouch.

The farmer's face brightened at the sight of the coin. He tucked it in a shirt pocket, and said, "Hop in then."

The five of them squashed into the cart. The splintering wood was strewn with malodorous straw and it gave ominous creaks as the donkeys pulled off. Kat doubted it would carry their weight all the way to Anestra.

"Fetching a new sow today," the farmer informed them. "From market in 'Nestra."

The ride was long and uncomfortable, but at least the drizzle stopped. Kat heard more than she ever wished to know of the breeding of pigs, of fodder and pasture, of rains and climate, and the livestock market prices. She was grateful that Ruis and Armus were in the front, doing their pastoral best to show interest in the farmer's conversation. Where did they find such infinite patience? Kat wished that Sigzay would hide her amusement, her giggles and grins at the farmer's expense.

Hedger seemed like her: miles away. He looked upset too, anguished or conflicted about something. He kept rubbing his eyes, and couldn't sit still.

Kat hated the long hours with nothing to do but think. It gave time for the Abbot's news to sink in. And with each mile nearer to Anestra, that cold finger touched her heart again. That sense of dread seeped into her soul; a whirlpool that had caught her—already she felt the tug of its current—to suck her down to her doom.

Was this the worst she'd ever felt?

They'd taken the Crown. A hundred points to them.

It was over. The game was finished, and she'd lost.

She blinked and wiped away the tears, but guessed that Hedger had seen them.

Kat hugged her knees, but it gave less comfort than it might have done. She felt cold, and it wasn't the weather.

Was there any point now in hoping or trying to make things better? Was there nothing she could say or do that would make any difference? Should she resign herself to being Queen, and surrender to the Duke, however much she hated it? And let her Aunt and Uncle do what they wanted and have their own way? Never mind that Aunt Sirika wanted to break her; she was crushed and broken already.

So she'd smile, serene, through all she had to do, even if inside she was dying every day. Lasseny would have lordship over Anestra, she'd marry Count Bassilius, and they'd worship Ilbassi instead of the Divine.

There was no more light in her eyes, no strength in her

will, no energy, no life, no hope. It had seeped from her like the blood from the monks. What did it matter now if she cried and everyone saw it? Every heartbeat was a drum marking out the final moments of her life.

Kat wished the donkeys would walk slower, and take longer to get there. Like a month. Or a lifetime.

But still ... she couldn't manage to wish herself to roll off the cart into a muddy ditch and lie still and cold forever.

By late afternoon the cart had rolled, still in one piece, through vineyards, orchards, farmlands and villages, to the outskirts of Anestra city.

Kat hadn't been out this way for a while. She lifted her eyes and made herself look as they passed. She'd been in the wilderness for only four days, but now it felt ten times longer. After the browns of the desert, it was green again, with fields, hedges and trees, beside the lanes and cottages of her homeland. She'd forgotten how beautiful it was, in a warm afternoon light. It was as though the landscape itself were trying to offer her comfort.

It was nearing sunset as they approached the North Gate of the city. They disembarked, stretching stiff limbs but uttering no complaint. The aches were different from the long days of walking, and they'd achieved their destination. Ruis and Armus gave a blessing on the farmer and his family, his lands and livestock, not to mention his new sow, and the farmer departed to the market.

Ruis turned on Sigzay. "Young lady, you may be amused by the smallness of the farmer's concerns, but it is unkind to laugh at him." Sigzay shrugged, and looked away.

Ruis went on, "Armus and I will report to the Under Father at the Temple. We'll lodge there, and perhaps we'll meet again soon. We bid you a good night. The power of the Divine for each of you." The clerics headed off across the fields along the city wall, towards the Temple and the sunset, under a fiery sky.

"We get you here safe then, Kat," Sigzay said. "And in time."

Weariness had caught up with Kat. She knew she ought to be more grateful for their help, but needing to be back here was different from wanting to be.

"Yes, thank you," she said. "I'd better return to the Castle. You may stay with me there, if you wish."

Her aunt and uncle would not like it, but they could hardly refuse, so close to her coronation.

Hedger and Sigzay accepted her offer.

Kat sighed. It was time to revert from adventurer to Princess, from Kat to Katelin, a prospect she couldn't relish less. She fixed in place her expressionless face and eyed the guards at the city gate. "Time to announce my return," she said.

ANESTRA

A thick stone wall with towers and turrets encompassed Anestra city, and sometimes Katelin imagined that she knew every stone. High over the walls flew the Old Kingdom flag: her radiant silver Crown on dark blue. The North Gate opened onto the Lasseny highway, and through Cleric Gate in the northwest lay the Temple of the Divine on Temple Hill. The East and South Gates led to farmlands, with dirt and gravel roads to the Eastern Ranges, the Manniswood and the Caldunate. To the west, the Ocean bordered the city, and in the natural harbour of Anestra Bay stone breakwaters protected the quayside.

The city streets rose to a central hill where Anestra Castle stood. From this ancient seat, the generations of the Kings of Anestra had ruled the Western Coast, in the realm now known as the Old Kingdom. The central Keep watched over the city and a battlemented wall enclosed the Castle grounds.

In front of the Castle lay Crown Square, with a daily market where all manner of traders sold the produce of farm, Ocean, craftsman and smith. Most homes and workshops were of red brick or stone, with storerooms and outhouses of timber.

A freshwater spring emerged beside the Castle and flowed down channels to the harbour. Through Princes' Park the stream made pools and waterfalls, beside lawns where Katelin and her cousins had played as children. For Anestra was a city of gardens, with oaks and elms lining the wider cobbled streets. Most homes grew their own vegetables and fruit, and the frontages were adorned with spring flowers. The bushes, hedges and trees of the city were trimmed and pruned with diligence.

But Katelin had heard that many of the residents grumbled that the city was not as it had been. For years the people had dwindled and aged, with too few children being born. Houses stood empty, and the whispers told of Anestra as a fossilised museum. No new building or change was allowed, and the lack of a spark of life or hope led to a sense of stifled decay.

"Come here and identify yourselves," barked the guard at the gate.

Oh dear. Katelin had forgotten how suspicious they must look. And the weapons concealed by their cloaks wouldn't help. Trust her to fall foul of her own city's rules about mercenaries. They weren't in Lasseny now: no brandishing steel or taking the law into their own hands.

Katelin, Hedger and Sigzay approached the guard. He continued, "We'll not have troublemakers in our city, what with the coronation and all. There's no use trying to hide your weapons. To pass this gate you must answer to me and surrender your arms." He planted his boots in front of them, his muscled bulk blocking their way.

Katelin was torn between affront at his rudeness, and applause at his efficiency in keeping trouble from the city. "What's your name, soldier?" she asked.

"I'm Sergeant Rossick of the Anestran guard, so I'll have your weapons and names." His blue eyes challenged her from under his helmet.

"Well, Sergeant Rossick," said Katelin, "soon you will answer to me. You may not recognise me in these clothes, or under the dirt of the road, but I am Princess Katelin. You will allow me to enter my city."

The Sergeant's sternness broke into a grin. "Princess Katelin, eh? Very good, miss. And I'll be the Duke of Lasseny. But just for the record, I need your real name too."

Katelin's mouth dropped open and her hands became fists. She glanced at Hedger and Sigzay, and then said, "No, Sergeant … I am … Princess Katelin. I am."

"Hey, lads," the Sergeant called over his shoulder. Half a dozen guards ambled out of the gatehouse, eating and chatting. "Any of you seen what Princess Katelin looks like up close? Well, now's your chance. Seems like we've got the Princess herself turned up at our humble gate here." The guards laughed and gathered round, scrutinising her.

Katelin's cheeks burned and she gritted her teeth. "Listen," she said. "I've been away on a … journey … in the north. And I've returned in time for my coronation … the day after tomorrow."

The Sergeant regarded her with amusement. "You won't give it up, will you, miss? Anyone hear about the Princess's 'journey to the north'?"

The guards chuckled and shook their heads, except for one. "Yes, Sergeant. My brother's in the Castle guards, and he's been told that Princess Katelin is away." The others turned to him. "Only he's been told that the Princess is on some sort of pre-coronation retreat at Mannismill."

Katelin stared at him, incredulous. "What? I'm on … on a pre-coronation retreat? At Mannismill?" She shouldn't have said that. Of course, they'd have invented some story to explain her absence.

"So he says," said the Sergeant. "If the Princess returns today, then she'll come to the South Gate, won't she, miss?"

Katelin was too tired for an argument. She turned to

Hedger and Sigzay, and hoped that at least these two believed her. Or were they now thinking that she'd pretended the whole Princess story? She didn't like the smirk on Sigzay's face.

Hedger stepped forward and said, "We can settle the young lady's identity by finding someone who recognises her. Could you fetch a Castle guard to confirm if she's Princess Katelin? If she is, then your Princess will be grateful, but at worst, you can charge us with wasting your time."

"All right," said the Sergeant. He turned to the guard who had spoken. "Is your brother on duty today and would he recognise the Princess?" When the young guard nodded, he was dispatched at a run to the Castle.

Katelin murmured to Hedger and Sigzay. "I'm sorry about this." Now that she was here, she longed to get inside and hide in her room.

At last the two guard brothers appeared at a trot. The Castle guard slowed and stared at Katelin, who tried hard, beneath her sweat, grime and smears, to appear most Princess-like.

The young guard bowed. "Your Highness," he said. "Welcome back."

Katelin was almost too busy surging with relief to notice how the Sergeant and city guards stiffened. "Our humble apologies, my Princess," mumbled Rossick.

"No disgrace to you, Sergeant," Katelin reassured him. The moment she was vindicated, her outrage melted. Now she could see the funny side of this. "You didn't expect to see me so disguised. I'm comforted by your zeal in keeping troublemakers like me off our streets." She tried a grin, but he was too flustered to notice it.

"We'll escort you to the Castle immediately, Your Highness." Then the Sergeant barked, "Conduct the Princess

Katelin and her guests to the Castle at once. One of you run ahead to alert them." A guard ran off, and four others lined up beside Katelin, Hedger and Sigzay.

An escort wasn't necessary, but she appreciated that he was trying to make amends. Katelin laid a hand on his arm, and he stared at her touch. "Thank you, Sergeant Rossick," she said. "And just think: now you can tell the story of how the Queen of the Western Coast turned up at your gate, and what happened when you failed to recognise her." Her smile was teasing. His in return was tentative, but relieved.

The three travellers strolled up Queensway, while the soldiers marched alongside them. Dusk was falling, and the lamplighters were starting their rounds. It was the hour of closing the curtains, unfolding the workshop shutters and hurrying home to evening meals. Swallows darted overhead, snapping up insects in mid-flight. On evenings such as this, Katelin adored the fragrance and colour of the jacaranda blossom.

In a curious way, the exchanges with Rossick had encouraged her. He'd shown her how much being Princess and Queen meant to the people of Anestra.

They crossed Crown Square, where the market stalls had been packed away, and entered Anestra Castle. Lights shone from the windows of the South Tower and Keep, and a breeze rustled the leaves in the grounds.

Katelin stopped as her muscles tightened. Guards stood to attention in the gatehouse and servants rushed about. A frenzy of activity seemed to have broken out with the news of her approach. They were preparing a banquet in the Hall; that would be for the coronation's early arrivals. But why all this fuss? Why couldn't it feel good to be home, instead of this stifling panic?

Katelin closed her eyes for a moment. When she opened

them, it was all still happening. She reminded herself to keep breathing.

The hastily summoned Royal Steward, Yardles, met them. The lamplight glinted off his combed-back silver hair, and this small, neat man was Katelin's favourite among the staff. Without saying much, he'd always seemed to be on her side.

"Welcome home, Your Highness," said the Steward. "We're so delighted to see you again, back from your retreat. It looks as though your journey here was muddy."

Muddy journey? If only he knew. "Thank you, Yardles," said Katelin. "Yes, I've enjoyed my … um … retreat." Since everyone insisted on running about, she'd ask them to do something useful. "Rooms in the South Tower, please, for my guests, Hedger and Sigzay. And we'd be grateful for hot baths, food and drink in our rooms. Please notify the Regent that I'm here, but to excuse me from this evening's banquet. Yes, I need to clean up after my journey. From Mannismill."

"Very good, my lady. And we're all looking forward to the day after tomorrow!" he called, as he scuttled away to attend to her requests.

Katelin turned to Hedger and Sigzay. "Welcome to my home," she said, with a sweep of her arm across the Castle grounds.

Hedger nodded. "Impressive."

"The guest rooms are always ready in the South Tower," said Katelin. "Someone will take you there soon. If you want me, I'm on the third floor of the Keep. Ask the staff if you need anything, and Yardles will inform them that you're free to come and go." Katelin stifled a yawn. "I need an early night. Thank you for all your help in getting me here. Good night and sleep well."

Hedger smiled and said, "We're pleased to have helped

you. Have a good night, Kat." Sigzay murmured something Katelin didn't catch.

A servant escorted the other two towards the South Tower. Katelin stood alone in the midst of the bustle. At last she could hide in her rooms. But before that, there was someone she wanted to see.

As she entered the Stables, the grooms were brushing down the horses of the newly arrived visitors. They stopped as Katelin entered, but she told them to carry on. Why couldn't they ignore her until she asked for something? She headed for the last stall on the left, and there he was. The white stallion neighed and stamped his feet as she opened the gate and came in to him.

"Novita," she breathed, and hugged his neck. "Have they been taking you out?" He tossed his head. "Yes, it seems they have." She stroked his flanks. "I'm sorry, I've been away, but we'll go out again soon. Just you and me. I promise." He nuzzled her head and nibbled her shoulder. He looked well, and she'd missed him. She ran her fingers through his mane. "As soon as I can, Novita."

She gave him a last pat, and kept her eyes down as she crossed the courtyard. In the entrance to the Keep, she hurried past the doors to the Hall and trudged up to the third floor.

Her rooms were as she'd left them nine days ago, except they'd taken the rope from the window. How dare they remove her escape route? She un-slung her shortbow and quiver, and hung them—with sadness but respect—on hooks in the wall. She eased off the pack, unclipped her cloak and let them both fall to the carpet. She sat on the bed, prised off her boots and inspected the injuries. The stab wound and bruises were healing well. She undid her ponytail and shook her hair free.

Back here again. Had that 'little adventure' been worth it? She'd made some new friends. And the Crown ... she'd hoped to find more of it, but the situation had only got worse. She'd be crowned in two days' time with one third of the Crown; no more or less than she'd always expected. So much for that childhood dream.

Could they do anything about the invading Lassenites? Go out to meet them in battle? No, Anestra needed the defensive advantage of her city walls. All soldiers would be here for the coronation anyway, but if there came an assault on the city, then children, mothers and the elderly could take refuge here in the Castle. Yes, that might be the best she could organise in the time.

In the adjoining room, the servant girl Adisha prepared a bath. A knock at the door interrupted her thoughts. A messenger bowed and read out a note: "Your Highness. The Regent and Consort are in banquet with their guests and will not be disturbed. Since you are not fit to be seen in public, you are excused from the banquet. You will attend them at Court in the morning."

Katelin snorted. Not fit to be seen in public? They had no idea what she'd gone through. She wasn't going to tell them either. "Very well, thank you," she said, and the messenger disappeared. Her Aunt and Uncle had better enjoy it while they could, for she was under their orders for only one more day. How good it would be, for Anestra and for her, to be relieved of that burden.

Adisha tapped on the door. "It's good to see you, milady. Your bath's ready."

"Thank you, Adisha." There were advantages in being a Princess, and in being at home. Hot baths, soft beds and clean sheets were three of them.

Katelin bathed and dressed in a nightshirt and robe, and found that supper had been brought and laid on a table. And ample food and drink, ready served. The surplus from the banquet was more than she could manage: pheasant and guinea fowl in plum gravy, halibut in a white cheese sauce, spring vegetables, freshly baked rolls with butter, and her favourite cranberry pastries. She poured a glass of red wine from the decanter and took a sip.

But in the midst of comfort and luxury, why did she yearn for the wilderness, the freedom, the adventure? Instead of a hot, soapy tub, why might she prefer a pool among the mesquite trees in a cool canyon stream? Or instead of this tray of stuff, to hunt and cook her own roasted mountain gazelle? Why was that?

She thought she knew.

✷ XVI ✷

COURT

Katelin was chewing a mouthful of halibut when there came a gentle knock at the door. She swallowed and dabbed her lips with a napkin. "Come in," she called.

Princess Rashelin peeked around the door. "Katelin," she squealed, and rushed in for a tight embrace. They scanned each other's faces, giggled, and sat down on the chair and bed. "I couldn't believe it when Yardles told us you were back. It's such a relief to see you."

"I've missed you too," said Katelin. "You've escaped from the banquet, then?"

"Yes, Mother and Father excused me to come up. I see they've brought you some of what we're having downstairs."

"So …" Katelin's smile was teasing, "… a pre-coronation retreat at Mannismill?"

Rashelin laughed. "Well, I had to think of something and that seemed plausible enough. Have you enjoyed your 'retreat'?"

Katelin bit her lip. What could she say?

Rashelin changed the subject. "And you owe me for making speeches on your behalf. Mother and Father made me cover for you."

"Oh, Rashelin, I'm sorry. I know you hate doing that."

She brushed it away. "Never mind, since you can do it yourself now." She looked Katelin over. "Any injuries this time?"

Katelin lifted the hem of her robe to reveal the stabbed leg and bruised foot.

"Ouch. Go on, then, where have you been? What have you been doing?"

"Ah, Rashelin." She wagged a playful finger. "Trying to winkle the truth out of me? Haven't you investigated my 'unscheduled departure'? Isn't that what your mother calls them?"

"Well. There was the rope from your window, of course. The trail led to the harbour, and a Caldunate vessel—the *Oyster Shell*, was it?—bound for Lasseny. That's as far as I could get."

Katelin nodded. "Not bad." Then her face fell. "I guess that if they'd let you go to Lasseny, you'd have come after me yourself." After a pause, she added, "How angry are they about this?"

Rashelin's nod was slow and deliberate. "Very. Katelin, ten days to the coronation and you disappear. What were you thinking?" There was no upset in her voice, only trying to understand. "That evening—polishing the silver—can't have been too much. Did you need to get away again?"

Katelin sighed. "Yes, I did. Your mother made it clear that my 'lessons in service to others' would become humiliating and painful. You know how hard they make it for me. But this time there turned out to be more to my going, like my last chance to do something before the coronation. Can you understand that?"

"I'll try to," said Rashelin. "You make it sound like some heroic race against time."

Katelin half smiled. "At times it felt like that. But now I'm not so sure …"

"Why? What happened?" Rashelin's face was all concern. "Go on, tell me."

Katelin hesitated. "Remember when we were younger, how we used to make secrecy promises?"

Rashelin took her hand. "Katelin, I promise that this will be secret: not a word, not a soul."

Katelin smiled. She'd almost forgotten that promise they'd used. Then she whispered, "I tried to find some more of the Crown."

"Oh, Katelin, I know it means so much to you, but ... we've been searching for years."

"Yes, I know." Her voice was small and quiet. "It seems that part is in Lasseny, as we guessed. Then I came so close to the final fragment. All these years it's been at the Timajet monastery ... but the Lassenites got to it first."

Rashelin frowned. "What do you mean, they got to it first?"

"Have you got time for me to explain?"

Rashelin nodded. "I have for this."

Katelin summarised what she'd been through over the last nine days. Rashelin leaned forward, intent, as she listened to the slaver capture, the escape from Lasseny, the slaughter at Timajet, and the news that Bassilius had taken the Crown fragment.

At the end, Rashelin said, "I can only say how relieved I am that you're safe and back at home."

Katelin could trust Rashelin enough to discuss the impending invasion. "Worst of all is that the Duke of Lasseny is moving against us. We need to warn the Council that his army is on its way."

"They know," Rashelin said. "I'm not supposed to mention this, but you know it already. I can't believe that Bassikrin would do this after his oaths to my parents to keep peaceful relations with Anestra. The Council asked me what I thought you'd do in response."

"Rashelin, the rule of your parents ends tomorrow night. As my birthday dawns, the Duke has chosen not to extend those promises into my rule. What did you say, and what do the Council think?"

"I said that you'd resist. That you'd call on Anestra to stand up to the bully and fight. The rest of the Council agrees with you. My mother wants you to surrender, wait for the Duke to send his army away and then go back on your word. But still to marry Bassilius."

Katelin snorted, and then shook her head. "Once the Regency ends, and I make the decisions, I'll be glad of your help with the Council."

Rashelin held her gaze and nodded. They both stared at the carpet.

In the silence, Katelin hesitated. She needed to tell someone about this, and Rashelin was the one to understand it. "There's one other thing, Rashelin; another secret. You've always had more faith in the Divine than I have. Well, I want to tell you … I met her."

Rashelin's eyes couldn't have gone wider. "You … met …"

"Yes," Katelin said. "She was invisible, but I felt her presence."

Rashelin swallowed hard. "You … she … when? Where?"

"On a hilltop, by myself. After Bassilius captured Armus and Hedger." She couldn't help smiling at Rashelin's amazement. "I heard her voice in my head. She spoke to me."

"She … spoke?" Rashelin jumped up and began to pace the carpet. "Katelin, that hasn't happened for decades. Centuries, for all I know. It must have been something crucial."

Katelin shrugged. "Well, it wasn't. I was trying to decide about rescuing Armus and Hedger from the Lassenites. That went all right. Then we went to Timajet, and saved Abbot Ruis's life, I suppose. But that's all. I think the Divine was trying to encourage me. To teach me to trust my heart."

A wave of weariness swept over Katelin. Last night's few hours of rest before going to Timajet seemed so long ago. She tried to hide her yawn behind her fingers, but Rashelin saw it.

"I'm sorry, Katelin, you're tired," she said. "I'll leave you to get to bed. But we'll talk about this again, soon after the coronation."

Katelin nodded. "Yes, sleep will be welcome. Thank you for coming to see me, Rashelin. I wanted to talk to you. Do you forgive me for disappearing without telling you?"

"Of course, and even more so now that you've told me what's happened. You've had a hard time of it. You know that I'll help where I can. Have a good night, Katelin, and I'll see you at Court in the morning."

They embraced and Rashelin left for the banquet. Katelin finished her supper with a cranberry pastry, and drained the glass of wine.

What would she do without Rashelin? And how did Rashelin cope with that den of lions, the Court? She'd need an ally there too.

Katelin woke to the sound of Adisha moving in the room. She screwed up her eyes at the assault of sunshine as the servant girl folded back the shutters. She'd been exhausted from her travels, but that hadn't stopped The Nightmare.

The clutching hands were back.

She should have expected it now that she was here. Would it continue once she was Queen, and it was real, and she was living The Nightmare every day?

She stretched, yawned … and her heart sank further. This morning she faced the consequences of her escape. Why couldn't her last day of freedom have been a good one? Instead it was her Uncle, Aunt and the Court. Today, a Princess; tomorrow, the Queen.

No, she wouldn't think about it. The weight in her stomach was heavy enough. Time to get the unpleasantness over with.

She washed and dressed, smoothing and braiding her dark-brown hair. The watery porridge at the Treasure Trove had been too salty, but the bowlful Adisha brought, with the crunch of almonds and the sweetness of honey, was better. She fastened on the emerald necklace that had been her mother's, which matched her dark green, richly embroidered gown.

She smiled with sudden mischief. How might the Court appreciate her dusty and travel-stained tunic, trousers, boots and cloak? She sighed at the tempting thought. At least if she looked like a Princess, they couldn't criticise her for that too.

Katelin swept down the wide stone stairs to the Hall of the Court, saying, "Good morning," to servants on the way. It contravened etiquette, and Aunt and Uncle didn't do it, but it was only human to greet people.

The nerves set in as she approached the double doors to the den of ravening lions. She kept filling her lungs so as not to hold her breath. Expressionless mask on. The door-wardens swung them back, and the herald announced her: "Her Royal Highness, the Princess Katelin."

It was an effort to take the first step. That was it. Just walk forward. What should she look at this time, during her long entrance? To appear calm, relaxed, nonchalant, unconcerned? To glide like a swan: serene on the surface, while hiding frantic paddling underneath.

Katelin had always imagined the Hall of the Court to be pleased with itself, with its high timbered ceiling, blue-bannered stone walls and roaring fires. Sunshine streamed through mullioned, leaded-light windows, onto the marble statues of her ancestors, across the tapestries of their victories in battle and the blue silk banners with her radiant silver Crown.

Katelin ignored the side aisles: the tables and chairs where ministers and officials lurked behind pillars, pretending at the business of city and state. She avoided the stares of the ever-present courtiers, envoys and lords, prowling by the tables, exerting influence and currying favour. She looked straight ahead: to the steps leading to the lair of the head of the pride.

And why did they do that? They were talking before she entered, so why was there silence now? Couldn't they cover the echo of her shoes on the flagstones? Why must they stop what they were doing, to watch and assess her? How could she look like a Queen-in-waiting, when her stomach was turning somersaults?

But they'd better watch out, all of them. Tomorrow this young lioness would take over the pride.

"Ah, my favourite niece has returned!" Regent Ethabos's roar greeted her from the end of the Hall. Favourite niece? Only niece.

"Welcome home, Princess Katelin," the Regent went on. "We pray that your retreat at Mannismill has helped you to focus your thoughts for the future."

So had Uncle Ethabos sobered up yet from last night? Did he know that behind his ample back it was debated how much his chairs were widened and strengthened?

And had Aunt Sirika tried her fiercest glare, down her long, sharp nose, to see if she could melt a candle or break a glass?

At least Rashelin was there as a source of comfort. With her parents so ugly and their daughter the opposite—was this when two wrongs made a right?

But why did Katelin always fight with her Uncle and

Aunt? Was it her reaction to being attacked? They insisted on strict public politeness, but she despised their hypocrisy. If the unity of the Family meant so much to them, they should curb their personal disdain for her. They didn't have to force out gracious smiles, when these never brightened their eyes.

"Your Royal Highnesses." Katelin curtsied. "My Lord Regent, Lady Consort, Aunt, Uncle, good morning. Yes, thank you, my *retreat* has been most helpful." Did they like that insolent emphasis? Apparently not, judging by the acid stares. If they wanted to play games, then she could play them too.

"Council Chamber," Consort Sirika hissed. "Now."

Rashelin helped her father to his feet and accompanied his waddle from the Hall. Sirika paraded out next and Katelin followed with a determined step.

Behind her in the Hall the conversations resumed. It was better that the Royal Family wasn't overheard, lest the truth of their relationships became known.

Ethabos took his chair at the Council table, with Sirika on his right. Katelin seated herself opposite them. Rashelin took a diplomatic chair halfway in between.

"I've a mind to give you a good thrashing," the Regent began.

Katelin stared him down. He wouldn't dare. Not today.

Sirika's voice was quiet, dangerous. "I suppose you think yourself clever to have done this now. But no, you're a foolish little girl and a stupid, useless runaway. Were you trying to make us worry, to despatch soldiers and ships all over the Coast to search for you?"

Katelin wondered whether they'd done any of that, but said nothing.

"And don't think for one moment that you've avoided any of our plans. Your breaking will be different now, that's all. In the meantime, we do have a coronation to arrange, you know. And you disappear, without a word, and leave us to prepare the whole thing."

They would never have let her interfere with the coronation arrangements, but this wasn't worth pointing out. She waited for Sirika to finish. They tried to make her feel like a naughty little cub, but she wouldn't have it. Always they tested her self-control, to stay calm and polite, as the only way to deal with their constant bullying.

"You remember that it is tomorrow, or had you forgotten? Well? What do you have to say for yourself?"

At last Katelin could say, "I'm sorry if my journey caused you trouble or concern, my Lady, but I'm back home now, safe and in time for tomorrow."

The Regent was at his most gruff. "Where did you go and what have you been up to?"

It was time to stretch the truth, of course, with no need to go into details. "I sailed to Lasseny and walked back by way of the desert," said Katelin. "I've made some new friends, who have returned with me."

"More scroungers to abuse our hospitality," said Regent Ethabos. "So you've made your peace with the Duke?"

"Peace with the Duke, my Lord?" said Katelin. "No chance of that. Not after what I've learned. I was in Lasseny city but had no contact with the Duke or the Count. And our hospitality is a small reward to thank my friends for assisting my safe return."

The Regent jabbed a finger at her. "If you hadn't run off in the first place, you wouldn't have needed help to return. So what were you doing in Lasseny?"

What did they think? Getting away from the two of them, of course. But she knew better than to say it. "Just one of my little adventures, my Lord," said Katelin. "You know how I love the outdoors, and to travel ... to see new places ... meet new people ..."

"Enough! We're tired of your insolence. At least you're here. You can go, and we'll send for you when we need you." The Regent dismissed her with a wave of his hand. "And don't forget the rehearsal this afternoon."

Katelin could tell that her coronation was close because her telling off had been short and light. But oh no, they couldn't dismiss her like that. If they weren't going to mention the subject, then she would. "But, my Lord." Katelin forced him to look at her again. "I have to report that the Duke of Lasseny has mustered his forces to attack us."

Sirika's tone was even sharper than usual. "What do you mean? The Duke has maintained a friendly peace with us for years."

Katelin drew a deep breath. "Duke Bassikrin has gathered his army from his northern and eastern borders, and they march here as we speak. And on our way south, we found that Count Bassilius and his men have destroyed the monastery at Timajet. They killed all but one of the monks."

The Regent and Consort glanced at each other, and there was definite alarm in their eyes. "You will remain silent about this," Sirika said. "We will not have your rumours unsettling the people before the coronation. If and when the Duke arrives, then your Uncle and I will meet with him. You may go."

"No," Katelin stated. "You will not meet with him. Not if it's after today." But inside she was trembling. She glanced at Rashelin, who was looking between them with a pained expression.

"Get out," Sirika hissed.

Katelin glared at them. Was it even worth saying anything more before tomorrow, when she became responsible for everything? She'd get the coronation over first, and then deal with the Lassenites.

She knew she shouldn't antagonise them, but couldn't resist it. She looked around the Council table, tapping her chin. "Hmm, I wonder. Which chair shall I sit in … when I preside at Council meetings?"

Sirika's eyes narrowed. "Be careful, little girl. Remember that after tomorrow your Uncle and I will still have powerful allies and friends. The Council and the Court will still listen to our wisdom and experience, and not to your selfish whims. Because who will you have on your side? The commoners?" Her smile was sneering, nasty.

Katelin swallowed. Her Aunt was right, because Katelin had no idea yet how much weight being Queen carried in here.

She stood and curtsied. Her Aunt and Uncle had already turned to each other, no doubt to discuss further the intimidation of their niece. Rashelin gave Katelin a sympathetic look.

"My Lord, my Lady," Katelin said. She had to have the last word. "I'll leave you to your packing then, to vacate my apartments." Before they could react, she turned away and hurried to exit the Chamber and Court.

✷ XVII ✷

BALCONY

It was only when she reached the third floor landing that Katelin realised how much she'd stomped up the stairs. There was momentary remorse: she shouldn't have been spiteful to them. But they drove her to it. They brought out the rebellious girl in her. But after all she'd been through, and with the coronation so close, perhaps she should have tried harder to hold her tongue. At least those wretched audiences with the Regent and Consort ended tomorrow: no more answering to them. But then she'd need to fight them for everything.

Waiting for her on a chair outside her door was Hedger. Her anger melted. He'd come to see her.

"Bad morning?" he said. "It sounded like half the army were climbing the stairs."

"I've had better," she said. "I was attending our beloved Regent and Consort, and we always manage to fight with each other. Was I really that loud?" She laughed, and it was a welcome relief. "Come in."

Hedger followed her in, and looked her up and down. "It's a pleasant change to see you looking like a Princess, my lady," he teased.

"Now don't you start." She wagged a playful finger at him. "I get enough of that from the Court. I wondered about appearing in my travelling clothes, but reckoned I was in enough trouble already. Is Sigzay all right?"

"She's fine," said Hedger. "She felt it stuffy in the Castle, so she's gone out to the market."

"I know what she means," said Katelin. "Come out onto the balcony."

She pushed open the casement windows which led onto a wide, stone balcony with a cast iron rail. "That's better," she sighed. "The Castle air stifles me. With a breeze on my face, I can breathe again. Sometimes I need this view across the city, to Temple Hill, the harbour, the mountains and the sea."

"Quite a panorama," said Hedger. He joined her at the rail. "It smells fresher than Lasseny too."

"It does. My private window on the world," Katelin breathed. "That's the Temple of the Divine; and to the left of the mountains, there's Hermit's Isle." She indicated the landmarks. "I don't see any slavers there today."

"Oh yes, you told us about that." Hedger smiled.

She pointed to her bedroom window with a sheer drop to the grounds below. "From that window I made my escape from the Castle. I thought of descending from this balcony but it overhangs too much. When I'm Queen, I think I'll keep a permanent rope through a window, to escape whenever I wish. Or maybe a rope ladder."

"Kat, when you're Queen, you can walk down the stairs and out the front gate, you know."

"Yes, I suppose so. But it won't feel like a proper escape unless I climb out of a window and scale a wall." She grinned. Then she added, "Although I won't be able to run away on any more adventures, will I? No more being an irresponsible Princess."

"No, I guess not." Hedger paused. "Talking of becoming Queen, what do you have to do tomorrow?"

"Not much." Katelin shrugged. "I wake up, turn eighteen and get Crowned. That's it: Queen. Of course, my Aunt and Uncle have organised everyone and everything, to ensure that it all runs to plan. They don't trust me one bit, and are convinced that, given the chance, I'd ruin the whole palaver."

"What will the Regent and Consort do after tomorrow?" Hedger asked.

"I'd like them to disappear off to their country estate at Mannismill, but I doubt that will happen. They're moving to other rooms in the Castle, to keep an oppressive eye on me, while I move one floor down from here into the royal apartments. My Uncle will eat and drink his way to oblivion, but my Aunt will plot and scheme to try to keep power and influence. Of course, it's been she, not my Uncle, who's ruled the Kingdom during the Regency. She tries to bully me into becoming her puppet or figurehead Queen. It's only her obsession with tradition and appearance that's kept her from murdering me these last fifteen years. She'll try to sabotage whatever I do as Queen."

"You don't like them much, do you?"

Katelin sighed. "No, I've never known anyone irritate each other as much as we do. They're stuck in the past, so nostalgic, old-fashioned, traditional. They've no sense of the future … or even of the present for that matter. Their biggest fear is that I will change things, and for them 'change' means 'spoil'. It's as though a breath of fresh air is the worst that can happen."

"I understand," said Hedger. "A Regent is a caretaker for the throne, entrusted with maintaining the Kingdom until you come of age. It isn't their place to change things."

Katelin turned mock accuser. "You're not sticking up for them, are you? I thought you were on my side."

"Of course I'm on your side, Kat. But I try to understand different points of view."

"I'll let you off." The breeze stirred her hair where it had escaped from the braid. "They do everything they can to annoy me. They've brought me up since I was two, and we've never seen eye to eye. I rebel against their assumptions, while they try to make me the Queen they want me to be. All my life they've told me I'm useless."

"Kat, from what I've seen, you're far from useless. You'll never be anyone's puppet or figurehead. You'll be a better Queen than anyone expects."

Katelin flushed at the compliment. "Why, thank you, but I'm sure you're the only one who thinks so."

"I guess it was hard on them too when your parents were killed. They never expected to have to rule Anestra. They enjoyed a grand, luxurious, irresponsible life as members of the Royal Family. All of a sudden they were in charge, with a two-year-old niece to bring up, who would take power away from them the minute you turned eighteen."

"I suppose you're right, but they could have been nicer about it. They've enjoyed their power too." Katelin's gazing at the horizon turned wistful. "I wish I remembered my parents, but I was too young when they died. My best friend has always been my cousin Rashelin. Have you met her: the Regent's daughter, three years older than me?"

Hedger narrowed his eyes, as if remembering. "I guess I saw her when I was little boy here in Anestra."

"Oh, you'd remember if you had," said Katelin with a laugh, "as she's the charming and beautiful one. But what about you? We spend all this time talking about me and the Royal Family. Do you have family in Anestra? And how did you end up as a mercenary in Lasseny?"

Hedger drew a deep breath. "I was born and brought up here, and was eight years old when my parents were killed in the Crown War. I was taken to Lasseny and sold as a slave boy. That life was hard; that's when I got these." He indicated his scarred hands and forehead. "I became a talented swordsman, so my master put me in for the city entertainment. The prize was freedom and I won it. I've travelled much since then, even back to Anestra, but based in Lasseny."

"That sounds a hard life. And lonely too, until you met Sigzay." Katelin looked at him. "But you and I have one thing in common."

"Orphaned by the Crown War? Yes. War makes too many widows and orphans." Then his seriousness broke into a teasing smile. "But I'm not sure that 'Princess' counts as hard and lonely."

"Fair enough," said Katelin with a laugh. "I know I appreciated the hot bath, ready food, clean sheets and soft bed of last night." Then she was serious again. "But lonely? Castle life can be lonely amid the crowd. How many of these people can I call friends? I've never known who to trust or confide in, or what they're after."

"What about Rashelin? You called her your best friend."

"Yes, we grew up together; more like sisters than cousins, I suppose." Katelin returned her gaze to the horizon. "I love her; she's so kind, gentle, thoughtful. She avoids the attention or standing in front of crowds, but prefers to work behind the scenes, helping out, smoothing things over. But then, we can't be like normal sisters. She's older than me, yet inherits little, while I'm younger and inherit the Kingdom. That isn't fair, is it? She never makes things difficult, but I always feel it there in the background."

"There's plenty that doesn't seem fair," said Hedger.

Katelin gave a sudden laugh. "When we were younger, Rashelin and I had this joke. If ever I complained about having to be Queen, she'd tell me to abdicate on my eighteenth birthday, and she'd help her parents to look after it for me. I'd forgotten about that. And now here we are at that point. I wonder if Rashelin still thinks that I'll abdicate and her father will ascend to the throne."

"Abdication is a drastic and irreversible decision." Hedger's tone was grave.

"Now you sound like Brother Armus," Katelin chuckled. "He said something similar." She paused. "No, I could never abdicate, for that would leave the Kingdom languishing under the rule of Uncle Ethabos and Aunt Sirika. I couldn't do that to Anestra. But I've always thought Rashelin makes an excellent Princess. Not only is she young and beautiful, but she doesn't mind all of that Court stuff. You know: tact, diplomacy, making nobles and courtiers feel important and listened to, understanding how they think and what motivates them. She does that without even trying."

"That's a rare gift." Hedger nodded. "So the Regent and Consort resent you for becoming Queen instead of their daughter, and also think she's more suitable than you."

"That may be," Katelin said. "It's a cruel twist of fate: I inherit a Kingdom I don't want, while others want it more and might rule it better. I can't see how I'm suited for the role, or how the Divine's will and purpose is served in all this."

"The Divine requires patience and time to work out, but Armus and Ruis seem to understand her. I take comfort in this: the Divine kept you safe in your travels, Kat, and returned you in time for the coronation."

"Maybe," she said, "but so much went wrong. And it's tomorrow and the days after that worry me. I may be the Queen, with one part of the Crown, but that doesn't mean I can defend the Kingdom from invasion."

"You won't be alone, Kat," said Hedger. "You have generals and ministers, and Rashelin is capable and willing. I'm sure that Armus, Ruis, Sigzay and I would be happy to stay and help too, if you wish."

Katelin turned to face him. "Would you?"

Hedger nodded. "Of course. We never expected to be friends with the Queen of the Western Coast. We're no experts at ruling a Kingdom, but if you need common sense or someone to talk to, then we could do that."

Katelin smiled. "Thank you. I'd like that very much."

After a moment, Hedger added, "Although, now that you've told me how charming and beautiful Princess Rashelin is, I can't see Sigzay approving of my meeting her."

Katelin laughed. "Oh yes. She's the most eligible Princess there is."

"Second most eligible," corrected Hedger. "You hold your own in charm and beauty, Kat, and have better prospects than Rashelin ..."

"Why, I thank you." Katelin flushed again.

"Or, at least, Count Bassilius of Lasseny thinks so ..."

"Ugh, don't remind me."

They chuckled, then stood in silence, but it was a comfortable, not an awkward, one. Below them, the guards were changing shifts at the Castle gatehouse.

Hedger's scarred and pitted hand was beside hers on the rail. She remembered saying to Sigzay as they walked in the desert that she didn't fancy him. Now she'd begun to see what Sigzay had: behind his impressive physique was wisdom and strength. He was thoughtful, with an enviable calmness. So he and Sigzay had captured each other's hearts. Katelin didn't dare to broach that subject, to interfere in their love.

But what did she feel? His scarred forehead no longer seemed ugly, but was simply the way that he looked. He had a companionable presence; he made her laugh and feel safe. She'd grown to trust him; she was fond of him. What was that then? A friend? Yes. Or maybe this was like one of those relationships that she would never know, with a father. Or a brother.

"It shouldn't have been me, you know." Katelin cringed to realise that she'd said this out loud. Oh no, now she'd done it. A brother. To think of him again, today of all days.

"What do you mean?" said Hedger.

"Um ... well ..." If she trusted him, could she confide her grief to him? "It shouldn't have been me becoming Queen. When my parents were killed, my elder brother died too. We seldom speak of him now, as it's painful. He was the one preparing to succeed my father and assume the throne of Anestra. If he'd lived, since he was older than me, he'd have saved me from all of this. The Prince Edgaran," she said. The wistful tone was back.

"Ah, yes," said Hedger. "I remember."

"I was only two when he died, so I don't remember him. As the sole survivor of my Family, it all came down to me. I've resented the situation ever since I was old enough to understand it."

"I've often wondered about something," said Hedger. "A Kingdom should be ruled by someone worthy, who will serve and defend it, and not be weak or selfish. But inheritance is like drawing lots. So when a ruler dies, the most deserving of the role should be chosen as successor. Do you think that would work?"

"Um, I don't know." What was he suggesting? "Would the Council or Court choose? Or the people? But in that arrangement, I could avoid becoming Queen. Or at least, Anestra could choose between, say, Rashelin, the Regent, the Consort, me ... and you. Given that list, who is your choice?"

"Hmm." Hedger stroked his chin. "I know the Regent, the Consort and Rashelin only by reputation. If I can't choose myself, then Kat, I'm afraid it has to be you after all."

"Oh no," Katelin cried. "If I can't choose myself, and I wouldn't *ever* choose the Regent or Consort, then the next ruler of Anestra is … Rashelin … or you." They both laughed.

Silence fell between them again. Katelin enjoyed the view, the breeze, the sunshine … and the comfort of Hedger's presence.

He drew a deep breath. "Can I ask …? You're still dreading becoming Queen tomorrow, aren't you?"

There was no point trying to hide it. "Yes, I am," she said. "I can't avoid it, and it's what's best for Anestra. My fate was decided when I was born to be privileged and responsible. So they'll lock me up in my ornate and comfortable prison, with my lifelong battle against my Aunt and Uncle and the Court. And it'll start, unless there's some way to prevent it, with defeat by Lasseny and marriage to Bassilius." The words tasted bitter.

"But …" Hedger hesitated, then said, "… if there were a way for you to avoid becoming Queen, without abdicating, but to stay as a Princess in the Royal Family, what would you do with yourself?"

"Um …" She didn't see how that could happen. But in the years of not wanting to be Queen, she'd longed for what else she might do. "I'd live in Anestra, if there were ways I could help the Kingdom. I'd continue as an irresponsible Princess, with my riding, hunting and travelling. Maybe they'd let me command a company of the Royal Archers, and be a roving 'Princess-at-large', up and down the Coast. But my heart lies with the people of Anestra, and I'd love to get out of the Court and Castle, and away from the stuffy, self-important nobles and ministers. I want to help and serve Anestrans. And who knows? If I'm really that eligible, someone might marry me and settle me down with children." She laughed.

But now Hedger seemed both nervous and serious.

"Kat," he said. "I came up here this morning to tell you something."

His tone made her heart stop, leap upwards and start pounding.

She stared into his conker eyes, which now had a strange uncertainty about them, and tried to swallow her heart back into place. What was this?

Hedger drew, and let out, a long breath. "A few days ago in the desert you told us who you are. You said that, if we wish, we've a right to keep secrets. You've trusted me, so I'm going to be honest with you. I've told you the truth, but I haven't told you everything. There's something I need to tell you … before tomorrow."

What was he saying? Never mind the speech. His voice quavered, but he could still get on and say it.

"You can't see how to avoid becoming Queen unless you abdicate," Hedger went on. "You don't want the throne, so how is the Divine will and purpose served in that? But there is a way out. I've kept this secret for fifteen years, since I was a boy of eight."

He paused. "You know me as Hedger, but that's only a nickname, a shortened form. My full name is properly … Edgaran."

XVIII

TEMPLE

Katelin stared at him.

"Edgaran ..." she whispered.

"Yes, Kat." Hedger's voice was gentle. "The Prince. Your brother."

She didn't understand. What was he saying?

He smiled, and reached a hand towards her.

Katelin shrank away. Her reeling thoughts had darkened. "My brother? You're the dead Prince Edgaran? I don't believe you."

"But, Kat—"

Katelin's hands had balled into fists and she flung the words at him. "How dare you? You come here and claim to be my long lost brother? You exploit my sorrow and grief? You're a complete stranger ... and you claim the Kingship of Anestra? You expect anyone to believe you?"

"Listen, Kat—"

"You have evidence or proof for your claim?"

"I don't know how to prove this." Hedger crossed his arms, looked down. "I could tell you about when we were children, but you say you don't remember that."

"And you could have made it up," Katelin snapped. "I'm told that imposters are clever. If you're Anestran and about the right age you could try it. When did you come up with this 'lost Prince Edgaran' plan? As soon as we met in Lasseny, or after I told you who I was in the desert?"

"No, Kat." Hedger uncrossed his arms, his voice rising too.

"I haven't lied to you, and I've only ever tried to help you. I'm loyal to Anestra, and I thought we'd started to trust each other."

"Oh yes, very well done," Katelin sneered. "Excellent job of winning my trust. Now I remember: it was you who pushed me to reveal my identity. Then you could work on me to claim the rule of Anestra?"

"I'm telling you the truth, Kat," Hedger yelled. "Can't you even consider that?"

He grabbed the rail, his knuckles white. Katelin's blood ran cold. She stepped back from him. As well as being an imposter, he could be a spy, an agent of Lasseny. The Duke trained his spies to infiltrate Anestra, and to impersonate or befriend the powerful.

She was in danger.

He carried no sword, but could be hiding a poisoned blade. How better to cripple Anestra on the eve of the coronation than to assassinate the new Queen?

Beneath her gown, Katelin's legs shook. She gripped the rail to steady herself, and glanced up. Hedger watched her, but hadn't approached or threatened her. What could she do? First, she needed protection. Katelin pretended calmness, turned from the balcony and re-entered the room. Hedger followed, but not too close behind.

She feigned confusion and forced a smile. "Well … yes … I ought to consider that you might be truthful. I need to think about this. We should talk with someone—perhaps our Family, downstairs, in the Hall? Will you come?"

She didn't wait for an answer and left the room. She needed to stay ahead of him down the stairs. And find the guards. She refused to hear any more from him, as she couldn't trust a word he said.

At the foot of the stairs, Katelin didn't turn to the Hall but ran outside. Two guards were on duty at the entrance to the Keep, with others at the Castle gatehouse.

"I need your help," Katelin shouted, and they leapt forward. She couldn't let Hedger wander in freedom. She had to stop him—and Sigzay too, if she were his accomplice.

Hedger emerged through the Keep doors, but halted on the threshold at the sight of Katelin and the guards.

"Arrest this man," Katelin ordered. Two guards grabbed Hedger and secured his arms behind his back. "He's a suspected Lassenite agent and spy. Take him to the dungeons and confine him." But he made no attempt to resist or run. What was that she saw in his eyes? Anger, frustration, sadness, betrayal? As the guards led him away, she added to the others, "When his accomplice returns from the city, imprison her too. That's Sigzay, a young barbarian woman."

Katelin stood in the midst of the courtyard and wished that the guards weren't watching her. She stared at the flagstones. What a silly, naive girl she'd been, blinded by a charming rogue. Now he'd churned her up inside.

She needed to discuss this with someone. She'd talk to Rashelin, but didn't want to face the Hall of the Court again. There was someone who'd known Hedger for a while though, and that was Brother Armus. She trusted a cleric not to be a Lassenite agent, and he'd be at the Temple. She said to the guards, "Two of you, come with me."

Katelin left the Castle and crossed Crown Square, ignoring that the two guards struggled to match her urgent pace. With everything else, she'd forgotten: they were preparing the dais by the Castle wall for that afternoon's coronation rehearsal. She couldn't bear to think about that now.

She tried to calm down enough to think. Had Hedger given any sign of being a Lassenite agent? She couldn't think of anything. But maybe she'd been too preoccupied with her own worries to notice. Armus could tell her of any suspicions from while they were captives of Bassilius.

But it couldn't be true, could it, that Hedger was her long-dead brother? Could he have survived in secret all this time? But why hadn't he declared himself before now? And on her coronation eve too. Even if she believed him, no one else would, not without firm evidence or proof. So what difference would that make?

Katelin and the guards turned into Temple Approach and exited through the city walls at Cleric Gate. As they climbed Temple Hill, the building's white marble columns gleamed above them in the noontime sun.

A low wall surrounded the complex and they were admitted at once through the main entrance. An initiate went to fetch Brother Armus while Katelin and her guards waited in the wide vestibule. A pool of water rippled in a whisper of breeze through the coolness of the high vaulted building. Echoes of voices and footsteps wafted into the vastness.

Two female clerics approached, bowed and wished her well for tomorrow. Katelin returned their greeting, then entered a side room to avoid further disturbance, posting the guards outside the door. She pulled a chair up to a large wooden table, but couldn't stay seated and paced the room instead.

How much should she tell Armus of their balcony conversation? Before she could think further, Brother Armus entered the room, chatting away with Abbot Ruis.

"A thousand apologies, Princess Katelin, Your Highness," said Abbot Ruis, as he closed the door. "I didn't recognise you yesterday at Timajet, and Armus only told me about you last night." He bowed and took her hand.

Armus's smile was hesitant. "I hope that's all right, Princess. Now that we're back in Anestra, your identity would soon become obvious. I've related to the Abbot all that's happened since we met in Lasseny."

None of that seemed to matter now. Katelin nodded, and realised that she'd no more than glanced at them. She sat down, stared at the table and sighed. Where to begin? The clerics seated themselves opposite her.

"I trust you've had a good night's rest after our journey?" said Ruis. He was making conversation, covering her distracted silence. She nodded, still focused on the grain in the wood.

Armus said, "I've good news of our friend initiate Prento, by the way." The young man's name poked at Katelin's heart. Was he here? Could she see him?

"He arrived two days ago," Armus went on, "and delivered the judgement. Because he was captured by bandits on the highway, they've sent him by ship with the goldens for Daytose's release. He should reach Lasseny tomorrow."

So he'd gone again. She couldn't afford to think about Prento now, but his lordship would have been a welcome diversion.

Ruis said, "We've reported the atrocity at Timajet to the Under Father and the council of clerics. We're devastated to have lost so many good people, but they're with the Divine. Some sisters and brothers will return there soon to bury the dead."

There was an awkward silence.

Armus leaned forward. "Princess, are you all right?"

No, she wasn't. And she hadn't said a word since they'd come in, had she? She placed her hands flat on the table and cleared her throat. "I need to discuss something with you."

The clerics looked at each other. "Of course," said Armus. "What is it?"

She'd better come straight to the point. Katelin drew a

deep breath, looked up and met their concerned gaze at last. "Hedger came to see me this morning and claimed that he is Prince Edgaran."

The clerics stared at her. "What? Prince Edgaran?" said Ruis. "But the young Prince died as a boy, in the Crown War."

"Yes, of course he did," Katelin snapped. Her anger had resurfaced unbidden. "There's no evidence to support his claim. All I can think is that Hedger's trying to deceive us, as a Lassenite agent and spy."

"A spy?" said Armus. "So what have you done?"

"My guards have secured him in the dungeons. We can't let him wander about to spread unsettling rumours. I've ordered Sigzay's arrest too, assuming she's his accomplice. But Armus, you've known Hedger longer than the rest of us. Have you ever had reason to doubt him?"

Armus thought, and then shook his head. "Not at all. I can't say I know him well, but he's come and gone from Lasseny in his mercenary work. He's always seemed loyal to Anestra."

"But if you're a spy, then that's how you're supposed to seem," said Katelin. "What about when Bassilius captured you in the desert? Anything suspicious then?"

"Yes, I remember something now," said Armus. "Bassilius recognised him. The Count mentioned seeing him outside the Duke's Palace, when we were all in Lasseny. The two of them were antagonistic and rude to each other, but perhaps that was part of the act."

"And remember how Hedger spared those Lassenite soldiers who guarded you?" said Katelin. "That infuriated Sigzay. She must have been afraid that he was giving away his true allegiance. So Hedger may have guessed who I was from the start. He seized the chance to accompany me, and won my trust after I revealed my identity that morning in the canyon."

Armus frowned. "But Hedger and Sigzay were the ones who warned us about the muster of the Lassenite army. Why would they do that, if they work for the Duke?"

"I don't know," said Katelin. "Even with the warning, we've made no difference to Anestran defences. Come to think of it, it's only their word that those were the supply wagons, and that the Duke's withdrawn his forces from the north-east. So maybe some of that's a lie too ... except that I saw something with my own eyes. Oh, I can't worry about that now. It'll all have to wait until after the coronation."

"It seems harsh on Hedger and Sigzay," Armus mused, "after all they've done to help us, to languish in your dungeons. But I suppose you have to be extra careful until the coronation is over."

Katelin stood up to leave.

"One moment, please, Princess," Abbot Ruis said. "There's something else, if I may."

Katelin sat down.

Ruis looked like he was about to deliver a speech. "Our situation might seem bleak, Your Highness. What you've told us may be a last, desperate act by the Duke and his spies to unsettle Anestra on the coronation eve. Whether or not the Duke attacks us, already Count Bassilius has ransacked my monastery, slaughtered the monks and pillaged the Crown fragment. I understand, Princess, if everything seems against you ... but I assure you that isn't the case." To Katelin's surprise, the Abbot smiled. "For I know something you don't."

Katelin stared at him. He'd grabbed her full attention.

"Yes, part of the Crown was at Timajet," he continued. "It was a third of the whole, so the fragments at Anestra, Lasseny and Timajet make up the complete Crown. There's been a fragile truce for fifteen years between the cities of the

Coast. The attack on Timajet shatters that: a devastating blow. And yes, I think that the Duke will use what he has of the Crown to try to conquer Anestra."

Ruis paused and frowned. This much Katelin knew. Couldn't the Abbot get on with it? But he spoke as someone who knew more than any of them guessed. It was as though he were uttering prophecy, inspired by the spirit of the Divine. Katelin's muscles went rigid at the thought.

"The time for the return of the Crown has come," declared Ruis, his voice rising. "Two parts are reunited and war breaks out on the Coast. The balance of power between Lasseny and Anestra shifts. The Duke reveals his intentions, with terrible consequences for us all."

A chill washed over Katelin's skin and the hairs on her arms stood. She couldn't take her eyes from the Abbot.

Ruis paused for maximum dramatic effect, and his frown melted into a smile. His voice softened. "But the Divine is good to us beyond all human reckoning. Princess Katelin returns to Anestra and tomorrow becomes our Queen. The Regency is over, and she for whom we have waited so long will ascend to her rightful place on the throne." His voice rose again. "She will lead us in the defence of our city to counter any threat from Lasseny. The Divine has ensured that we have you, Princess, and that we have the Crown of Anestra."

Katelin's insides had clenched solid at these confident words of the Abbot. "But I don't know how to do any of that," she blurted out. "And we've only one part of the three!"

The Abbot's smile remained assured. "Duke Bassikrin guessed that a fragment of the Crown was at Timajet. His son ransacked the chapel, and stole the contents of the reliquary behind the altar. But all that was there was a replica; an exact copy of our part of the Crown, but a fake nevertheless. The true fragment of the broken Crown was hidden in the vestry, in a floor safe, in a battered metal box. Princess Katelin, the second part of your Crown of Anestra is safely in my pocket."

XIX

CROWN

Katelin sat speechless. As Ruis's words sank in, a sudden lightness grew into a deep giggle inside. Jumping stars! The Crown … was here … in this room? She could only stare. Then grin.

The Abbot's smile was broad and his eyes shone. His finger tapped the box in his pocket, and it gave a dull thud through the folds of his garment.

Armus burst out laughing. "The Divine never ceases to surprise me." He shook his head. "The way she brings victory from defeat is stupendous."

"No, not victory," corrected the Abbot. "I fear there is still a war to win before that can be claimed."

At last Katelin managed to gasp, "You … you have the second part of the Crown right here? We've searched for years—and it's in your pocket?" It was more of a squeal than she would have liked.

"Right here, safe and sound," said Ruis, grinning, his hand on it. "So you see, Princess, the situation for Anestra is not as bleak as we thought."

He'd enjoyed to the full his moment of revelation, hadn't he?

Realisation overwhelmed Katelin with relief, and tears washed into her eyes. In the carnage at Timajet there had been one redeeming spark: Bassilius had made off with a fake. They'd been right to go to the burning monastery, because they'd saved this man and the secret that he kept. She would be Queen, and war might come, however much of the Crown she'd gained. But for the moment, the joy quenched her dread. So this game wasn't over yet. A hundred points to her; thank the Divine!

"Does anyone else know about this?" Katelin asked.

"No, Princess," said Ruis, "not any more. Only a few of us at Timajet knew. I thought it best kept secret, as it's your business alone. It's your decision how and when you make this public. Would you like me to show it to you?"

It was an unnecessary question. Would she like to see it? Yes, of course she would!

Abbot Ruis pulled the battered metal box from his robes. He placed it on the table, and Katelin's eyes were wide and popping. "Behold the Crown of Anestra," he said, and prised the lid from the box.

Similar to the fragment in the Royal Treasury, the box contained a cushion of dark blue silk on which rested an ornate piece of silverwork. The fragment was about seven inches in length, and curved to form part of the circle of the Crown. Its working was intricate, and the silver was inscribed and studded with gems.

At the sight of the piece, unobstructed by oak panels, glass doors, locks or safes, Katelin felt herself drawn to it even more. Again, it was as if this silverwork called to her. As though it had always belonged to her. Or she to it.

From a distance came Ruis's voice. "Some consider the chief worth of this piece to be in the metal and stones; or that this is ancient, a part of the long history of the Old Kingdom of Anestra. Yes, it is beautiful and beyond price. But far more important is that this is sacred." His hand hovered over the box, but didn't touch it. "Here most of all dwells the power of the Divine, in the most sacred relic of our realm. Those honoured to wear it receive the guidance, glory and power of the Divine in a way no others can. I've touched it, of course, but few others have. I presume the fragment in the Royal Treasury is also untouched?"

Katelin nodded, entranced. "That's right," she said. "It's in the strongest safe, and guarded these fifteen years. The Royal Treasurer wears gloves to polish it."

"Good," said Ruis. "Now I deliver this most precious object to its rightful owner at last." He pushed the box across the table to rest in front of Katelin. "It is yours now, Princess. You may pick it up."

Katelin jumped in shock. She stared at him, a shiver dancing down her spine. "I can touch it?" she squeaked.

"Of course." Ruis's smile was reassuring. "You will wear it in its circlet on your head from tomorrow. Those who love the Divine, as you do, have nothing whatsoever to fear from it."

Katelin wiped her hands on her gown. She'd never been allowed this near to the part in the Treasury. Let alone to touch it. But now she wanted to, more than anything. Her stomach knotted, and her arm trembled as it stretched towards the box. She held her breath as her fingers touched the silver. Then they curled and picked it up.

It wasn't cold. It had an inner warmth as though it were alive. It was lighter than she'd expected, and her fingers tingled. She examined the silver: the exquisite designs and fine tracery of ancient writing all over it. She was no expert, but was sure these were sapphires, emeralds, rubies and diamonds embedded. She ran her fingers over the large, priceless gems and gazed into their depths. Her heart was galloping, and an ecstasy ran through her body.

The Crown.

Her Crown.

At last she came back to herself, to notice her fingerprints all over the highly polished silver. She returned it to its box.

She looked up. Armus was beaming, watching her. Ruis was frowning, in thought.

"What is it, Abbot Ruis?" Katelin asked. "What's the matter?"

Ruis paused before answering. "It's all right," he said. "It's that I've long wondered about something."

"About what?"

The Abbot took a deep breath. "Can you describe the flag of Anestra, please, Princess?"

As soon as Ruis said this, she knew what he meant. "Of course," Katelin replied. "It's a dark blue flag with a silver Crown in the centre and radiance around it; like rays coming out of the sun."

"Indeed," said Ruis. "I saw the Crown on the head of your father, King Etharan. I've heard these days that some don't believe it, but I know what I saw. The Crown of Anestra shone on the head of the King. Some call it magic, but the Crown radiates with Divine glory for the King or Queen alone. Our ruler receives the power of the Divine so our Kingdom never falls to an enemy."

"I remember it now," said Katelin. "The Crown glows when touched by the ruler of Anestra. But I've never been allowed to touch it before." She frowned. "So why didn't it shine just then?"

"I can think of two reasons," the Abbot replied. "For one thing, you're not yet Queen. The Divine knows all things: that you're not yet eighteen, nor Crowned till tomorrow. And for another, this is only a broken fragment and not the whole Crown. But still, I wondered whether we'd see anything if you touched it before becoming Queen."

"So we wait for tomorrow, and then the Crown will shine when it's placed on my head?"

"Yes, it will," said the Abbot, and smiled. "Everyone is so

excited to see that, as it hasn't happened for fifteen years."

Katelin had often wondered too: how it would feel, when she became Queen, to experience the power and glory of the Divine, the radiance of the Crown from her own head. She gazed at the metal box, lying open on the table, with the Crown fragment resting on its dark blue cushion. She couldn't believe that this Divine object, this sacred relic, was here in front of her. A bashful smile crept over her face. "What will it feel like?"

Ruis and Armus laughed, and the Abbot said, "There's no one alive who knows. So perhaps, after tomorrow, you'd be kind enough to come back and tell us?"

Katelin laughed too. "Yes, of course. Well, so far I can tell you that it was warm and light, and my fingers tingled; it was as though the Crown called to me."

The clerics' eyes were shining, enraptured.

"You thrill us more than you can know, Princess," said Ruis. "Many clerics have studied the Crown, but none can say the effects of breaking it. How will that affect its glory and power? But now, you remember what I told you on the highway, about the tiny Crown fragments repairing themselves?" Ruis indicated the perfect silverwork before them, and Katelin nodded. "Well, that may answer another question for you."

"Which is?" said Katelin, when there was a pause.

"How do you incorporate this piece of the Crown with the part in the Treasury in time for tomorrow? The answer is that you don't have to. Give this box to the Royal Treasurer, and when she places this piece into the circlet of the Crown it will fuse together as new."

Katelin said, "So this fragment will fuse with the existing part, making two thirds of the Crown and leaving one third as circlet?"

"That is correct," said Ruis. "For so long we've awaited what tomorrow will bring. Anestra needs you, Princess, and the Divine and the Crown, to restore our glory as in the days of your father. From those who are given much, much is expected."

Katelin swallowed down her unease at the responsibility. "I'll arrange good seats for you, my friends. You won't miss a thing."

"This is a highlight of our lives," said Armus, "and we're honoured that you call us your friends."

An idea popped into Katelin's head. "Can I ask that nothing of this is mentioned to anyone before tomorrow? I'd like to keep this part of the Crown secret, to see the expressions on their faces."

Armus and Ruis looked at each other. "I can understand that, Princess," said Ruis. "But not even the Under Father?"

"No, not even the Under Father, please," she replied. "Once someone else knows, I wouldn't know where to draw the line. It can be a pleasant surprise for him too."

"As you wish." Ruis smiled. "The Crown has a whole volume of The Tome to itself, you know. I guess that after tomorrow we'll be adding a few extra lines to the end of its history." He stood up. "Now then, Armus and I need to stay here at the Temple and help to prepare for tomorrow."

Armus frowned. "And after the coronation, as soon as I've time, I'll ask to see Hedger and Sigzay."

Ruis nodded. "But Princess, I think you're required for the rehearsal about now?"

Katelin groaned. "Yes, of course. With everything else, I'd forgotten about that. It must be time for it." She reached for the lid of the battered metal box and replaced it. She hesitated, and then handed the box back to Ruis, enjoying his look of surprise. "I can't walk around with this in my hand for the rest of today, and expect no one to ask me about it. Would you look after it for one more day, back in your wonderful pocket? And please be ready when I ask for it tomorrow?"

"Of course, Your Majesty," Ruis replied, and bowed low. "My Queen."

Katelin smiled. It would take a while to get used to that title.

The box disappeared into his pocket, and Ruis said, "You could give me no greater honour. One last thing: after your coronation, we hope you'll allow us to continue your training in the ways of the Divine. Armus tells me that your education has been lacking with regard to your powers and those of the Crown."

She didn't understand—her powers? The Crown had powers, but she didn't. But she had no time to ask. "Yes, of course," she said. "I'll need to learn all that I can. I have to run and my guards will escort me. Thank you both and I'll see you tomorrow." She embraced the clerics and hurried from the room. She was halfway to the Temple entrance before the guards caught up with her fast pace towards Crown Square.

Katelin's joy vanished through the afternoon as she endured the coronation rehearsal. She fixed in place her mask of expressionless smile for the Court ceremony that she found so pointless. And why did her Aunt and Uncle insist on being so critical? Still, there were two consolations: she had to repeat this only once—tomorrow—and she had a surprise to spring on them all.

Katelin escaped to her rooms when the rehearsal concluded, relieved of any duties until evening. She rested on her bed for a moment.

She awoke at sunset to activity below her window. A carriage had brought from Mannismill Rashelin's three younger brothers, Tajion, Agabos and Ethnir. They oozed arrogance, as they resented having to wait in the courtyard. No doubt they'd objected to coming for her coronation at all. They preferred their country pursuits at Mannismill, and taking advantage of tutors less strict than their parents. Not Katelin's favourite boys. Yardles appeared and escorted them inside.

Katelin groaned. She needed to get ready for the evening: Guest of Honour at the Eve of Coronation Banquet. Couldn't she have a quiet evening and an early night—it might be her last for a while? No, she had to get this over with—placid, emotionless face; pleasantries and politeness—and so to get through it. If this was her fate for the rest of her life, then the Divine and the Crown had better help her.

Katelin was dismissed from the banquet before 'Her Birthday' started at midnight. She climbed into bed.

So this was it: her last night of freedom. When she awoke, her life as she knew it would have ended. That was if she got to sleep at all. She tugged the blankets tighter.

Ever since she'd been old enough to understand, she'd known this night would come. The moment she'd dreaded all her life: the eve of her eighteenth birthday. She should have been excited, or eager, or something. But she was too wound up to know how she felt. And there was no escape from feeling crushed, small, alone.

Stop it. She disliked self-pity, didn't she? And no need to strangle the pillows. She lay on her back and stared into the silent, lonely darkness.

She'd been touched by what Ruis and Armus had said at the Temple. They'd be willing to assist her. Rashelin too. But what about Hedger and Sigzay, locked in the dungeons? They'd helped her so much in the last few days ... but she couldn't worry about them now.

And—as if by a miracle—she'd gained what she'd sought:

the second part of the Crown. Perhaps it had indeed been the Divine who had met her on the hilltop, and led her to Timajet, to Abbot Ruis and the Crown fragment.

Yes, she had a few friends, but needed to pin her hopes on the Divine and the Crown to see her through. That was one thing to look forward to: the radiance and power of the Divine, on her and through her, at noon tomorrow. Were these consolations enough to sustain her through the coming weeks and years? She wouldn't find an answer to that one tonight.

So … was something magical supposed to happen overnight, to change her from a child to an adult? It was a silly notion that one night's sleep could mean so much.

✴ XX ✴

CORONATION

The royal attendants woke Katelin early. They congratulated her on her eighteenth birthday and wished her the power of the Divine for the day.

Katelin accepted that she should spend some of the morning getting ready. But she had to resign herself to being closeted all morning, with them fussing over her bathing, hair, face, nails, garments, shoes, jewellery, headdress, bouquet and everything else that they thought was required. The greatest fuss was whether the gown and shoes would cover her injured leg and foot. Was this to be her daily endurance in order to appear like their Queen?

Patience, Katelin. This was a special day for them too. For today at least, she would present a courageous face to the world. Besides, she couldn't wait to relieve the Regent and Consort of their authority.

Whenever she could, Katelin went to a window to watch the preparations in Crown Square.

Coronation Day dawned overcast and it had rained during the night. The sun soon broke through, burned away the early clouds and dried up the ground. Servants finished off the dais that backed onto the Castle wall with carpets, furniture, hangings and arrangements of flowers.

The harbour was undoubtedly full, and the streets were beginning to throng with joyful Anestrans and the visitors who had come to be part of this historic day. All morning the people gathered in Crown Square, where musicians took turns to play and entertainers moved through the crowds.

Katelin guessed that much excited chatter centred on being first-hand witnesses of a miracle. Today, for the first time in fifteen years, the legendary glory of the Crown of Anestra would be displayed. Parents would tell children, and Anestrans would tell visitors, of the brightness and beauty of the radiance they would see.

Guards and soldiers marshalled the crowds and prepared to salute her as their new commander. Sunshine glinted off specially polished arms and armour, and a breeze fluttered the banners on tower and turret. The multitudes were dressed in their finest, and the air below would be filled with a conversational hubbub and the fragrance of lily and rose. Katelin half wished she were down there among them.

Half an hour before noon, Katelin was alone at an upper window, twisting her fingers. She wore a plain cream gown of rich silk, adorned only by exquisite embroidery at the neckline, cuff and hem.

She watched the clerics of the Divine process from Temple Approach along pathways across the Square. At the rear came the doddering and much loved Under Father, confounding the doubters by living long enough to Crown her as Queen. A jewelled staff supported his unsteady shuffle, and his silvery white robes and headdress shone in the sun. He grinned and blinked between his bushy white eyebrows and beard. Abbot Ruis and Brother Armus took the envied positions by the dais that Katelin had arranged for them.

By a quarter before noon, Katelin had descended to watch from a shadowed corner of the Castle gateway. The first to process through were the Regent's Family. Half-hearted cheers went up for Regent Ethabos as he waddled with assistance to his place. Consort Sirika paraded across the dais as if trying to look more regal than a Queen. A warmer welcome greeted Princess Rashelin and her brothers, the three young Princes swaggering to their chairs. The Regent and Consort shifted with discomfort in their seats, displaced from prime position for the first time in years. They eyed the vacant royal throne.

At ten minutes before noon, a fanfare sounded from the gatehouse battlements and the people hushed. Quevelle, the Royal Treasurer, in her dark blue uniform and white cotton gloves, marched through the Castle gate. On a blue silk cushion she carried the silver Crown of Anestra from the Treasury. The crowd burst into applause and their cheer rose clear across the city. For some minutes they drowned the music with their chant: "Crown of Anestra, Crown of Anestra." The Treasurer placed her cushion on a table beside the throne and withdrew.

Katelin had been allowed to choose her escort and had requested the Royal Steward, Yardles. As he held her hand in the gateway, she heard him say, "Princess, this is the proudest moment of my life."

But Yardles never referred to himself! And it was the first time that Katelin had seen emotion moisten his eyes.

She squeezed his hand and gave him a nervous smile. "Yardles, thank you for doing this for me. It's the proudest moment of mine too. Come on, and let's show our faces to the world."

The great bell of the Castle Tower struck noon and the crowd fell silent. As the last chime faded, the trumpeters on the battlements burst into a thrilling fanfare. At their final note, Her Royal Highness the Princess Katelin stepped through the Castle gate. The shout of the people rose to split the sky asunder. The roar must have echoed off walls, through windows and doors, along deserted streets, over hedges and fields, and for many miles beyond.

This couldn't all be for her. But it was. No one could mistake that Anestra welcomed their new Queen.

Me.

The nerves intensified. Katelin tried to swallow. She hoped that Yardles couldn't feel too much of the shaking in her arms.

The musicians began a stately introit, and the crowd took up a new chant: "Katelin, Katelin, Katelin!" Little could be heard above it.

They chanted for her. But they didn't know her. All this enthusiasm—it was for the position that she was to occupy. Could she meet any of the expectations that they had for their new Queen?

They began with a procession to each corner of the Square, Katelin winding back and forth through as many of the crowd as she could. This was one tradition that she liked: a young Queen, her clothes plain, came forth from among her people, for the Divine to lift to her new authority. Yardles represented Anestra's people, to escort and present her.

Katelin stopped. The Nightmare: all these hands reaching for her.

But this was different. Yes, the hands were eager, but restrained and respectful too. She could reach and touch them if she wished. And she did so. It was contrary to etiquette, but it sent the crowd into ecstasies of delight.

The crowds danced and sang as Katelin moved among them. Some blew kisses and strewed flowers on the cobbles as she passed. A few young people were perched in the trees of Princes' Park, and Katelin waved to these also.

In the tumult of the moment, her nerves were almost forgotten. Katelin wondered whether she might even enjoy herself today.

She remembered now the forced and phoney devotion to Count Bassilius in the streets of Lasseny. How precious to know that this welcome by her people was heartfelt and genuine.

At the Bay Road corner, two dark faces caught Katelin's eye and she stifled a squeal. Captain Farag and Jersull! From the *Oyster Shell*. They looked dumbfounded to see her—even more than she was to see them. She reached and squeezed their hands, as the crowds prevented an embrace. "Welcome to Anestra," she said with a laugh. "Sorry I missed the voyage south."

"We heard that Anestra Crowned a new Queen today," Jersull called back, "but now we discover it's our own Kat the archer!"

"That might not be today's only surprise," she said, with a smile. "Enjoy yourselves," and Yardles had to lead her away from them.

Katelin arrived at the dais and took her chair beside the throne, framed by the hangings on the wall. From her conspicuous position, Katelin smiled at Rashelin, and at Armus and Ruis. What about Hedger and Sigzay in the dungeons? If only the turn of events had been different.

The ceremony continued with readings and songs, and an address from the Under Father. Katelin could settle for a while in her chair. She tried to remember this, to take it all in, to fix it in her memory: her Coronation Day.

At last, the moment of enthronement and coronation arrived. Yardles led Katelin to the front of the dais, and the crowds cheered their consent that she should be Queen.

Huh. Most would be terrified to have so many watching them. But the Court had watched Katelin all her life.

Now that the time had come, she felt almost confident. It was Anestra's welcome that made the difference. But would the crowd still love her when they knew her, discovered what she was like? Maybe she could rule Anestra, if she could earn the people's loyalty, with a few good friends, and with the power of the Divine and two thirds of the Crown. If she could get the Regent and Consort out of the way, she might even cope with the annoyances of the Court. Learn a little lion taming. She'd be a different sort of Queen from any before, but she could only be herself. Maybe she could improve the fortunes of Anestra. And now she could reveal the glory, the power ... and her little secret.

The Keeper of the Robes came forward. The dark blue robes of the Queen of Anestra, trimmed and traced through with silver, covered over Katelin's plain cream gown. Katelin lifted her head, smiled and raised her arms in a gesture of embrace. The people murmured and sighed, and she caught glimpses even of awe in their faces at her majesty revealed before them. Those who'd prepared her all morning had done their work well.

The Royal Steward and Keeper of the Robes took Katelin's hands and led her to before the throne. The Under Father shuffled forward and gestured for Katelin to sit. As she did so, the trumpeters sounded the brief fanfare of enthronement. Then silence fell across the Square.

The Under Father's movements were deliberate, but it wasn't because of age. The dear old man was savouring the moment too. He turned to the side table where the single fragment of the Crown of Anestra with its silver circlet lay on its dark blue cushion. He picked it up in both hands, and paused with the sacred relic aloft to glint in the midday sunshine.

He positioned the Crown above Katelin's head. Everyone strained to see. Katelin braced herself, her knuckles turning white on the arms of the throne. And she wasn't the only one holding her breath.

This was it.

In a slow, loud voice, the Under Father cried: "O White Goddess, our Life Weaver, hear us! In the name of the Divine, and with her power upon you, I Crown you, Princess Katelin, Queen of the Western Coast and of the Old Kingdom of Anestra!" In a firm but gentle movement, he lowered the Crown and placed it onto Katelin's head.

Right on cue the royal trumpeters sounded and Katelin's trembling erupted.

Nothing happened.

There was no power and no glory. Not even lightness, warmth or tingling. The Crown felt heavy, cold and lifeless. Katelin's insides lurched. No! Why had nothing happened? She wanted to run and hide.

She needed the help of the Divine and the Crown … she'd been relying on them …

Wait. She had the duration of the fanfare in which to think. Never mind that the floor had fallen away from her world. She mustn't show the panic. She could do this. She needed to control herself enough to betray no inner turmoil. There were still things for her to say and do, as planned. But every eye was upon her.

As one, the people frowned and gasped. Queen Katelin sat in her robes on the throne and the Crown rested on her head. But it looked the same as the moment before. It did not sparkle, shine, glow or radiate. In an instant, the mood of the crowd turned. A ripple of confusion and disquiet swept across the people. Katelin could almost hear them: wasn't this now their Queen? Where was the Divine seal of approval? What had happened to their Crown, their Kingdom, their Queen? Many looked cheated of the promised miracle.

The trumpeters finished, and the crowd's mutter and shuffle of feet became unmistakeable. Officials and dignitaries turned to each other in consternation, whispering to ascertain the cause of the problem. Scattered clapping broke out in the crowd and a forlorn chant of: "Long live the Queen." But it soon died away.

Of course. The Crown was broken. That had to be it. She had to tell them. But would they believe her? And did she believe it? Or was something else wrong?

This had to be the moment. She had to summon her courage and do it. Never mind the shakes and that her stomach had sunk through the floor. She couldn't hide, weep or run away now. She was eighteen, Crowned Queen, and this thing should have been shining on her head. It was time to explain why it wasn't. It was time to act.

Katelin took a deep breath and stood up.

The restlessness of the scene froze. The mutter subsided to nothing as Queen Katelin stepped forward on the dais. Yes, she knew: she wasn't supposed to stand up, move or say anything now. She averted her gaze from her Uncle and Aunt. Her mind raced: how could she say this? She looked every bit the Queen—except for the persistent dullness of the Crown. So her face and voice mustn't betray her shaking. The Square was on tenterhooks for her every word.

"People of Anestra, my fellow citizens," she called. Katelin started as her voice carried to each corner of the Square. It was as though she spoke to each one in person. Was it the absolute silence, or an effect of the Crown?

"I thank you for your welcome today as I come of age on my eighteenth birthday. You have waited long years for this day, and I have waited too. I have been your Princess and now I become your Queen. I thank my Uncle and Aunt, the Regent and Consort, for their years of rule in my place, and I wish them a long and happy retirement."

The Regent snorted, the Consort scowled and the people shuffled with unease. How the mood of the crowd had changed. This was no time for a speech. They wanted an explanation—any that she could give them. She could only be open and honest.

"But my people, I sense that you are disappointed. You expected to see the glory of the Divine revealed in my Crown. Do not be concerned, good people of Anestra. Please allow me to explain some things to you."

Silence. This had better be good.

"Two days ago I returned to Anestra with some new friends and a gift for you." Across Crown Square no one stirred, afraid of missing something. "First of all, my new friends. I introduce to you Abbot Ruis of Timajet, and Brother Armus, clerics of the Divine." She indicated for them to stand where they were, and they did so. "These two have been helpful to me, and have achieved something wonderful for Anestra. Please welcome and thank them."

The crowd clapped, but it was muted, and they still looked mystified. The Regent, Consort and dignitaries did not clap; their faces were thunder.

Katelin resolved to ignore them. "I ask Abbot Ruis to come forward," she continued. Ruis stepped onto the dais in his plain grey robes and stood beside her.

Every eye was fixed on her. She mustn't mess this up. Katelin lifted the Crown from her head and held it in front of her. The intake of breath on all sides was audible. Their concern had become alarm. What was she doing? And what was she about to do? Katelin forced calmness. This was her surprise.

"Fifteen years ago this sacred relic, our Crown of Anestra, was broken and two parts of it lost. One third of our Crown was recovered, as you can all see." She raised and rotated the Crown for all to inspect and be sure. "The reason it hasn't radiated Divine glory today is because our Crown is broken.

In the long history of the Old Kingdom, this has never happened before, and not even the clerics knew for sure that it would still shine."

She cast Abbot Ruis an anxious glance and he gave her a reassuring smile. But the crowd shuffled their feet and remained silent.

She pressed on. "We have all longed for our Crown to be restored. So today, in honour of my coronation, I present to you, my people of Anestra, this gift."

Katelin turned and gave Abbot Ruis a nervous nod. He drew from his pocket the battered metal box, removed the lid and offered her the box. Holding the Crown in one hand, Katelin picked up the Crown fragment with the other. Ruis bowed, stepped back and sat down. So that everyone could see, Katelin lifted her hands.

"Kept secret and safe these last fifteen years in the monastery at Timajet, I give to you, my people, the second part of the ancient Crown of Anestra!"

A murmur of approval and surprise swept the crowd. A glance at the dignitaries showed that even they were impressed. As they applauded, many squinted at the silverwork in her hand, but apart from a glint of reflected sunlight, it wasn't shining either.

Katelin examined the Crown and the fragment. It was obvious how they fitted together, which was a huge relief. But would anything happen now? And what was that? Her fingers were tingling at last. Did the fragments long to be reunited?

She raised her hands, held the parts together and cried, "Behold! By the power of the Divine, two thirds of our Crown is restored!"

A burst of white light sprang from the Crown as the fragments fused together. The crowd gasped in wonder and delight, and even the guests and officials approved. Applause and cheering swept the Square.

Jumping stars! That nearly made her drop it. But what a relief. Divine glory had been revealed at last.

Then the flash and excitement faded.

Katelin held a more complete Crown, but it remained dull in her hands. What else could she say or do now? She replaced the Crown on her head. They'd better continue with the homage and the feast.

A trumpet blast sounded from the North Gate of the city. The notes came clear and urgent across the crowded Square. It was no fanfare or salute. It sounded more like … an alarm.

Katelin was struck rigid. No, not now. Not right this minute. She stared, vacant and afraid, as her face drained of blood. The signal finished, and the agitation of the crowd and officials became obvious.

Why couldn't she think or move? And her mouth had become dry and cold. She felt sick. Because she knew that signal.

Invasion.

And of all times for it to sound, in the middle of this.

"That will be the Lassenite army." Consort Sirika had risen from her chair and sidled across to her. "A report came yesterday that they were forced marching," she was saying, "but we didn't expect—"

"What?" Katelin rounded on her. "And you didn't tell me? You knew they might come today, but didn't warn me?"

Sirika sniffed in defiance. "Yes, of course, we knew they might arrive today. We're not stupid. But we had to proceed with the coronation and now we can negotiate—"

"Shut up!" Katelin snapped. And it felt good. "You don't rule here now. *I* do. So *I'll* decide what we'll do."

The Queen had told her. And for the first time ever, Aunt

Sirika backed down before her. In public at least, she had to be seen to obey her Queen.

That was it. Katelin had finished with mistreatment from those two. And from the Lassenites. Sirika had fired her for what they must do.

Queen Katelin stepped forward to face her people. She raised her arms and cried over the growing hubbub: "All Anestra, hear me!"

Every eye turned back to her. Every ear listened.

"To battle! Soldiers to your posts! Prepare to defend the city! Those who can't fight can take refuge in the Castle. We fight for our homes and families, for our freedom! For the Divine, for the Crown, for Anestra—for your Queen!"

DUKE

A bank of cloud swallowed the sun and a shadowed chill fell across Anestra. The Keeper retrieved Katelin's robes, while soldiers and guards made for their posts and the crowds dispersed from the Square.

Katelin turned to the Regent's Family. It was time to make them do something useful. "Uncle, Aunt, escort our distinguished guests back into the Castle and look after them in the Hall." She paused long enough to register their dropped jaws and outrage at being ordered about.

"Rashelin," she went on, "open the Castle grounds to any elderly, women and children who may wish to seek refuge there."

Her cousin nodded, and then took Katelin's arm. "I'll get everyone to pray," she said. Their eyes met, before Rashelin turned away.

The Family started to direct the dignitaries, courtiers, nobles and officials towards the Castle gate. Yes, that was the safest place for visitors and the vulnerable as war came to Anestra.

Katelin's whirling mind seemed cocooned amid the bustle, but she was trembling inside. She was proud of them all: calm, resolute, responding to her call.

The clerics were leaving for the Temple. Ruis, Armus, Temple guards and initiates escorted the lagging Under Father.

What about Farag and Jersull? They'd make for the *Oyster Shell* and find refuge on the water.

Katelin stirred herself to move from the dais and to join those streaming into the Castle. Once inside, she detached herself from the throngs and stepped onto the grass of the grounds. Events had piled on top of her and she needed to think.

She leant back against a tree. She was Queen. She was eighteen, and Crowned. But the Crown had failed to shine on her head. That was because it was broken. Or was it? There had been that tingle and flash as the fragments were reunited. Was the Divine trying to tell her something?

There was so much more at stake now than her own fate. It was the future of the Kingdom. It had never been a game, had it?

General Bolas approached her, stroking his walrus moustache. He bowed low.

"General," Katelin said. "Where do you want me? My bow is at your disposal."

The old General smiled. "No, no, my Queen. I think you misunderstand. It is we who are at your disposal. Command us."

Katelin gulped. She hadn't caught up with jumping from the bottom to the top of command. But she needed to leave the details with those who knew what they were doing. "Um … thank you, General. Please defend the city in the best way that you know how."

General Bolas nodded. "Thank you, Your Majesty. The Lassenites are approaching the North Gate, but they're not here yet. I suggest we face them there."

Katelin nodded, and Bolas hurried from the Castle.

She lifted the Crown of Anestra from her head and looked at it. Why couldn't it have shone? She'd been relying on Divine glory, wisdom and power to help her to rule. And to defeat her enemies. But here it was, this sacred relic, dull and lifeless in her hands. What use was it now? If it didn't work for her …

Katelin stood up straight, her whole body trembling. Now that she had it in her hands, she had the means to test his claim …

Did she dare? Could she spare the time for this?

Through the Castle's clamour, Katelin headed for the dungeons. If two thirds of the Crown still didn't shine for her, would the glory come for Hedger?

As she descended the steps, walls of stone muffled the din outside. She reached the passage where gates of iron glinted in the flicker of torches.

In the first cell on the left, Sigzay leapt to her feet and yanked on the bars. "You dare imprison us," she yelled. "After all we do for you?"

"Not now, Sigzay," Katelin snapped. "I don't have time to explain."

The barbarian's glare was fire and ice, with a fury to cut through both iron and stone.

Katelin ordered the guards to unlock the next gate, and they waited in the passage as she went in to Hedger.

He rose to his feet. "What's happening, Kat? I heard the trumpet."

She had to tell him everything. "The Lassenites have arrived—in the middle of Coronation Day." Her words came out between shuddering breaths.

Hedger nodded, his face grave. "I see you carry the Crown. And two parts of it."

Katelin had to swallow before saying, "Abbot Ruis had the second part hidden at Timajet and Bassilius made off with a fake. But it didn't shine when I was Crowned." She wanted to sound clear and commanding, but knew she wasn't managing it. Hedger said nothing, but watched her. "You claim to be Prince Edgaran, my elder brother."

"What?" Sigzay exclaimed from the next cell. "What you talk about?"

Sigzay, shut up! She needed to talk to Hedger. Either he'd told her nothing of their balcony conversation, or else she was expert at pretending. Katelin raised the Crown in front of her.

"Now we can test your claim. Would you touch this?" She held the Crown towards him. "Please?"

His eyes were fixed on it, then rose and met hers. Go on, Hedger, please. She didn't know if she believed him, but was desperate for his help. "I dare you to prove you're not an imposter," she whispered. "This is no trap. If nothing happens at your touch, then we'll sort this out once the battle is over. But if it's true ..."

Hedger stepped forward. He held Katelin's eyes as he reached for the Crown. Her arm trembled as his fingers met the sacred relic that she held.

The light in the cell changed. The guards in the passage gasped. Her eyes darted downwards to his hand—to a steady glow ... of gentle white.

Hedger's fingers shone as though held in front of the brightest of lamps. He curled his hand around the silverwork and the light grew until the cell was filled with radiance.

Katelin's arms and face tingled with warmth, and her heart leapt with delight. Her head swam and she closed her eyes as the brightness bathed her. Through her eyelids, the white light danced into more colours than she'd ever imagined. The world paused, time suspended, awed, silent, beautiful ...

... until at last Hedger uncurled his hand and released the precious silverwork. The glory faded, and the world of time resumed, drab and dim.

It was some moments before Katelin returned to herself. Jumping stars! She opened her eyes, which let the tears fall down her cheeks. "Edgaran ..." she whispered.

"What—what was that?" Sigzay cried from the next cell.

Katelin threw herself into Edgaran's arms. She buried her face and sobbed on his shoulder. "I'm sorry, I'm sorry."

He cradled her head. "It's all right, it's all right," he murmured, and kissed her hair. "I'm relieved there was a way to show you."

"Show what?" demanded Sigzay. "What goes on? Someone explain to me!"

They let go of each other and Katelin wiped her face. She stepped into the passage. "Yesterday Hedger told me that he is Prince Edgaran of Anestra; that he survived the Crown War, but only as a slave in Lasseny. I thought him an imposter, an agent of the Duke, sent to assassinate me. The proof was for him to touch the Crown."

Sigzay glared at Edgaran, and she looked about to explode.

He said, "It's true, Sigzay, and I longed for Kat to believe me."

"Believe you?" Sigzay spat the words. "You lie to me all the years?"

"I didn't lie," said Edgaran, "but I didn't tell you the whole truth. It was safer that no one knew who I was."

"But why?" asked Katelin. "Why keep your identity secret? Why not return to Anestra and become King?"

Edgaran shook his head. "I like my freedom too much. In one thing we're alike, Kat: I wasn't ready to rule, either. And I'm still not." His smile was grim, resigned. "As I said yesterday, Kingdoms should be earned, not given. I needed to become a man, before being a King as well."

"But why now?" Katelin pressed him. "After all this time, why reveal yourself to me yesterday?"

Edgaran drew a deep breath. "For you, Kat. You're not the two-year-old little sister I left behind. You're a young woman, living in dread on the threshold of your destiny. I'd hoped you'd enjoy being Queen, and I could stay unknown and free. But it's tearing you apart—and I'm your way out. I had to act, for your sake, and for the good of Anestra."

Katelin's thoughts were catching up. "So all that's happened today … is a message. The glory of the Crown—or lack of it—indicates that it's not me, but you, who should rule Anestra. It wasn't that it's broken, but that it's showing the right person to rule."

She began to understand. Her destiny was changing. Could she dare to believe that she might be free?

"That's right," said Edgaran, "but now we have work to do. Kat, you are Queen, I am Prince, and it seems that the power of the Crown works through me as Anestra's true ruler. This is not the day to worry about titles, but to stand together to defend our people. Kat, it is time to earn our Kingdom."

"Hedger—Edgaran—my brother," Katelin declared. "I give you the Crown as my rightful King." She'd never been more relieved at any previous words. She reached and placed the Crown on his head. It sparkled. The Crown had been made for him. It covered the scar on his forehead, and his face looked whole and handsome again.

Katelin turned at last to Sigzay. The barbarian's explosion smouldered, for the moment held in check. "We've talked long enough and we need to go. Sigzay, will you help us?"

Sigzay bit her lip. She looked to have a thousand accusations.

Edgaran touched her arm. "My brave wolf," he said.

Sigzay glared at him, then nodded. The guards unlocked her cell.

Katelin led them out of her dungeons. Her tread felt lighter as she climbed the steps. She went to war, but the responsibility for the Kingdom was shared.

As they emerged into the Castle courtyard, Katelin smiled

at how the hubbub ceased. She didn't blame them. Soldiers, dignitaries, servants and guards all stared and pointed at the glittering Crown on Prince Edgaran's head.

Katelin raised her voice. "My people, let me explain. This is my brother, Prince Edgaran, long thought dead and lost. The Crown's glory confirms that he will rule. But today we defend our city. So shout abroad this message: Prince Edgaran has returned and stands beside our Queen! Divine glory shines from the Crown, and we have seen it! Anestra has Queen and Prince, Crown and Glory—our city will not fall!"

The soldiers roared and clashed their arms. Runners set off to streets and squares, to walls and gates, to spread the wildfire throughout the city.

Katelin turned to Edgaran. "We need to fetch our weapons."

"And we should go together," he said.

"Agreed. General Bolas said to meet him at the North Gate. I'll join the Archers on the city wall."

Edgaran nodded. "I'll go wherever we need a sword."

Edgaran and Sigzay hurried to the South Tower and Katelin entered the Keep. They met again in the courtyard, hurried across Crown Square and down Queensway. People stared as the rumour was confirmed: their Queen had a warrior Prince at her side, his Crown radiant with Divine glory. Bewilderment turned to cheers and hope.

As they passed, even some of the elderly and older children were helping to construct barricades, and seeking such armour and weapons as they could find.

Katelin, Edgaran and Sigzay came to the North Gate, and it was shut. Sergeant Rossick stood among the troops and Katelin couldn't resist a smile at him. He bowed in return.

They climbed to the gatehouse parapet, where General

Bolas stood among the royal longbow men and women. The afternoon light was fading fast as heavy banks of cloud streamed in from the west. Katelin looked to the north … and gasped.

The whole countryside was moving. It was an angry sea— and the tide was coming in. Fires burned, dust and smoke rose, drums and war-chants carried on the breeze.

Everywhere troops marched towards her. The Duke of Lasseny's organised battalions came under black banners with crimson stars. Others were mere rabbles, mobs of thugs and ruffians. Sigzay cursed as she pointed out northern barbarians among the enemy ranks. There were green and gold flags of the Autarch of Unta, and other banners Katelin didn't know.

Breath succeeded breath, thin, laboured, choking.

The Lassenites had force-marched into sight while they were in Coronation Day festival in the Square. The Duke's display of power was timed for the Kingdom passing to her, an inexperienced girl now made Queen. His plans to crush her might yet prove effective.

General Bolas was pointing out to Katelin the approaching hordes: cavalry, crossbowmen, archers, horse-drawn catapults, siege towers, battering rams, ladders.

"There's no way we could have prepared against this assault," he said to her. "Even with the warning of two or three days, our full strength was already mustered. We're outnumbered many times to one. This is no idle skirmish or medium-strength show of force. All Lasseny is emptied. The Duke intends to conquer our city once and for all; to pillage our treasures and enslave us."

"Not during my reign, General," Katelin stated. "Not if we can prevent it."

But the trembling in Katelin's bones couldn't be quelled.

Around the Lassenite army a faint crimson haze rolled along the ground, enveloping them in unearthly light under darkened skies.

"Ilbassi," muttered Katelin. "The mages are coming—perhaps the Archmage himself. They've invoked their god and summoned a storm."

Edgaran laid a hand on her arm. "Kat, I don't know how much you ask for the Divine's aid, but we both need to do so today. If we're willing, the Divine and the Crown will take and use all of us: heart, body and spirit. Do you accept that we could die today for the sake of Anestra?"

And that was it.

Katelin swallowed hard. In this one question, her brother had stated the dilemma that had dominated her life. If she were willing to give her life in battle for Anestra, then why not in a lifetime of service as Queen?

But now that she'd been asked, there was no hesitation.

Katelin fixed her eyes on his, and nodded. "Yes, we must do all that we can. I am willing." She heaved her deepest breath and turned to face the coming storm.

A Captain came to them from the cavalry, the men and women of the Knights of Anestra. With her consent, General Bolas ordered them to hold position near her, behind the gate. When messengers came from other Captains, they bade each defend the city to the best of their ability and as each saw fit. While they might hope in walls and gates, and in the Divine Crown, it was fifteen years since the defenders had been tested.

Katelin prayed that her people would find strength in their Queen and Prince atop the gatehouse tower, and in the glory of their Crown.

Now she called together her longbow Captains. "My shortbow is no match for your longbows, but I ask to join you as a fellow archer. And I'm sorry I'm an inexperienced general."

A Captain spoke up. "Queen Katelin, you have our loyalty and our love, and we're honoured to serve you. Our bows are at your disposal: command us."

Katelin tried to draw on their faith in her. "Our foes are numerous and will seek to overwhelm. Every arrow must count. So aim for the leaders; find their Captains and take them first. Target those who bring siege towers and ladders. To the wall! The Divine speed each arrow to its mark!"

The Captains shouted, took their positions and bolstered the courage of their Archers with a chant: "For Katelin and the Crown, for Anestra and the Queen."

The leading ranks of the Lassenite army stopped.

A single horseman rode forward, his right arm raised in token of parley. A dozen mounted bodyguards followed him and halted in front of the gatehouse.

Katelin held up her right arm in answer. No arrow flew and a nervous silence fell. Katelin, Edgaran and General Bolas descended from the gatehouse and mounted horses from among the Knights. The guards opened the gate, and a troop of Knights escorted them through to the parley.

As they advanced, the crimson haze retreated before them, shredded by the shimmering white of Edgaran's Crown.

The single horseman wore full armour with a crimson star on a black breastplate. A crown sat among untidy grey hairs above a stern, wrinkled face.

Katelin's stomach clenched further. A chill flowed before this old man and she felt her skin crawl. She flinched to meet his unblinking black eyes, but an indignant fire burned deep inside her. Face to face with her adversary at last: Duke Bassikrin of Lasseny himself had come.

Her eyes flickered up to the old man's crown. It was an

assembly of several different pieces. Did it include now that fake piece from Timajet? And even the last true fragment of their Crown of Anestra? She couldn't tell from here.

Katelin's gaze strayed to someone else among the mounted bodyguards: Archmage Gaitox of Ilbassi. He recognised her then, from his curious stare.

She straightened her shoulders and faced the Duke. His eyes had travelled from Katelin, to Edgaran, to the Crown, and back. So he hadn't expected this, had he?

"Ah, the Princess Katelin," Duke Bassikrin said, in a casual tone. "Or is it Queen now? Well, well, see how the little girl has grown. I've come to wish you a happy eighteenth birthday." He tried to force a smile, but it came out as a grotesque leer.

Katelin cleared her throat. "Queen, if you please. Your birthday wishes are very kind." But she doubted he could have made them more patronising. "You—you've gone to considerable trouble to deliver them." She indicated the army behind him … and tried to swallow her stutter.

"Yes, I wanted to do it in person," he said. "You see, I have come for your allegiance."

"To *swear* allegiance to Queen Katelin, you mean," cut in Edgaran.

Duke Bassikrin turned to him. "Who is this?"

"This is Prince Edgaran of Anestra," Katelin replied.

The Duke's eyes widened, his mouth opened and closed. His surprise was there, before he managed to mask it. "Prince Edgaran?" he snorted. "These fools have upstarts and imposters leading them. It matters not. Will you surrender and give me your allegiance?"

"The surrender has terms to it, I presume," said Katelin. "What are they?" There was no harm in discovering the Duke's ambitions.

Duke Bassikrin's face slipped into a greedy smile. Did he

think even for a moment that she might accept? "You will accept me as overlord of Anestra. You will convert to the worship of Ilbassi. And to seal the agreement, you will marry Bassilius, my son."

Now she would make his grin falter. "Unacceptable," Katelin declared. "We have the Crown of Anestra, sacred relic of the Divine. Our Goddess will never let this city fall."

"Ah yes, the Divine," Bassikrin mocked. "The Great Nanny Matron of us all." His bodyguards sniggered. "You insult my intelligence with feeble superstition and old wives' tales," he retorted. "This city falls to me today and you know it."

"I see you wear a crown, Duke," Katelin answered, "but it gives no radiance. You steal part of our Crown, but gain neither glory nor power."

"Radiance, glory and power," Bassikrin sneered. "Is that what you call the conjurer's light tricks on the imposter's head? So you persist as a foolish little girl. You refuse to surrender, and spurn my generous offer of the hand of my son?"

Katelin was phrasing a reply when her brother answered.

"Queen Katelin is a brave and noble servant of the people of Anestra," Edgaran said. "And she is a far greater person than you will ever be, Duke Bassikrin."

The Duke scowled. "We shall see. I will take great pleasure in sacking your city. This parley is over." He turned and spurred his horse back towards his ranks, the bodyguards and Archmage hurrying after him. Katelin, Edgaran, Bolas and the Knights retreated through the gatehouse, and the gate was shut and barred.

A volley of arrows and catapult barrage filled the darkening sky.

"Return fire!" Katelin shouted, as she dismounted behind the gatehouse. The air became thick with missiles.

Edgaran and Bolas stayed with the Knights, while Katelin raced to join her Archers. By the time she reached them, the Lassenites had surged forward, covered by their own archers and crossbowmen. Siege towers approached the walls, battering rams the gatehouse, and ladders were being raised.

Anestra would be overwhelmed hand to hand, unless they could use the advantages of height, battlement, superior weapons and training. But Katelin still couldn't think how to prevent this assault proving decisive.

The siege towers reached the walls and the best of the Lassenite army spewed forth. They moved to engage the Archers, so that those below could attack the gate without arrows from above. Anestran soldiers and guards tried to defend the Royal Archers on the walls, but the combat was desperate and failing. The climbing Lassenites were too many and too fast.

Katelin saw no alternative. She called her Archers back, and they scrambled down to join the Knights behind the gatehouse.

The battle raged on the walls. Katelin jumped as a sudden crash echoed across the city. The Duke's battering rams had begun to slam into the gate. Sigzay stood alongside Katelin's Royal Archers, near Edgaran and the Knights, but there were too few others as they waited for the gate to breach. The soldiers held the walls, but couldn't defend both walls and gatehouse.

"Those are barbarian arms that ram gate," Sigzay muttered.

The reinforced timbers shuddered and splintered—the gate was about to break. Katelin raised her shortbow and gave the call: "To me, to me! Defend the gate! Fall back from the walls and hold the gatehouse!"

Anestrans retreated from the walls, and in their place

Lassenites swarmed up ladders and out of siege towers unchecked. The crimson haze came with them.

And the gate broke.

Timbers crashed, dust billowed, and a vast horde of Lassenite soldiery crushed to surge through the gate. "Fire!" Katelin shouted, and a hail of arrows cut down the first ranks of incomers. Then Prince Edgaran and the Knights of Anestra charged.

The cavalry assault swept the attackers back to the ruined gate. But the momentum was lost and the advance stalled. Katelin directed her Archers to fire at the Lassenites descending from the walls, but they had to fall back to avoid being engaged. General Bolas formed the soldiers into a shield in front of them, but they were too few. Edgaran called the cavalry to re-form, but all around them Anestrans were falling.

Katelin's eye caught the glimmer of the Crown in the gloom. Now was the time they needed Divine help through the relic, but how could they call on her? How had the Divine helped her against the Archmage at the Shrine of Ilbassi?

Divine, please help us?

As if in answer to her thought, Edgaran cried, "Divine, send your power through your Crown!"

The Crown blazed. White light flooded the gatehouse, blinding the invaders. The crimson haze was blasted apart. Katelin's shout was echoed by many Anestran voices: "For the Divine, the Crown, the Prince and the Queen!" They charged forward and held the gate.

A cry on their left rose above the tumult. "The Temple, the Temple! They're attacking the Temple! The Temple burns!"

Edgaran stood in his stirrups, raised his sword and called, "Knights of Anestra, with me! Knights with me to the Temple!" At the head of the cavalry, Edgaran sped off along North Side.

He was gone. The defence of the city now fell to Katelin and Bolas alone. As the Crown's light departed, the crimson tide rolled in. The battle lines looked bleaker, but what else could they do? Lassenites fell and others took their places; Anestrans fell and there were none to replace them.

They were going to lose the gate. Katelin tried to focus on each shot and not give in to despair. More than anything now she longed to save Anestra, to hold back the invading Lassenites. But how? What could she do? She'd offer her life to save them, if only there were some way to do that. She'd never felt so helpless.

Sigzay sprinted towards her, re-loading her crossbow. "Kat," she called, "we find safer place than this. Order Archers back."

"We have to hold the gate," Katelin shouted back. "We can't abandon the guard."

But Sigzay had already gone, disappearing up Queensway. Katelin turned back to the gate to see that Sergeant Rossick stood alone in the breach. Under the gatehouse arch, he swung his sword like a madman. Katelin couldn't look away, until a Lassenite spear impaled him, and Rossick fell to the oncoming crush.

Katelin shook herself from horror into action. She turned to General Bolas. "Fall back, fall back!" she cried. The General nodded and repeated her cry. Archers, soldiers and guards rallied to their position, and they led the rearguard action towards Crown Square.

Behind them, the North Gate was taken and Lassenites poured into the city.

✳ XXII ✳

SACRIFICE

Heavy clouds rolled in from the west, overshadowing the Temple, as Brother Armus, Abbot Ruis and the Under Father passed through Cleric Gate and climbed Temple Hill. They entered through the low wall that surrounded the complex where guards and initiates had begun to gather.

Armus surveyed the plain. Already it was alight where the Lassenite army marched on the city's North Gate. But a large rabble had broken off from the main horde and was heading towards them.

Armus was grateful that his years in Lasseny had taught him self-defence, for many of the clerics had vowed never to use violence. So while the Captain of the Temple guards ordered his troops to line the wall, Armus organised the initiates to support them. The guards had arms and armour, but the initiates had only staves and clubs. The young clerics had fire in their eyes, though, the same outrage that stirred in Armus's heart that their sacred place might be attacked.

Armus went for his mace. By the time he returned to the entrance, a troop of horsemen approached, keeping a ragged pace in front of a mass of hooligans, ruffians and thugs. The banner under which the cavalry rode was familiar enough to Armus.

"Count Bassilius," he muttered to Ruis and the Under Father. "So while the better troops storm Anestra's North Gate, the Duke dispatches his son against us with the dregs of

257

Lasseny's backstreets. We're no match for them in weaponry or numbers."

The Count of Lasseny looked wary as he rode up among his mounted bodyguards, his right hand raised for parley.

Armus stepped forward, smacking his palm with the shaft of his mace, and spoke first. "Hello again, Bassilius. Remember me?"

The Count's face twitched. He ignored Armus and addressed the Under Father. "You will surrender this building or you will all be killed."

The Under Father bristled, and the strength of his voice belied his great age. "This is no parley," he said. "That is an ultimatum."

"You are correct," said Bassilius. "You can save your lives and become our slaves, or sentence everyone here to brutal and senseless deaths. In either case, we'll ransack this building and use it for the worship of Ilbassi."

"Never!" cried the Under Father. But it was the last word he spoke. A throwing axe thudded into his head. A ruffian seemed to have lost patience that the parley had lasted this long. Ruis caught the old man's body and dragged it into the Temple.

As though the axe were a signal, the whole Lassenite rabble roared and erupted forwards. They crashed into the defenders like a breaker to the shore, and were checked at the wall. But the next wave, with the power of a storm surge, overwhelmed the breakwater and gushed through to the sacred place behind.

Armus fell back with the Temple guards. He stood by a pillar and swung his mace like an incense burner in a bruising arc in front of him. The better arms and armour of the guards could not compensate for being so far outnumbered. Many initiates were cut down, but only after taking a Lassenite with them. Thugs threw torches into the building, kindling fabric, hangings and furniture. Abbot Ruis left the Under Father's body, snatched a bronze basin and scooped up pool water to extinguish fires.

As Jersull followed Captain Farag to the harbour, he began to see smoke and flame upon the water. The logjam of anchored ships formed undulating platforms of wood, like giant floating stepping stones to the Ocean. But blockading them all was a fleet of slaver ships, strung out across the Bay.

Jersull and Farag hurried along the harbour wall to their rowing boat. While other sailors jumped and swung from deck to deck, they heaved their oars against the strengthening wind to the *Oyster Shell.* Slavers were also crossing decks and setting fires, and the slaughter had spread to the harbour wall and quayside.

Thunder rolled across the Bay, and lightning flashed down as the storm swept in.

The *Oyster Shell* was adrift. "They came to us first," Jersull muttered to Farag, "and have raised anchor to steal her, cargo and all."

They raced up a rope ladder to the deck, sword and scimitar in hand. Bodies were strewn about, both slaver and crew. "They think they've won this battle and moved on," said Jersull.

A shout from the poop deck whirled them around. Then two slavers emerged from the forecastle, cutlasses drawn. Farag ran astern, yelling, "You commandeer my ship!" The slaver leapt on top of him, but the Captain's upraised sword impaled him and they fell to the deck.

Jersull parried the lunges of the slavers and kicked one in the chest. The man staggered backwards and toppled over the side. The other fell to a sweeping scimitar slash. With neither sight nor sound of other slavers on board, Jersull ran to drop anchor.

Prince Edgaran and the Knights of Anestra thundered through Cleric Gate. In the fading light he willed the Crown to brightness, and it shone across the eastern slopes of Temple Hill. Bands of thugs and ill-disciplined hordes swarmed around the Temple, and the building was alight.

Edgaran led a charge of the Knights against the ragged groups on the hillside. The Knights' onslaught had been checked at the North Gate, but here they could gallop against scattered, ill-armoured enemies. They drove wide swathes through the Lassenites, breaking the siege of the clerics and guards in the building. Many thugs turned and fled north-eastwards at the swift onset of the cavalry.

Edgaran reached the Temple entrance, where Brother Armus leaned against a pillar, gasping for breath. He raised his sword, and the cleric's mace rose in answering salute. Armus wiped his brow on his sleeve. Then he disappeared into the building to tackle stray invaders and extinguish fires.

A Captain of the Knights rode up. "Prince Edgaran," he said, "Count Bassilius is here with his bodyguards. They're re-grouping, and rallying their rabble for a fresh attack. And there are reports of fighting in the Bay."

Edgaran's breathing was heavy. "The Duke attacks us on all sides, but he will not succeed today. He engages our army at the North Gate and Temple, and must have told his allies of easy pickings among ships in the Bay. Captain, I'll see to the harbour. The Knights must defend the Temple against Bassilius. Then, if you can, ride outside the city wall against the Lassenites at the North Gate."

Edgaran dismounted and left the Captain and the Knights. He ran alone down Temple Hill to a harbour full of cries and smoke, and battles on the ships and quayside. To encourage the defenders he gave a blast of glory from the Crown. The flash caught the attention of all in the Bay … but it winded him. Using the light and power of the Crown was draining his strength.

With a shout and his long sword raised, Edgaran leaped onto the harbour wall. He drove against the slavers and engaged them hand to hand among the sailors and guards on the waterside. His anger made the light of the Crown blaze forth, and the defenders took up a new shout: "For Anestra, for the Crown!" None could stand against the swing of Edgaran's sword and the fury of his wrath.

Now he understood: his energy flowed into the Crown and joined with that of the Divine. It made him invulnerable … but how long could his strength last? And the battle had robbed him of self-control.

Slavers jumped into the water to evade him and swam back to the ships, where a ferocious melee surged across the decks for the dominance of the Bay.

Sigzay crawled across a roof that overlooked Queensway. In the street below, a few knots of defenders from the Anestran army made last stands in doorways, but Queen Katelin, the Archers and guards had fallen back to Crown Square. A stream of Lassenites ran up from the North Gate, pillaging and setting fires as they went.

Sigzay ignored the battles below and watched the North Gate. Mounted bodyguards waited this side of the gatehouse as Duke Bassikrin himself rode through. Archmage Gaitox entered behind him, and they congratulated each other on the capture of the city.

Sigzay waited. Her crossbow had only two remaining bolts.

The entourage set off up Queensway and the first of the bodyguards passed. Sigzay's patience was cold and steady as the Duke rode beneath her hidden vantage point. With the right moment for ambush selected, Sigzay fired.

The bolt thudded into the back of the Duke's neck where the armour was weakest. He slumped forward on his horse, which walked on with its stricken load. The bodyguards clustered to shield him, but not before Sigzay reloaded and emptied her last bolt into the Duke's back.

The bodyguards scanned the skyline to mark her position, but Sigzay had already fled. She leaped from roof to roof until thwarted by a gap too wide to jump. She slid and fell to a heap on the ground. Lassenites approached and she sprinted away, until she came to a shadowed doorway into which she disappeared.

Queen Katelin and the Royal Archers stood besieged on the coronation dais. The scattered remnants of the Anestran army formed a final stand around her, led by General Bolas, who was protecting the Castle gates. But it was a decreasing semi-circle of soldiers and guards against the constantly replenished Lassenites. Katelin and her Archers tried in vain to turn the tide, as they fired down their remaining arrows into the enemy phalanxes.

Then into Crown Square rode Archmage Gaitox. Katelin wondered where Duke Bassikrin was. No doubt he skulked outside the walls, she thought, leading from the rear. So the Archmage commanded here, and he looked to be glorying in the slaughter of each worshipper of the Divine.

Katelin felt hot and sick. Gaitox's presence brought tendrils of the crimson haze that now floated across the Square. It was as though they emanated from the Archmage himself; that he breathed out visible, noxious fumes. The tendrils seemed to seek Katelin, grope for her, to entangle, throttle and kill. And against them she could think of no defence.

She tore her gaze away, to the Archers around her. Despite the desperate courage with which they fought for Queen and Castle, the last stand of Anestra couldn't persist. Without the presence of the Crown, could she still summon Divine help? Ilbassi's Archmage had invoked his power in a ghoulish crimson light, but Katelin didn't know how to call on her Goddess, now that they needed her.

Without understanding how she knew, Katelin sensed that Rashelin was praying for her. In fact, all the Anestrans who cowered within the Castle walls would be imploring the Divine for aid. Katelin tried to draw on her people's faith and hope.

"Divine, please help us."

And then louder, stronger: "Divine, if I met you on that hilltop, then you said for me to trust you. We need your help now!"

A white glow enveloped her. It was dim and tentative, but spread along her line of Archers, keeping the crimson tendrils at bay. But if the White Goddess were to fulfil her promise to save her city and people, then there had to be more than this.

The first heavy drops of rain began. They grew into soaking torrents as the full weight of the storm lashed Anestra city. As if that were his cue, the Archmage ordered forward every last soldier, barbarian and thug at his disposal into a final press against them.

In the torrential gloom, a white spark to her left turned Katelin's head. Hedger and the Crown! Her brother was back. But wait … he hadn't come down Temple Approach, but up Bay Road from the harbour.

She saw Edgaran bend over in the corner of the Square,

hands on knees, struggling for breath. Anestra was in desperate plight. They needed him … but he was exhausted.

What had he said to her? If they were willing, to win this battle, the Divine and the Crown would take all of them: every last breath of their spirit and strength. Was that what was happening?

The brightness of the Crown reflected off the wet cobbles and lit up the Square. The crimson tendrils blew away and the Lassenite soldiers faltered.

Archmage Gaitox roared with rage. On the verge of his victory, the sight of Divine glory sent him insane: he leapt about, cackling, flinging his limbs in wild frustration.

He threw his arms up to the darkened skies, and his voice boomed with a terrible incantation. What was this? Did he have some ultimate power to crush the enemies of his god?

"Ilbassi!" Gaitox screamed. "God of truth and justice, see this Anestran upstart's blasphemy. Come and claim this city. Take these wretches, these followers of the Divine, and make them your own. You promised to come when your Archmage calls. Hear me now! Come, Ilbassi, come!"

He'd gone mad. He couldn't summon his god.

But above the Archmage's outstretched arms, the outlines of a great, grey door appeared in the heavens. It cracked open, and then began to swing wide. Inside it, the boundaries of the planes of existence were breached.

A pinprick of crimson light appeared. Katelin stood transfixed as it grew brighter than any star. The light was painful, searing, but she couldn't look away. It grew into the form of a man, but greater and more terrible, wreathed in crimson flame.

Ilbassi was coming.

The god approached the planar threshold and the city was bathed in a ghastly light, as though drowning in blood.

No! How could they fight him? Katelin shook and wept, her body cold, gripped in a fist of iron. Her sanity began to unravel.

Around her the fighting froze and weapons dropped from strengthless hands. Anestrans, Lassenites and barbarians alike fell to the ground and covered their heads. But it was the Anestrans who buried their faces.

Katelin couldn't even make herself move.

But one man fought on. Edgaran's voice carried from the corner of the Square. "No!" he shouted.

The cry cracked a chink in Katelin's cocoon of terror. Edgaran raised an arm towards her and gasped: "Divine, help her! She needs your aid!"

The Crown flickered ... and brightened. A white beam sped towards Katelin on the dais, enveloping her in its glow—and banishing the crimson.

Katelin's senses reeled, but her will was free. No longer frozen with terror, her mind raced. What could she do? She had to decide fast ... and act faster. She couldn't touch their god, but the Archmage ...

The terrified dread became a spark of new resolve. She'd met him before, matched wits with this bully, and defeated him. What had she ever done? An arrow? Their leader? But was Gaitox even in range of her bow?

Her hands trembled as she nocked a last arrow, and aimed. "Divine, speed this missile to its mark."

A flicker of white shimmered along the shaft. With a scream of effort, Katelin let the arrow fly. As a lightning bolt across the Square, the javelin of white raced towards the mages and plunged into the Archmage's chest.

She got him!

Gaitox gagged and shuddered in mid incantation. A white glory engulfed him, a dazzling brightness against the crimson in the rest of the Square. The Archmage writhed and collapsed.

The summons of his god was incomplete.

Katelin looked up. Ilbassi paused on the celestial threshold, his eyes of fire regarding the scene below. The doorway above Anestra city lay open before him. He moved to step through it into the Western Coast, to conclude the battle of crimson against white.

Katelin's hope vanished. The chill terror flooded back, undiminished. What else could they do? Hedger? The Crown? She screamed, "Divine, save us from Ilbassi! You promised Anestra wouldn't fall. What more can we do? By the Crown, help him! I give myself. Now!"

A great drain of energy left her, and she staggered. The light erupted from Prince Edgaran's Crown, and blasted into Ilbassi. The threatening figure of the foreign god recoiled, halted … but then resumed his relentless advance.

Edgaran fell to his knees. She heard him yell, "Divine, I have nothing more to give. Save my people! I give myself for them. Take me, and let them be spared!"

The glory of the Crown exploded upwards. Thunder boomed, the ground heaved and lightning forked down into the Square. The brilliance rose above the city, a radiance that was oppressive to the Lassenites … and anathema to Ilbassi.

The brightness formed into a finger of the Divine: white, slender, strong. It touched the great, grey doorway in the heavens, and the door began to move. Ilbassi tried to stop its closing, holding it with a hand, and then bracing it with his shoulder. But with sure and agonising slowness, the finger of the Divine pushed closed the planar door. The crimson that bathed the city was shut out.

The Divine had kept her promise.

There was silence except for the rain.

And then pandemonium. With the battle in the skies over, the grip of terror vanished. Soldiers, guards, Archers, mages, barbarians and thugs picked themselves up and grabbed their weapons. Swords and shields clashed. Arrows flew.

But Katelin could only stare in horror at her brother. From the corner of the Square, a final burst of light from the Prince's Crown surged across the city.

Edgaran collapsed forward, twitching, twisting, as his drained and lifeless body sprawled upon the ground.

And then the Crown went out.

Hedger! No!

An arrow thudded into Katelin's thigh. She screamed, clutching at the shaft in her leg. Too late she saw the mages pointing at her, the one who had felled their Archmage.

Her mind was working as if down a long tunnel: too dim, too slow. She'd stepped forward to shoot … she was far too conspicuous …

It was over now …

A second arrow plunged into her left side. She crumpled backwards onto the dais and was lost to the battle of her city and people.

✶ XXIII ✶

AFTERMATH

Katelin became aware of floating in darkness. Strengthless, helpless.

Her body was nearby … somewhere … but it was too weak and painful to inhabit.

Then with dizzying speed she rushed back into it.

If she'd had the breath, she would have gasped. Someone was driving needles into her right thigh, her left side, the back of her head. The nerves writhed, crawled, shrank, screamed.

She tried to move, but couldn't. She tried to speak, but no voice came. She tried opening her eyes, but they wouldn't. The agony was excruciating, but could only be endured.

She tried to whimper, but not even that would sound. She couldn't see, but tears still came. At length she gave up trying, and lay there. Cocooned in painful darkness, all she could think was to pray.

The Divine had to save her. Now.

Where was she? What had happened to her?

Was this death? No, she refused to believe it. It was too painful for that.

Please, please, please help her. Now.

At last, the beginnings of a weak strength returned. It seemed an improvement when her whole body ached as well as the particular sharpness. Her muscles were lead, her head on fire. She breathed: shallow and weak. Her heart pumped, blood flowed. She listened: there were sounds around her. Were they voices?

Her mind was clearing. She tried her eyes again, and a blurry light appeared between teary, flickering eyelashes. She tried licking her lips and her tongue moved.

A voice: "She's waking up, milady. Quick now, come and see."

Her head swam for a while, but then she realised she was in a bed. A face loomed through the tears. She tried to focus.

Rashelin.

"Katelin, it's me," she was saying. "You're all right, you're safe. It's Rashelin, can you hear me?"

Only one desire filled her mind. She ungritted her teeth long enough to gasp, "Stop—driving—the needles." She screwed up her eyes, but the tears still flowed.

Rashelin said something else, but she didn't take it in.

In the silence that followed, one memory seared her mind, one last image stabbed her. Katelin opened her eyes and mumbled, "Hedger. Where is he?"

An unmistakeable shadow crossed Rashelin's face. A pause. She said, "He's here beside you."

Katelin tried to turn her head. She couldn't, so Rashelin helped her. She struggled to focus on the next pillow ... and her heart stopped cold.

Edgaran lay next to her. His face was deathly pale and turned to the ceiling. His eyes were closed, like a marble effigy. He looked waxen, drawn, haggard, old.

A corpse.

Tears flooded back. Her physical agony was nothing compared to this.

Oh, Hedger, no.

No, Divine, no. She had to send him back.

Katelin tried to reach for him, but her hand only twitched. Seeing this, Rashelin lifted her hand and placed it into her brother's. It was cold and clammy.

Dead.

He had to come back. Not leave her.

With all her remaining strength, she squeezed his hand.

Come back ... Hedger ...

And the darkness took her once more.

Katelin awoke to a damp sponge moistening her lips. It was good—cleansing, refreshing. She swallowed, licked her lips, opened her mouth and received some bitter liquid. She was stronger; the sharp, stabbing pains were now a throb.

The room was dim, the night lamp gentle on her eyes. Rashelin sat beside her bed with a bowl and sponge. Katelin tried to move again ... but she held a hand.

And it was warm.

She turned her head—and Edgaran slept beside her.

He was transformed.

Colour and warmth had returned to his face, and he looked no worse than asleep.

He was alive.

The relief washed over her, and a laugh began deep in her stomach. But it was too painful to let out. She turned back to Rashelin and breathed as much as she could manage.

"So we're not dead," she whispered, with a faint smile, "and you aren't an angel. And I'm not asleep, so you aren't a dream."

Rashelin laughed. And its refreshing music tinkled down into her soul and mingled with the joy inside. "No, my dear Katelin, you are neither dead nor dreaming. We've all been so worried and praying for you. We've longed for you to wake up."

"Rashelin?"

"Hello." She smiled. "Yes, it's me. How are you feeling?"

Katelin thought about that. "Weak," she breathed at last, "and sore. Where am I?"

"Anestra Castle, of course. A bedroom in the royal apartments. You lost a lot of blood, and we've been desperate for you both. I can't tell you what it means to talk to you."

Rashelin held a spoon to her mouth and she sipped. "Rashelin," she murmured, "what happened to Hedger?"

Rashelin frowned. "We don't know. He has no obvious wounds. We found him face down in the Square after the battle. He was stone dead … but now he's alive."

Katelin hesitated. "So … did we win?"

"Yes, we won," said Rashelin, "but it was close. We lost many good people and there's a lot of damage. But we can repair things, so don't worry about that for now. Sleep and rest, recover your strength and we'll ask the Divine to heal you."

Katelin sighed and closed her eyes. She had no energy to argue, and Rashelin's hand was warm and gentle on her forehead. She drifted back to sleep, with Rashelin's prayer echoing into her dreams: "The Divine heal you and strengthen you. May she refresh you, renew you and raise you up …"

When Katelin woke again, it was morning. She flinched against the brightness, licked her lips and swallowed. She stretched, winced, and remembered that she'd been holding Edgaran's hand.

She turned. He was sitting up in bed, watching her.

Katelin spluttered and coughed. When her breathing settled she looked around. The two of them were alone in the bedroom.

"Good morning." Edgaran smiled. "I wondered when I'd see your green eyes again."

"Hello," Katelin croaked. She sounded as weak as she felt. "You're feeling better then?"

"I'm a little stronger, yes." He called, "Rashelin." In a few moments she came through the door.

"Hello, you two!" Rashelin squealed. "You're both awake." The delight across her face was medicine in itself, but her eyes were dark from lack of sleep.

"Can I have a drink, please?" Katelin whispered. "I don't think I can sit up."

"That's all right," said Rashelin. "I'll spoon you some water." The servant girl, Adisha, hurried in with two cups.

"Thank you, Adisha," Katelin managed.

"Milady," she said, and couldn't hide a tearful smile as she went out. Edgaran drank from his cup and Rashelin spooned the water for Katelin. It was bliss to her scratchy throat.

Katelin asked, "Hedger, what happened to you?"

Edgaran stared at the bed-clothes. Rashelin stopped spooning to listen. "It's hard to describe." His voice was quiet. "I fought at the gate, the Temple, the harbour. I ran back to the Square, but with no strength left. Anestra needed me or we would lose. Ilbassi had come ... but I was afraid of what I had to do. I asked the Divine to save our people, and for her to take me instead. And she did. She took all of me and used it to save Anestra. But the price was so high." A ghost of loss and sadness passed across Edgaran's face. "It killed me."

"But you're alive now." Katelin frowned. "The Divine sent you back?"

"Yes, she did." Edgaran looked up at her. "I was sleeping deep enough never to wake. But then you called me, Kat, and the Divine let me go. You said my name, you tugged my hand. The Divine took me in the battle, but she wants me here from now on. Abbot Ruis said it at Timajet: 'The Divine takes to her those whom she loves, and leaves behind those with work still to do.' So Kat, she has work for us to do."

Katelin took a spoonful of water from Rashelin. "Armus said that Divine power flows through the Anestran Royal Family. That's true, then."

"Yes, it's true," said Edgaran. "The Divine is in the Crown, and in you and me, for all that she wants of us." He paused. "Kat, I'm so sorry. All these years, I've been a runaway too, hoping that you would thrive as Queen. I thought that with Rashelin here, and your advisers, you could order everything as you wished. So I hope you can forgive me … for my absence."

Katelin sighed. Could she forgive him? All those years of dread that she'd borne alone, when it should have been his? But he was here now, and perhaps it was the future that mattered more.

She nodded. "Yes, I forgive you," she breathed. "On one condition. That you promise me that you'll stay here from now on, and live up to your responsibilities."

Edgaran stared at her, and swallowed hard. "You ask a high price, little sister." Then he sighed. "Yes, I'll stay. I promise."

"I'll help you both too," said Rashelin. "If there are ways in which I can serve."

Katelin smiled and squeezed her cousin's hand. "Thank you, Rashelin, and yes, please. We'll need your tact and experience, your relationships with people at Court." She looked between the two of them. "So what shall we be? King, Queen and Princess? Between the three of us, do you think we might manage a Kingdom?"

Rashelin sent out the good news that the Queen and Prince were both awake and recovering. Yardles came in with Sigzay, and the Steward seemed overcome as he took Katelin's hand. She managed a weak smile and squeezed his hand in return before he bustled off to his duties.

Sigzay, who had suffered only grazes and bruises in the battle, brought them more of her medicinal herbs. The leaves were fragrant when crushed, but when infused in hot water, became the bitter drink that Rashelin had been giving them. Sigzay insisted that they drink it, to heal their blood and energy, their wounds and strength. Now Katelin recognised that her recovery was due to herbs, attentive care and widespread prayer in her favour. Her leg and side remained bandaged, and she was shocked to learn that she'd lain wounded and unconscious for more than a day before waking.

Rashelin related to them the outcome of the battle. Duke Bassikrin had been killed by Sigzay's crossbow bolts and Archmage Gaitox by Katelin's last arrow. At the Temple, the Knights had unhorsed and captured Count Bassilius. In the Bay, the slavers had been repulsed, but several vessels had been stolen, plundered, burnt or sunk, and their crews slaughtered.

Edgaran's final sacrifice had given the power of the Crown to Anestra's soldiers to overcome the leaderless Lassenites. The Knights had prevented much of the Duke's army from escaping, but many of the attackers had fled north or been killed. The fighting had ended with the Knights riding through the North Gate, up Queensway and into Crown Square.

The Duke's crown lay in the Anestran Royal Treasury, awaiting Katelin's instructions. It was assumed that it incorporated the final part of the Crown of Anestra, along with the fake part from Timajet. Katelin ordered Count Bassilius, despite his many crimes, to be moved from the dungeons, to be guarded with dignity in a guest room.

The former Regent and Consort had kept a low profile since the battle, overseeing the departures of visiting dignitaries.

Rashelin reported to Edgaran and Katelin her parents' relief at the Prince's return, but had to add how overjoyed they were that he had taken the rule of Anestra away from Katelin.

Edgaran was alone in the royal apartments when Sigzay came to see him. "I speak with you, Highness?" she asked, as she entered the drawing room.

"Of course," he replied. "We haven't had a chance to talk since the dungeons, have we?" He understood the point that she made, by not calling him 'Hedger', and that an awkward discussion was in prospect. She'd been at his bedside when he woke, but had since been an intermittent visitor.

He was sitting at one end of a long sofa and she sat down at the other end. Her knuckles were white as she gripped the arm, and her face was as inscrutable as ever. He moved to sit next to her and took her hand, but sensed her reluctance at his touch. Her hand was trembling.

"What is it?" he asked.

"You have more lies to tell, more secrets to devastate me?"

"Sigzay." He linked his fingers through hers. "I'm so sorry. We've known each other for a long time, and I didn't know what else to do."

"You know me a long time, but I not know you at all."

Edgaran felt the hurt in her eyes and voice. "I'm sorry I kept who I am from you all this time. Can you understand why I had to?"

"No. You understand I feel lied and betrayed? You destroy all trust I have in you?" Her bitterness cut into him.

Edgaran sighed. "Yes, I can see how you feel that. I hoped you could be happy for me, and share this with me."

"Happy for you? Share it? How I share this? I not Princess, not royal. I not abbot, not cleric. I not follow Divine, not Anestran. What here for me to share?"

"I know you're none of those things." He took both her hands and looked straight into her grey eyes. "You're more than those to me. You're my friend; my closest, dearest friend. You're my love. We've been through so much together. I love you. I need you. I can't do this without you."

"You need me?" Her voice rose. "How does mighty Prince of Anestra need young barbarian woman?"

He tried a smile. "You could keep my feet on the ground."

She took a deep breath. The trembling had spread to her whole body. Returning his gaze, she said, "You say you love me, but not tell me truth. How I trust you?"

Edgaran looked at the floor, and said, "I knew that if I told you, it would change everything. I didn't want anything to change. I wanted to be with you, just the two of us, and not have to deal with all this." He waved his arm around the sumptuous room.

She nodded. "Hedger, I not mind who you are. I mind you not tell me truth."

Edgaran swallowed. Then heaved a breath. "Sigzay ... I'm sorry for how much I've hurt you. I hope that one day you'll be able to forgive me."

"Maybe," said Sigzay. "One day. But not today. And not here. Not with all this." She indicated the room. "Come away with me? Back to north?"

Edgaran winced. "I can't. I have duties and responsibilities here. I promised Kat that I would stay and become King. Couldn't you stay here?"

Sigzay bit her lip. There was too much in her eyes: grief, hurt, anger, loss.

He put an arm around her, but she remained tense, not sinking into his embrace. The lights of the chandelier glinted like diamonds in her white hair. He traced his finger around the wolf tattoo on her shoulder, and kissed her hair. "My brave wolf," he breathed. "We've been together so long. We've been through so much. But I understand that I need to earn your trust again."

She sat up and regarded him. "You do. But you ask too much of me, to stay here, to leave home for you, to sacrifice my freedom too."

"Maybe I could fit in two or three days soon for us to go away together. To talk and think."

"Fit in? Two or three days?"

Their eyes met, and Edgaran understood. This would be hard. If not impossible. They dropped their gaze. He nodded, and they sat in silence.

Sigzay stared at the wall. Then she turned tearful eyes to him and tried to smile. "You remember us in wilderness together? In Ironbore Hills, at my home in north and explore to east? I have you all to myself. If we stay here, everyone wants bits of you. How much left for me?"

"I don't know," he said. "All this is new to me too. Believe me, I wish we could go back to that. But I can't, not now. Sigzay, my love, whatever else goes on, you have all of my heart."

"What about Kat? She have none of your heart, your love?"

Edgaran frowned. "Well … of course, I love her too, she's my sister—"

Sigzay took back her hands, and an icy control returned. "Always thought Kat wanted steal you from me. Was right. She has."

Edgaran stiffened. His voice trembled and his finger was pointing. "No, Sigzay, don't. It's not like that. Don't blame her. This was my choice."

Sigzay stood up, her face unreadable again. "Much has

happen. I need think and decide what I do. I here for few days then go away. I go back to north for fresh air and clear thoughts."

"Sigzay, wait, please." Edgaran rose too. "It's not only your life that's bound to mine. I'm bound to you as well. Please don't say that you want to be free, that you want your life back."

"No," she said at once. A cloud of anguish shadowed Sigzay's face. "That why I never walk away." Her voice became a whisper. "That how you know I come back."

"Sigzay, don't go. I see that you need some time to think. Can we talk about this again soon?" Sigzay was at the door, and she left the room without answering.

Her boots faded down the corridor. He sank back onto the sofa. He'd hurt and betrayed his friend, his love. Now he was losing her.

He sat there in silence for a long time.

Katelin realised that someone had saved her life by carrying her from the battle before she bled to death. She wanted to thank and reward him, so she sent for the Captain of the Archers. He entered her third floor drawing room looking as though what he had to say would displease her.

"Your Majesty," he said, "you asked to know how your life was saved. When you fell on the dais, the Archers closed ranks to protect you. One of us ran to your body, lifted you and stumbled into the Castle."

"Thank you, Captain." Katelin smiled. "So do you know who performed this heroic deed?"

The Captain hesitated. "I do, milady. But the man in question … has asked to remain unknown."

"What? Why?"

The Captain sounded as if this were a rehearsed statement.

"He said, milady, that any of the Archers would've done the same. Although he was the one that rescued you, he reckons he deserves no special thanks for something any of us would've done."

Katelin stared at him. A warm lump was growing in her chest. "Any of the Archers would risk their lives for me?"

"No, milady." The burly Captain looked almost shy. "Not risk. Any of us would give our lives for yours."

Katelin was stunned. "You would? But … why?"

The Captain looked blank. "You're our Queen, milady."

Simple as that. The warm lump now filled her throat. She didn't deserve this devotion. But she seemed to have it anyway. She managed to say, "Does our secret hero suggest what I should do?"

"He suggests," replied the Captain, "that any thanks you think are right and proper should be shared by the whole company, milady."

She hoped he couldn't see that her eyes brimmed with tears. "Thank you, Captain. I'll do that."

"Very good, Your Majesty." The Captain bowed and left the room.

Katelin turned to gaze out of the window. The sky was blue and the fluffy clouds were well broken. The shadows of leaves danced across the sunlit lawn, like fairies in their merry-making.

Any of the Archers were willing to give their lives for her. The warm lump burst, and she could no longer restrain the tears.

These people loved her.

How had she earned their devotion? Being their Queen was special to them. She wanted to return their love, but didn't know how. Edgaran had the task of ruling them, but she'd think of other ways to serve. She'd get out of the Castle and meet them, get to know them, fathom what she meant to them and what they desired of her.

It was some time before she thought to blow her nose and wipe her face.

These people loved her.

Later that day, a messenger from the Castle gate reported to Katelin that two Caldunim asked to see her.

"Farag and Jersull," Katelin exclaimed. "Of course. Prince Edgaran and I will receive them in the royal apartments."

So Yardles led the Captain and first mate of the *Oyster Shell* to where the Queen and Prince of Anestra sat in the finest drawing room on the Western Coast. The look on the southerners' faces as the Royal Steward announced them was priceless.

As they shuffled through the door, Katelin pushed herself to her feet and waved them over. She explained that her wounds were still healing and embraced them with care. Before Yardles went out, she asked him, "Would you fetch eight goldens from the Treasury, please? I have a debt to repay."

Yardles's eyebrows shot up, but he nodded. Farag smiled.

Katelin said, "Hedger and Jersull have met before, but Captain Farag, meet my dear brother, who is Prince Edgaran of Anestra."

"We are honoured, Your Majesties," said Farag.

Edgaran held up his hands. "Please," he said, "any friend of Kat's is a friend of mine. So you may call me 'Hedger', as she does."

Jersull still looked gloomy, even as he said, "It's good to see you again, friend Hedger. And to think that one evening at the Treasure Trove in Lasseny I had mutton stew and ale with the Queen and Prince of Anestra." The others laughed.

They sat and Katelin asked them, "How is everyone on the *Oyster Shell*? I heard there was fighting in the harbour."

Farag and Jersull looked at each other. Farag said, "I'm sorry to say that only few of our crew survived. The slavers killed many and almost escaped with the ship. We were lucky to get back to the harbour in time."

No! Katelin hadn't spoken with many in the crew, but she remembered some faces. She whispered, "Only so few of you left? I'm afraid to ask, but what about your cabin boy, Moxee?"

"He's fine," said Farag. "He and a few others jumped overboard and swam to safety. We're recruiting new hands but it's a slow business. So many in Anestra are injured or bereaved, and have other matters to see to."

"Is there any way we can help?" said Edgaran.

"We wondered if we might entice a certain young archer to another adventure," Jersull said, straight-faced.

Katelin's heart leapt and she wondered if the excited glint showed in her eyes. "You know," she said, "I'm tempted. I need to recover, and I promised Hedger I'd help him here for a while." She looked sideways at Edgaran and said to the Caldunim in a loud whisper, "But if you send me word when you're next in port, I'll climb down a rope, jump a wall and sneak off to a boat by the quay." They laughed again.

Edgaran said, "You may abscond from the Kingdom whenever you like, Kat. But this might help you. We can place the *Oyster Shell* under royal protection, and entitle you to assistance from Anestran soldiers and ships. And you can have the freedom of Anestra, to exempt you from docking fees. Will that help?"

Katelin could almost see Farag calculating how much he would save. The man was in merchant Captain heaven. He managed, "Yes, indeed, my lord, thank you."

Jersull looked thoughtful. "We've won a battle or two

against the slave traders," he said, "but not yet the war. Now with you two in charge of the Western Coast, you might just make me an optimist." And he gave Katelin his third smile.

She grinned. Edgaran said, "We're happy to help after all you've done for Kat. And besides, the next time she goes missing, we'll know where to start looking."

✳ XXIV ✳

FREEDOM

Katelin asked Edgaran to accompany her to speak with Count Bassilius. It was not a meeting she relished and she put it off for several days. She knew that the Divine was merciful, and that she ought to reflect this in her dealings with Bassilius. But she struggled to stomach forgiving him, and decided that would depend on whether he was willing to amend his ways. In the meantime she made sure that the captive Count was well looked after.

At last the two of them went to the South Tower and the guards unlocked the guest room door. Bassilius was on the window seat, watching the activity outside. Katelin felt her hackles rise. He looked Katelin up and down, and started when he saw Edgaran.

"Queen Katelin," he said. "But who are you?"

They drew up chairs near to the Count and Edgaran spoke first. "Yes, Bassilius, it's me again. We've met a few times in recent days: outside the Palace in Lasseny, and you tied me up as a brigand and spy in a canyon. I've been known as Hedger, but my full name is Prince Edgaran of Anestra."

"Prince Edgaran," Bassilius whispered. His face twitched. He stared at him, then at Katelin, and back. "You led the Knights at the Temple … with the Crown."

"Yes, that was me," said Edgaran. "The defence of our city from your concerted attack prevented us from meeting face to face."

Bassilius said nothing.

Katelin forced herself into politeness. "Is your room comfortable?" she asked. "Are you getting enough to eat?"

"I wouldn't call it adequate," Bassilius replied. Angry discomfort radiated from him. This was not going well.

"You will notice," said Edgaran, "that we've refrained from binding your ankles and wrists." Bassilius glared at him. "And Queen Katelin ordered your move from the dungeons to this room. We trust you agree that your position deserves some civility?"

"Thank you very much," Bassilius sneered.

Edgaran concluded his list of charges with: "And I can reassure you, Count, that I won't kick you in the stomach."

The full memory of their desert encounter seemed to come back to him. Bassilius nodded, wiping his hands on his trousers. "What do you want?" he murmured.

"Well," said Katelin, "if we can talk as civilised people without sneering or sarcasm, we should discuss what might happen to you."

Bassilius swallowed. The lofty disdain vanished from his face, as perhaps he realised how much he was in their power. "All right," he said. "I suppose you want me to apologise for how I've treated you."

"That would be a good start," said Katelin.

"Sorry," Bassilius said. It wasn't heartfelt, but she guessed he'd seldom had to say it before.

Edgaran seemed to give him the benefit of the doubt. "Apology accepted," he said.

"Now," said Katelin. "You know that your father was killed in the battle. Many think you should be executed for your part in the invasion. What do you say to that?" The words came out with a sharpness she only half intended.

Bassilius twitched again. "I'm not afraid to die. I've been a faithful follower of Ilbassi. He'll be just with his reward when I stand before him in judgement."

"Your devotion does you credit, Bassilius," said Katelin, "even if your choice of god is misplaced." She heaved a breath and tried to swallow away her distaste. "However, those who are learned in Old Kingdom law inform us that, whatever the crimes of your father, you stand to succeed him as Duke of Lasseny."

Bassilius's eyes widened. She allowed him some moments to think. Was that a first inkling of his way out of this?

"Yes, it wasn't my idea to attack Anestra," Bassilius blurted out.

"I see," Katelin said. She fixed him with her gaze. "And the slaughter at Timajet?"

"My father's orders," Bassilius stated. "He told me to retrieve what he wanted from the monastery, and execute any who resisted."

Bassilius hadn't fooled her for a moment. He might hurry to shift all blame onto his deceased father, who could no longer contradict him, but he'd enjoyed the power of his role. He'd followed orders with enthusiasm, not reluctance. "You can blame your father as much as you like," said Katelin. "The question is whether you will work with us in the future." She tried to put as much challenge into the words as she could.

Bassilius licked his lips and Katelin watched him. Yes, he was afraid of losing wealth and power. And his life. So was this now his greedy hope of regaining it all? "What do you have in mind?" he asked.

Katelin hoped they weren't making the biggest mistake of their lives. "The Old Kingdom used to stretch the length of the Western Coast. In those days Lasseny was subject to Anestra and the Duke was a vassal of the King. Would you accept that arrangement again?"

"Under what terms?" Bassilius was guarded.

Katelin was careful too. "When you swear a public oath of loyalty to the two of us, we will confirm you as the new Duke of Lasseny. You will apologise, and your city will pay compensation, for the damage and loss of life that you've caused. As part of the Kingdom, you will stop slave traders from using your harbour, and allow faith in the Divine to be taught in your territory."

Bassilius picked at the stitching on the window seat cushion. He muttered to himself, "Many of our people have been killed. It will take time to gather the money you might ask."

"That your men died while attacking our city is not our problem," Katelin snapped. "If you agree to our overlordship, then we'll discuss the reparations later."

Bassilius stood up. "Agreed." He held out his hand.

So he'd realised this was the best deal that he'd get. Perhaps he wasn't stupid after all. Katelin stood and took the sweaty hand.

She looked him straight in the eye. "We've been merciful to you today, Bassilius. More than you deserve. We trust you'll never forget it."

He nodded, nervous, but said nothing. Edgaran stood and took his hand also.

"And just to be clear," Katelin said, turning to go, "I will never agree to marry you."

Repaying Captain Farag reminded Katelin of the Treasury's thousand goldens reward for the return of the Crown. She found it a happy task to divide it between the five of them who had journeyed back from Timajet. Katelin, Edgaran and Ruis donated their shares of two hundred goldens each to assist the injured and bereaved, and for repairs to the city and

Temple. Brother Armus's augmented share of two hundred and twelve goldens included the extra twelve to repay him at last for buying Katelin at the Lasseny slave market.

Sigzay took her share of two hundred goldens and left for the north before Katelin realised she was going. Katelin was sad to have missed the chance to say goodbye, but noticed the pain in Edgaran's face about it. He seemed to be consoling himself that Sigzay would be back before long in any case.

Armus enlisted some fellow clerics to return with him to Lasseny, to use his reward to establish there a new congregation of the Divine. Although she was sorry that Armus was leaving too, Katelin asked him to keep a gentle eye on the new Duke Bassilius. The cleric made it clear that he was not prepared to spy on him, but consented that his reports to the Temple could comment on how Bassilius was settling into his role.

Katelin was delighted when the Cleric Council announced Abbot Ruis as their choice to become the next Under Father. Now at least she could insist that he instruct her in all she wanted to know about the Divine.

And then it was time to celebrate. At the invitation of Queen Katelin, a banquet was to take place three weeks after the Coronation Day battle. It was to be a relaxed and informal day, the people bringing tables and chairs for all to be seated at a feast in Crown Square. The banquet should have been at royal expense, but in the end no bills were submitted to the Treasury for reimbursement. The city bakers, butchers, grocers and fishmongers, the taverns and wine merchants were happy to supply ample food and drink.

When the people were gathered, Ethabos, Sirika, Rashelin and her three brothers took their places on the repaired dais. Brother Armus and Under Father Ruis led the clerics of the

Divine to their seats beside the dais. Contrary to the tradition of his predecessors, Ruis had decided for his time as Under Father to wear nothing more elaborate than his plain grey monk's garment.

Musicians played popular tunes and the people clapped and sang. At the chime of noon, the royal trumpeters sounded from the battlements. Queen Katelin and Prince Edgaran came through the Castle gate. She wasn't as nervous as on Coronation Day, but they still had life-changing matters to address.

The sister and brother were bare-headed and richly dressed, Katelin in her royal robes of silver and dark blue silk. The multitudes rose, and the shout of welcome deafened them. Katelin still felt shaky, and was unable to walk too far or stand for long. They escorted each other to the dais, Katelin to her throne, Edgaran to one side. Long before the applause looked like ending, Katelin signalled for all to be seated.

Bassilius of Lasseny emerged from the Castle to rumbles of discontent in the crowd. He lumbered across the dais and knelt before the Queen and Prince. His voice was rough as he said: "In the name of the Divine and Ilbassi, here do I, Bassilius of Lasseny, swear allegiance to the Crown of Anestra, and obedience to your word. I acknowledge my guilt towards the people of Anestra and promise to pay reparations."

Katelin gave him credit for the attempt at humility in his voice, but couldn't help thinking that he lied.

Bassilius remained kneeling as Queen Katelin tried to mask the hesitation in her voice, as she said, "Bassilius, I confirm you as the new Duke of Lasseny, in succession to your father. In return for obedience, you receive our protection. Your allegiance to Anestra is witnessed by the Divine and Ilbassi. It is by your actions in the future that your words of today will be tested." She indicated for Bassilius to rise, and he did so, and withdrew. The mood across the Square lightened.

Using a wooden staff for support, Katelin rose and stepped forward. She felt herself a weakling Queen. But she wouldn't always be so, and she could give them a warm smile at least. A chant began, as on Coronation Day: "Katelin, Katelin, Katelin!" It spread across the Square, and the deafening roar washed over her. Weakling or not, they loved her anyway.

She let their welcome fill her. At the front, a toddler sat on an old man's shoulders, both cheering for all they were worth. The old man must have doubted that he'd live to see a new King or Queen wearing the completed Crown. And Katelin wondered if, in years to come, the toddler would tell his grandchildren of this day. She lifted an arm, and the people quietened for her to speak.

"My dear people of Anestra," she called, and the crowds erupted. Katelin collapsed into giggles, laughing until she ached. And she couldn't keep the tears in either. She grinned at Edgaran and Rashelin, who also laughed and dabbed their eyes.

At last, the people let her continue. "My fellow citizens, we have suffered much in recent days, but the Divine is always faithful. There is damage and loss, but we are free. We'll rebuild our city together. We'll restore our walls and gates, our homes and businesses, and replant our gardens and parks. Today, together, we commit ourselves to this work." The crowds cheered their approval.

"But for most of you," Katelin continued, "life can never be as it was. Too many have been injured; too many have been killed." The crowd became still. "To all who have lost someone, I say this: know that all Anestra stands with you in your grief. We will do what we can to help you, and never forget those who have fallen. As we remember in our hearts those who have died, please would you all stand?"

As a single person the multitude rose and stood in silence across the Square. On his grandfather's shoulders, the toddler was quiet and still. He looked in wonder at the mass of thoughtful, grieving, thankful people, and the tears that rolled down many cheeks.

Katelin thought of the old Under Father, and Sergeant Rossick, and countless others: the *Oyster Shell's* crew, guards, clerics, Knights, Archers, soldiers. While she'd wrestled with the dread of her destiny, everyone else had struggled with their own problems and grief. Could she learn one day not to be so selfish?

Then, unbidden, she remembered Duke Bassikrin … and Archmage Gaitox. She shuddered. An evil had been banished from the world, but how many innocent people along with it? How many Lassenites had she killed with her arrows? And what would her people think of her remembering their fallen enemies now? They had been enemies: Lassenites and barbarians, but they'd been people too. Someone in Anestra needed to remember them, so why not her?

She thought of her father, King Etharan, buried at Timajet. And her mother, Queen Emmelis. Both now with the Divine. If they were looking down, she hoped they'd be pleased. And proud of her.

The flags and banners fluttered in the breeze. Then Katelin concluded the minute's reflection. "Those whom we love and miss, we will always remember."

The crowd murmured their agreement, sat down and wiped their faces.

Katelin spoke again. "Today I thank those without whom our city would have been lost. I pay tribute to the bravery, the skill, the fortitude of you all. Soldiers, Archers, Knights; guards of gate and wall, of Temple, harbour and Castle: stand to attention where you are."

On the Castle walls, beside the dais and gate, across the Square, around the tables, they stood. Many were bandaged, but their posture showed their pride.

"Look at these brave men and women," said Katelin. "To these and many others, we owe our lives, our homes, our city and our freedom. True Anestrans all, we honour and thank you today." The people burst into prolonged applause. Those who stood swelled their chests, but struggled to maintain their composure.

When the clapping died away, Katelin smiled and said, "I have something personal to say." The crowd stirred. "You know that I was injured in the battle, and fell here on this dais. One of the Royal Archers risked his life to save mine. I asked for the name of my rescuer …" she paused, and then said, "… but no one will tell me who he was!" Laughter rippled across the Square.

"I owe that man my life. He has said that any of his company are willing to give their lives for me. So I have no choice but to reward them all. Once again you have earned your name. What can we offer you? Double pay for a year? From the depths of my heart, I honour and I thank … the Queen's Own Archers!"

The people leapt to their feet; they roared, whistled and cheered the Archers who had saved their Queen.

When at last all were quiet and seated, Katelin continued. "People of Anestra, my dear friends, we are gathered with two joyful tasks to perform. For fifteen long years our city has had neither King or Queen, nor its sacred relic of a Crown. But no longer. Witness today the final restoration of our ancient Crown of Anestra!"

The people wept for joy as Quevelle, the Royal Treasurer, brought the Crown onto the dais. It was alongside, but separate from, the final fragment from Duke Bassikrin's crown. The crowd chanted, "Crown of Anestra, Crown of Anestra!" as the Treasurer placed her cushion beside the throne.

Katelin paused. She remembered a childhood dream. Was this how she'd imagined it? Yes, close enough. She tried to hide her grin. And blink away the filling of her eyes.

She picked up the Crown and the final piece, lifting them high. The silverwork glittered in the sunshine. She called aloud, "O Divine, our White Goddess, the Life-Weaver, you have helped and saved us. Receive our love and worship, as we dedicate ourselves to you today. For the sake of your grateful people, restore your Crown! Glory to the Divine!"

Katelin brought together the broken parts of the Crown of Anestra, and with a dazzling flash they fused into a completed circle. White light spiralled upwards from the Crown in Katelin's hands. The people gasped and shielded their eyes as the brilliance erupted skywards. A thunderclap boomed over the Square, and a sunburst streamed down into the city. For the first time in years, the glory of the Crown followed its perfect ring and went on forever.

Katelin couldn't say how long it was until the radiance faded, and the brightness of the sun returned to its place in the skies. The Crown of Anestra rested complete in her hands, and had resumed its normal bright silver.

Jumping stars! That was even better than she'd expected!

The crowd came back to themselves. They broke into spontaneous praise to the Divine, hailing Queen Katelin and the glory of the Crown of Anestra. Some clerics had fallen on their faces. They picked themselves up, but many still streamed tears of joy.

Katelin laid aside the Crown. She drew Edgaran to his feet and led him to the front of the dais.

"People of Anestra," said Katelin, "on my Coronation Day, it became clear to me that the Crown of the Divine is not the only precious gift that we've received. Fifteen years ago we lost not only our Crown, but also my father and mother, our last King and Queen. We thought that we'd lost my elder brother too. But he wasn't killed, he was captured and survived. As many of you will have heard, my brother has returned. My people, I present to you … the Prince Edgaran!"

The crowd roared.

Katelin held up a hand. "Three weeks ago you expected to see the glory of the Crown from the head of your Queen— but nothing happened. As we have all seen today, the Divine has not abandoned us, nor has her power or glory waned. But she shows us the true ruler of Anestra. Here I am, your Crowned Queen … and yet my elder brother is here. What are we to do?"

The crowd looked uncertain, so Katelin smiled. "Please do not worry, because Edgaran and I have an offer for you, our people. We will not ask you to choose between us, my brother and me. In the long history of the Old Kingdom this has never happened before, but would you like to have the both of us? Would you agree if Edgaran and I rule as brother and sister, King and Queen, together?"

The people leapt up, erupting into cheered agreement. "King and Queen together!" they shouted. "Edgaran and Katelin! King and Queen together!"

Katelin said, "Then I will Crown my brother by placing our sacred relic on Prince Edgaran's head. When Divine glory shines forth, will you have him as your King?"

The roar from the crowd almost bowled her over. "Yes, we will! Glory to the Divine, to the Crown, to our King and Queen forever!"

Katelin smiled. "No King or Queen for fifteen years, then two come along together." The people laughed.

She bowed before them. She turned and beckoned to

Princess Rashelin. With Rashelin's help, Katelin removed the royal robes and, standing once more in her simple cream dress, transferred them onto Edgaran's shoulders. Rashelin sat, while Katelin took Edgaran's hand. She led him in front of Anestra's royal throne, and motioned for him to sit. All Anestra bent the knee, and silence fell.

Katelin stood alone before Prince Edgaran. She took the restored Crown and raised it high above his head. She wasn't the only one holding her breath, her gaze fixed, for this culmination of all things. Edgaran looked up at her and smiled. Oh, yes, hello, big brother.

Katelin called: "Hear us, O White Goddess, our Life Weaver. In the name of the Divine and with her power upon you, I Crown you, Prince Edgaran, as my King, as King of the Western Coast and of the Old Kingdom of Anestra!" She lowered the Crown to rest on King Edgaran's head. Then she too knelt.

The completed Crown sparkled. White flames flickered around its circle and gems. As the sun emerged from behind dark clouds, its brilliance grew. Before Katelin's upraised eyes a white light ascended from King Edgaran's head. It climbed to the heavens, and then soared upwards to be lost in the brightness of the afternoon sky.

As if in response, the whole sky flashed. A deluge of glory descended on Crown Square. Radiance hovered above the King as a halo, and his whole body shone. Then Divine love and power burst forth from him, overwhelmed them all, and filled every heart to overflowing.

✶ EPILOGUE ✶

Katelin spurred Novita towards the top of the hill. She and the white stallion were both panting and sweating from the ride. The sky was a deep blue, the summer air was warm and a gentle breeze stirred the grass. Katelin let Novita drink from the spring near the hilltop, and lifted her eyes to absorb the view.

The Eastern Range climbed before her. Foothills mounted shoulder upon shoulder to sheer cliffs and ragged ridges, until snow-capped peaks marched to the distant horizon. Wide fields stretched to her left, the country estates, groves and orchards of Anestra, fertile and cultivated, with the rich greenery of pasture, hedge and tree. It was as if a painter had used the countryside as a palette, to mix all the colours of green to find the right hue.

On Katelin's right lay the wide valley of the river Mannis as it swept through its final course to the Ocean. At the head of the valley the Manniswood began, the great forest stretching east and south of the mountains until lost in the haze of distance. Clouds on the horizon formed far away castles in the sky.

How many times had she seen this view, and yet it had never looked so beautiful? The colours were sharper, the air smelled sweeter, and the birdsong sounded more joyful. The place and the view hadn't changed, had they? It was her.

For the first time in her life, she felt free.

For as long as she could remember, she'd borne the heavy burden: that responsibility, those expectations, to rule the people of the Divine. The dread of it had chained her heart, but that was no longer her destiny. Edgaran had the ultimate authority, and that liberation was a whole new life beginning.

She was still the Queen, with a role in the life of Anestra, but that was all she was called to be. She had a new friend and brother, her saviour, her King. He would rule Anestra well, with Rashelin's help and empowered by the Crown. Katelin would help him too, serving among their people who loved her. At last she understood: ruling Anestra didn't have to be a heavy duty for one person alone. The tasks could be shared. The three of them together—King, Queen and Princess— could govern between them, each bringing their different gifts and experience.

Maybe true freedom wasn't about doing what she liked, but being willing for what she was meant to do. Now she could be herself. And no more Nightmare.

So had she cheated Destiny? She was the Queen, but had never expected to have a brother as King beside her. Maybe she'd dodged it … so far. And rebelling hadn't caused her too much harm … yet. Her injuries had healed, but she'd bear the reminders of her 'little adventure'—the scars of stabbed leg and arrow wounds—for the rest of her life.

She smiled, and then laughed out loud. Maybe she couldn't be an irresponsible Queen, but she could still reclaim some lost years of childhood. So the game was over … and she'd won. She didn't think she'd ever been this happy. "Thank you, Divine," she breathed, "and thank you, Hedger." Could it get any better than this?

"Hey!"

Katelin looked back for the source of the call. Two people rode towards her from Anestra city, and long before they reached her, Katelin knew them to be Edgaran and Rashelin.

She smiled: those two worked well together, as cousins and as firm friends.

"Hello there!" Katelin called. Novita cropped the long grass on the hilltop.

"Isn't it a beautiful day?" Rashelin called back.

Edgaran rode up and said, "We found you, Kat. We've a message for you, but that was only an excuse to come out for a ride." They reined in next to Novita.

"A message for me?" Katelin grinned. "You've chased me over valley and hill for a few hours then?"

"Not quite," said Edgaran. "Rashelin said this is one of your favourite spots, so we guessed you might ride this way."

"And can you see why?" said Katelin. She swept her arm at the panorama before them.

"Yes, I can," said Edgaran. He drank in the view. "Breathtaking."

"So what's the message?" said Katelin.

"You remember that young initiate we rescued from bandits in the canyons?"

There came a poke at Katelin's heart. Initiate Prento! She'd wondered where his lordship was, and whether she'd meet him again. But she hadn't admitted any feelings for him even to herself, so she had to sound as though she struggled to remember the name. "Initiate ... Prento, wasn't it?"

"That's him," said Edgaran. "I only met him once, but didn't you and Armus see him in Lasseny before that?"

Katelin nodded. A message from him? She maintained her casual tone. "What about him?"

"He came to the Castle gate this morning," said Edgaran.

Katelin gave an involuntary start. Rashelin noticed it, but Katelin told herself the movement was Novita's rather than hers. It was the thought of Prento at the Castle.

"He asked after you," Edgaran went on. "It seems that he's only just learned that you're his Queen."

Katelin laughed, and hoped it didn't betray any nerves. "That's right. In Lasseny I was just 'Kat', and we had little chance to talk in the canyons. I haven't seen him since. How is he?"

"He's fine," said Edgaran. "He's moved back here from Lasseny and is living at the Temple now. He wants to thank you for rescuing him ... or something."

Jumping stars! What should she do? She could gallop straight to the Temple, but that would indicate something to Edgaran and Rashelin. Maybe Rashelin already suspected, but that would only confirm it.

Besides, she wanted to be sure of how Prento felt before admitting any feelings of her own. She should make his lordship wait for a while, and then pay a casual visit to the Temple, for something else. But it would be intriguing to see if anything might develop, so should she invite him to the Castle?

"I have an idea," said Rashelin. "Why don't we invite Prento to lunch? We could swap stories about your 'little adventure'. I'd like to hear his version of events, as I'm sure there are things you haven't told us."

"Good idea," said Katelin with a laugh. So Rashelin had decided to act as matchmaker. If she couldn't keep this secret from her cousin, then she might as well tell her everything.

But later. The future could wait. For now it was enough that Anestra had peace, that she was content with her destiny and had good friends in Edgaran and Rashelin. And maybe Prento too.

She glanced at her brother and cousin.

Oh no. Now Edgaran was grinning at the looks going on between them. Time to escape.

"Race you to the forest!" Katelin shouted, and spurred Novita to a galloping head start down the hillside. Caught in laughter and surprise, Edgaran and Rashelin sprang off at full speed after her.

Philip S Davies came to faith in the Divine at the age of eighteen, and has served as a cleric since 1997. In his family home in Oxfordshire, his study overlooks fields and a valley like those around Anestra.

You can find Philip at philipsdavies.com.

Also available from Books to Treasure

The Village

Eleanor Watkins

The Village is beautiful, a place of order and security, but it harbours three outsiders—Ellen the tinker's daughter, returning with her father to the place where he grew up, a freewoman among serfs; William, whose father is Lord of the Manor; and Sam, who is 'different'. As each strives to find their identity and their place in a world where they can never fully feel accepted, they are unexpectedly faced with a bigger challenge: the Black Death.

How will they cope with the terror that is all around them? What inner resources can they find to make sense of life? In the face of such devastation, can things ever be the same, or what new world should they build? As each of them tells their story, we see the glimmerings of hope and new life in the midst of great uncertainty.

Ellen, William and Sam—three young people with an extraordinary challenge to face.

Find more books from
Books to Treasure at
www.bookstotreasure.co.uk
or our official online shop at
www.bookdragonbooks.co.uk/books-to-treasure-19-c.asp